GOLDEN EYES

NIKKI McCORMACK

ISBN: 978-0-9983765-4-7 print
978-0-9983765-5-4 ebook
First Edition 2017

Published by
Elysium Books
Seattle, WA

Written by Nikki McCormack (https://nikkimccormack.com/)
Cover Design by Heather Hudson (http://www.studiowondercabinet.com/)
Editing by M Evan Matyas (http://chimeraediting.com)
Interior Design by Brian C. Short

*To my Humma, for your love and support,
and for your laugh that always makes me smile.*

Gargoyles soared over the manor courtyard and around the towers, banking and spiraling, gliding effortless on the air currents. They had no obvious purpose beyond perhaps enjoying their ability to fly on a beautiful, breezy day. They were crude-looking creatures, with lumpy, hairless, gray-brown skin but their bearing in flight transformed them. Absolute contentment radiated from them. A serenity that made them beautiful.

The breeze blew a lock of hair across Mira's nose and she grabbed it, pinning it down with one hand hard enough to cause some minor pain. An air of tension stole away the calm this place usually brought her. It felt like change was on the way. Maybe, if she watched the gargoyles long enough, she could rediscover that well of serenity within herself.

"I would love it if you listened to me occasionally."

"Oh." She started and spun around to face Kashi, her cheeks flaring up hot. Bowing her head, she executed a small curtsy, more to hide the burn in her cheeks than out of any true commitment to propriety. "I didn't realize someone had joined me up here."

"Obviously."

Her heart was still racing as he strode past her to look out over the edge of the tower, as much from the thought of being up here alone with him as from the surprise of his arrival. His straight black hair was bound up in a warrior's knot, though the breeze had pulled loose a few shorter strands around his face, taking some of the severity away from the style. Those stormy grey eyes watched the gargoyles with the same indifference she saw in them when he looked at her. That indifference cut her to the core.

"All these years and my brother says you still come out every day to watch them." He shook his head. "At least I always know where to find you."

She could think of nothing to say in response to the edge of bitterness in his voice.

They first met eleven years ago when she and her older brother, Dannesk, arrived at the Arkesh manor as wards. The main portion of their family's manor had burned in a devastating fire that took their parents from them. Their family's remaining holdings were strong enough that an arranged marriage between Dannesk and Ina Arkesh earned them a place as wards while their grandmother oversaw the selling of some properties and the rebuilding of the manor.

Mira believed she had found in Kashi a kindred soul. For almost seven years it had seemed so. Then Kashi went away for four years to complete an intensive training program at the military academy in Beikang. He returned a few months ago a different man, now distant and abrupt with her, impatient with her flights of fancy. Their easy childhood friendship dissolved under the weight of responsibility and an inexplicable tension that she ached to understand. Perhaps if she had gone to Beikang, as he had, and taken to studying politics their friendship could have endured. But her job was to remain here and learn the details of running a manor so she could help rebuild their family by marrying well. A prospect she dreaded. One that loomed ever closer on the horizon.

She sighed and turned her attention back to the gargoyles. No point wasting energy on things she couldn't change. Age and the demands of society weren't content to steal only childhood friendships from her. They would take her dreams away as well.

One of the great beasts banked close to the tower and met her eyes. For a few seconds, everything around her vanished and her breath caught in her throat. The gargoyle had the most brilliant gold eyes. Their gold shone brighter and richer than any treasure forged by men. For the briefest of moments, when it looked into her eyes, the expression on its horned countenance changed from ecstasy to sorrow. As if, in that instant, it shared her sadness for the freedom and friendship of childhood that she had lost. For dreams she set aside to strengthen the future of her family. Then the beast was gone again, diving down out of sight.

Stepping closer to the edge, she peered after it, but the gargoyle had already become lost among its flock. She hadn't ever seen one of the creatures interact with someone, not even with such a brief glance. Normally, they barely expressed any awareness of the humanity around them, almost as if they existed in a separate realm. That disinterest, along with their tendency to drive off unwanted pests, made them tolerated residents on the rooftops of large manors and castles. Many of which even designed perches for the beasts into the architecture.

Kashi cleared his throat, drawing her back to their awkward encounter.

"I apologize, Kashi." She slipped unthinkingly into the familiarity of their youth. "Was there something you needed?"

"Why else would I ever come up here?"

She winced at the lash in his tone. Why indeed? Not to hide from tutors or make up stories about the strange beasts flying nearby. Certainly not for the simple enjoyment of her company, not anymore. Did the military academy train them to such callousness?

She sighed again and his face darkened.

"You spend a lot of time sighing and daydreaming, my lady. All the while, life goes on without you. Maybe you should start paying attention before it has passed you by completely." He emphasized the last word with a swipe of his hand, cutting through the air between them like a blade.

She drew back, startled by the fervor in his voice and more than a little alarmed by the intensity of his gaze. Something had his ire up more than usual. "What do you mean?"

"Your brother is here. It seems he may have found you a suitable husband."

Ice spread through the pit of her stomach. "I… But he…" She stopped and placed a steadying hand on the stone parapet.

"What? Did you think you could stay here forever? Languish in the generosity of Lord and Lady Arkesh until you died an old maid?"

His words stung. Daydreaming indeed. If she could not have his love, she fancied the idea of going to the city and entering into politics. Perhaps die an old maid having made a name for herself in government. It was an impossible fantasy, but that didn't make it any less attractive. Her agreement with her brother was for a different future.

She felt tears coming to her eyes and swallowed hard, determined to keep them at bay. "Why are you so upset with me? I didn't realize you wanted me gone so badly."

He looked away quickly, almost as if she had embarrassed him somehow.

Good. He deserves it.

He didn't though. She could remember sitting in the corner of this very tower, their heads close together, making up stories of how they would run away to the city to avoid this fate. He always despised the idea of her having no say in who she would marry. This news was likely a blow to him as well as a friend who wanted the best for her, if he still was such.

His storm-filled eyes swept out over the courtyard. "I don't want you gone. What I want…"

He stopped. After a long moment of silence, he gave a sharp exhale and shook his head.

"They are waiting for you in the front sitting room, my lady."

"Thank you, Captain Marikashi," she replied, hiding disappointment behind stiff formality.

She forced herself to walk away from him with her head high. The effort made her feel even more like crying. She put one foot down onto the top rung of the ladder and hesitated. Perhaps she could send him down in her stead to tell her brother she was unwell. It might delay things for a little while, if only an hour or two. Or it might not. Dannesk was a sweet, but stubborn man. Tucking her skirts around her ankles and down into the trapdoor, she climbed down the ladder.

•

Kashi gripped the edge of the parapet and his gaze drifted out over the gargoyles again. He knew she spent long hours watching them. More so now then she had as a child. They were magnificent in flight, able to maneuver with an almost bat-like agility, but he could never understand why she watched them as often as she did, climbing up to the towers almost every morning since the day she arrived. He sometimes wondered if it were some manifestation of an inner longing to leave Arkesh.

She had been a ward in the manor for a long time. It wouldn't surprise him if she wished to spread her wings and move on.

It appeared that her brother, now Lord of Yukori, came to give her that chance. Her reaction to the news, however, told him this still wasn't the future she dreamed of. It wasn't the future he wanted for her either. He hadn't been foolish enough as a child to pretend that they would end up together. Even then he knew he would never be a suitable match. Why did it upset him so much now that what he had always expected was coming to pass?

He should have been more kind, but his helplessness in this situation left him floundering and angry. Neither of them was happy with this end, but they had both known it was coming. It was why he never told her how much he cared. It would only make this harder.

Kashi received regular letters from Dannesk during his training. He had known for some time that her brother was garnering interest in her from a few favored suitors. The process had taken Dannesk longer than he expected. He had intended to marry her off at fifteen to begin forging a stronger bond with one of the more respected houses, but his own marriage and other obligations delayed his search for two years.

The news that Dannesk was close to selecting a suitor had prompted Kashi to come home when he did. He wanted to watch her, to memorize her smile and the sound of her voice before she left Arkesh. Then he would return to the capital and see if he could make a life of military service. Many men in the Arkesh family line made their names that way. Having excelled in his training, he saw no reason not to do the same. A bastard only had so many options.

He shook his head. Perhaps time in the practice ring would ease his foolish melancholy.

Turning his back on the sky dancers, he headed down from the tower and began to make his way through the manor.

The best he could hope for was that Dannesk had found a good match for Mira. She deserved someone who would treat her well. Perhaps that was what had taken him so long. There was no doubt Dannesk loved his little sister dearly. He would go miles out of his way to get Mira the slightest thing she passingly mentioned needing. Even as children, Dannesk protected her if he thought others got too rough. More than once, he and Kashi had gotten into fights with other boys in her defense. She railed against it, insisting that she didn't need to be coddled. But what decent man wouldn't want to protect her? She was a dreamer and so delicately built, like one of the fragile glass dolls his half-sister Ina collected.

"Captain."

He turned to see Sunai, his half-brother Shakari's wife, as she hurried down the hall after him, her skirts lifted off the floor so as not to trip upon them. He found an easy smile for her. Since she had come to Arkesh, she had been as much a sister to him as Ina had ever been, more in some ways. He stood politely to wait for her.

"Captain Marikashi." She greeted him with a quick curtsy for formalities sake, then followed it with a fond smile and a light kiss on one cheek. "Have you spoken with Lord Yukori?"

He nodded, doing his best to brush aside the part of him that wanted to reject the use of such titles. In their childhood, the man known now as Lord Dannesk of Yukori or Lord Yukori had merely been Danni. So much changed in the last several years. Childhood friendships faltering before the demands of adult life.

She nodded in turn and swallowed once. "It will be sad to see her go."

A small shimmer of moisture sparkled in her blue eyes. A luxury he could not afford. Perhaps she would shed a few tears on his behalf when Mira left.

A smile threatened at the corners of his mouth as an idea occurred to him. "Perhaps we could give her something to remember us by."

"Oh?" The shimmer of moisture dissipated before a teasing smirk. She winked at him. "And what token of your affections would you suggest we give her?"

He gave her a chastising look, though her knowing smile broke down the attempted severity behind the expression. "Behave, Lady. You know that mare she's so fond of, the one she calls Aiko?" He didn't have to say any more. Her eyes came alight and she clasped her hands before her excited smile.

"That's a fantastic idea. I'll suggest it to Shakari immediately." Her tone promised that the suggestion would be more along the lines of an order. That meant it would happen. Shakari cared for Mira too and he preferred to avoid arguing with his wife whenever possible.

Kashi couldn't hold back a satisfied smile.

She placed a hand on his arm then, her expression turning to the gentle pleading look that meant she intended to ask him for a favor he might not enjoy. "Kashi, would you please invite Lord and Lady Yukori to stay for supper with us this evening?"

He hesitated, dread forming a knot in his stomach. As much as he wanted to know that Mira would go to a good man, he didn't want to listen and pretend enthusiasm while they went on about her husband-to-be. Still, he could refuse Sunai nothing when she looked at him that way. Resigning himself, he inclined his head. "I will do this for you alone, my lady."

"Thank you, little brother." She patted his cheek playfully before turning to walk away.

A flame of panic lit in his chest. "Sunai?"

She turned and smiled, her eyes soft with under-standing. "Don't fret. I will not tell Shakari the horse was your idea," she assured him, reading his thoughts with uncanny accuracy. A big smile dimpled her round cheeks before she continued down the hallway, not waiting for his nod of gratitude.

She knew how he felt about Mira, or at least that he cared for her, if not the extent of those feelings. The woman proved too observant sometimes, but he appre-ciated having someone to confide in. Neither of them spoke of it to Shakari. His older half-brother was much too devoted to propriety to take such a thing lightly. He had always been that way, but he took a firmer stand than ever on issues of social standing since taking over management of the manor.

Kashi touched the hilt of his sword once, yearning for the simple demands of the practice ring. Resigned, he altered his route to go and speak with Lord and Lady Yukori for Sunai.

Mira had meandered her way through the halls, taking the long way to her chambers first. The wind on the tower always left her dark mahogany hair in wild disarray, so she stopped before her vanity mirror and brushed it into submission. The sadness in the green eyes staring back at her only deepened her melancholy, creating an infinite reverberation of sorrow. She turned her back on the bleak image in the mirror and left her chambers.

Kashi was right, she did spend too much time day-dreaming. Dannesk told her the last time he visited that he would find her a suitor soon. He even apologized for the delay, as if she minded. She promptly forgot about it, discarding it in favor of long hours watching gargoyles fly and imagining what it might be like to be a politician and warrior's wife living in the city.

All their roles were changing. Lord and Lady Arkesh had been kind to accept them as wards when the fire decimated the Yukori holding. Ina and Dannesk had honored that generosity by marrying soon after he took over the rebuilt Yukori manor. Shakari Arkesh married Sunai, the daughter of another strong family, and was taking over management of the Arkesh family holding from their father. As a bastard son of Lord Arkesh, Kashi would never inherit any part of the manor. Kashi's only hope of achieving legitimate social standing was through the military, which at least explained his interest in that, though she resented it for taking him away from her. Her own obligations would soon be taking her away from him regardless.

The five children grew up together, learning together, watching out for one another, teasing one another, roaming the vast Arkesh holding to find grand adventures and frequent mishaps as only children could. How time had changed them all, bringing them closer in some ways and making them as distant as strangers in others. Sometimes she felt as if the other four had left her behind, still so much a child living in a fantasy world of her own creation.

Dannesk, Ina, and Shakari sat waiting for her in the grand sitting room off the entrance hall. She brushed her hands over her green skirts to smooth them several more times than necessary before entering. She dropped in a graceful curtsy to Shakari and then to her brother. Though the two held similar rank, they were in Shakari's household so it was proper to give him precedence.

Dannesk stood, his hazel eyes sparkling with an open affection that lightened her sorrow when he opened his arms to embrace her.

He squeezed her tight, chipping away some of her melancholy with his warmth. "You don't need to curtsy to me, Mira."

She returned his embrace, trying not to let resentment of his purpose stiffen the gesture and blushing before the watchful eyes of Ina and Shakari. "Danni, it is good to see you." She leaned to one side to peer around him when they parted. "And you, Lady Ina."

Ina smiled, one hand resting on a belly heavy with child. Her gray eyes and perfect, warm-toned skin—traits reminiscent of their shared father—reminded Mira painfully of Kashi.

Shakari, on the other hand, had skin pale as new snow and narrow features like his mother, with neatly cut pale blond hair and eyes as blue as the sky on a clear summer day. He had developed a certain aloofness of late, a detachment from his emotions, which made her worry for him and Sunai, though he always treated her kindly.

Shakari offered her a polite nod in greeting and gestured to the empty chair on one end that faced between them. "Please sit with us, dear Mira. Your smile is always welcome."

She nodded in polite acknowledgement of the compliment and accepted the offered chair, positioned to give her a clear view of all her adversaries, for today they were such. Even so, she appreciated the cordial regard that Shakari gave her today. It felt respectful and considerate. So very different from the cold distance she had gotten from Kashi since his return.

"What occasion brings you here, Brother?" She played innocent, giving herself an opportunity to get a feel for the mood in the room.

Dannesk shifted in his seat, a touch uneasy now, confirming the dreadful news Kashi brought her. He made a gesture to brush his dark hair away from his face, apparently forgetting that he had recently had it cropped short in the current noble fashion. He dropped his hand back to his lap with a fresh hint of red in his cheeks.

"You know I have been searching for an acceptable suitor for you, Mira?"

Right to the point. "Yes." She kept her tone pleasant despite the seething denial burning below the surface. Her eyes wandered to the lace trimmed ivory curtains, embroidered in a moody darker blue that complimented her temper.

"I think I've found an excellent match. Lord Ander of Barik has long been ill. His son, Lord Valin, will soon take over the Barik manor in name. He is yet unwed because he has been overseeing his father's care and, unofficially, management of the manor for several years. His family is very powerful. We spoke in depth about you when Lord Valin passed through the area a few weeks ago. He has graciously invited us to Barik manor to see you and discuss a marriage arrangement."

See me. As if only my appearance matters. As he spoke, Mira's sorrow deepened again, the shallow surface opening to reveal a bottomless pit of misery beneath. Barik manor. Could he find her a place any more remote? The Barik holding was much further west than their family's manor and as far west as one could get from the Arkesh manor without leaving the kingdom. Even farther still from the capital city of Beikang. The hope she had harbored that her future husband would be comfortable with her spending part of her time studying in Beikang crumbled.

Some of her disappointment must have shown through. Ina leaned forward and smiled reassurance. "He is nothing like his father, Mira. Lord Valin is young and vigorous and really quite charismatic."

This is what I agreed to. I must not complain. How hard it was to force a smile. She'd entered into this agreement as a naive child. "I am sure he is."

"I think it's a brilliant match." Shakari stated as though declaring a final judgement. "As Mira has been a ward in this house for eleven years, I will send an honorary escort of warriors to accompany her. I will even send Kashi to lead them. His leave isn't over for a several more months. He'll probably enjoy the distraction."

Mira's stomach dropped to her toes.

"You are far too generous, Shakari." Dannesk inclined his head in polite appreciation. "I have my own warriors, but your men would be welcome. I'm sure

Mira will take comfort from the company of another familiar face on the long trip."

It was all she could do not to protest, but there was no logical reason for doing so beyond not wanting to have her unrequited love rubbed in her face while riding to meet her future husband. The last thing she wanted was to have Kashi in her escort, but she forced gratitude into her smile. "My Lord Shakari is much too kind." *Much.*

"And you are a silly, beautiful girl." Shakari chuckled, showing a hint of his old charm and dismissing her formality. "We will miss you in Arkesh."

Mira took a deep breath to steady herself. She could feel the sting of unshed tears threatening again. "Do not write me off so quickly, Shakari. Lord Valin might send me back." To her surprise, she even managed a playful smile. *I really should have been a diplomat.*

"I doubt it." Kashi stepped into the doorway, his grey eyes dark like thunderclouds. He offered a tight smile to Shakari and Dannesk. Ina, he glanced past and Mira began to wonder if he was cold to all women these days.

Shakari regarded the younger man for a long moment, scrutinizing him as if he were seeing him for the first time. "He would have to be a fool to turn away such a prize, wouldn't he, Brother?"

Mira wasn't sure if she was more offended by being referred to as a prize or by the stinging indifference with which Kashi shrugged off the question and turned his attention to Dannesk.

"Lady Sunai has asked that you grace us with your company for supper this evening."

"We would be honored," Dannesk replied and Mira watched with a twinge of envy the way he smiled at Ina and squeezed her hand.

Kashi nodded graciously enough then turned. He finally looked at her, but she lowered her gaze to the floor, unable to meet his eyes. She listened to his footsteps as he stalked from the room and fought the tightening in her throat.

Shakari cleared his throat and stood. "Dannesk, I would like a private word with you. Ladies, I imagine Sunai would appreciate your company. You'll be most likely to find her in the atrium. She must be pining for something other than my boring talk of finances and crops."

Mira only nodded, still searching for the equilibrium Kashi robbed her of with his disinterest. Indeed, much like a thief, he had long ago stolen her heart and clearly intended to give her nothing to fill the empty space in her chest. Even his friendship had slipped away.

Ina smiled and stood. "My lords," she nodded courteously to each then extended a hand to Mira.

Taking the offered hand and offering the most gracious smile she could manage for Shakari and Dannesk, she let Ina draw her from the room. The two men left behind them, heading toward Shakari's study.

"You seem quite gloomy today, especially considering the good news your brother brings," Ina observed as they navigated the long, shadowed hallways toward the atrium.

"I mean no insult by my mood," Mira offered hastily. "It is wonderful news. Truly, I am quite pleased. I just was not expecting it today." The words sounded weak. She refused to meet the other woman's eyes while she lied.

"Darling Mira, Valin is a good man and a fine match." she consoled. "Captain Marikashi is handsome, but he will always be a warrior and he has no name to offer. He is not the kind of man you make into a husband."

Mira sucked in a breath and stopped in her tracks, yanking her hand away from her sister-in-law. "Who says I…"

Ina cut her off with an indulgent smile. "Don't worry about it, Mira. A woman cannot hide such things from another of her sex, not like she can hide them from a man." She took her hand again and gave it a gentle tug, drawing her along. "Let us find Sunai."

•

Ina's words troubled Mira for the next few days as she prepared her things for the journey to Barik manor. How had the woman known of her interest in Kashi? Was it something in the way she acted around him? Was it in her eyes or her voice? Worse yet, was it something in her body language? If Ina knew, then who else knew? What about Dannesk? What would he think if he knew she fancied the baseborn son of Arkesh?

She couldn't ask him about it now. He and Ina had already returned to the Yukori manor to tend to other affairs. He had left four of his men to escort her along with the six Arkesh men Kashi would lead. They would stop along the way at Yukori manor where Dannesk would join them and continue to Barik from there.

It was the question of a fool anyway. A second marriage into the Arkesh family would net their family nothing, even if Kashi had been a legitimate son. The Barik family, however, was well known and well respected. They had an enormous holding and, if gossip could be believed, were nearly as wealthy as the queen herself. She knew she should be flattered that Lord Valin Barik would consider taking her as his wife, but she couldn't get past the feeling of remorse. Of something lost. Maybe when she was far enough away from Kashi and the places that reminded her of him it wouldn't seem so bad, though that parting wasn't going to come soon enough for her. The idea of parting ways with him at Barik manor with her potential betrothed looking on horrified her, though it might at least discourage her from saying anything to him she might regret.

When the day came to leave, she snuck food from the kitchens and broke fast in the early hours alone on the tower, watching the gargoyles. This would be her last chance to watch this group and they were most active at dawn and dusk.

She hadn't been there but a few minutes when one of the creatures banked toward the tower. She froze mid-bite, afraid to make any sudden moves as it swept down and landed on the tower top only a couple of yards from where she sat. Those same golden eyes from a few days ago regarded her for several seconds before it curled up on the stones in a rather catlike fashion and rested its horned head on large feet tipped with menacing black talons. Leathery wings folded over it like a blanket and a barbed tail wrapped around its feet, the tip coming to rest under the creature's nose.

There was no way to know for certain that it was the same creature that had looked at her the other day. Something inside her insisted that it was and that it meant her no harm. Despite the intimidating armament and musculature of the creature, she found its unprecedented company more comforting than alarming on this day that promised much sorrow.

After finishing her meal she stood, moving slow so as not to startle the creature. "This is our second encounter, gargoyle," she started in a soothing tone. "If I weren't leaving, I might have given you a name. Unfortunately, I won't be coming up here anymore after today. Fare thee well."

The gargoyle opened one gold eye and watched her. When she opened the trapdoor, it moved and she froze, but it only rose, stretched, and took to the air again. She watched for a moment. If only she could fly away with such ease. Instead, she turned and climbed down the ladder from what would probably be her last visit to that tower. She stopped by the chambers that had been hers for so many years and looked around to make sure she hadn't forgotten anything important. After a short time spent staring in the mirror, she realized she was only delaying the inevitable and made herself go down to the courtyard.

A carriage already waited, along with the group of mounted soldiers from both families. She approached the carriage, fighting a losing battle against a telling frown until she noticed the little bay mare, Aiko, saddled and tied behind it. Glancing around, she spotted Kashi mounted up among the men flanking the carriage and smiled her gratitude. He alone knew how much the mare meant to her. She didn't doubt that he was responsible for the animal's presence. His brief surreptitious smile, a quick flashback to their childhood friendship, brought a surge of delight that faded fast when she remembered the purpose of their journey. This wasn't some carefree romp across the countryside.

For Lord and Lady Arkesh's sake, she tried to hide her lack of enthusiasm and behave like a proper lady. They both hugged her warmly and wished her well, telling her she could keep Aiko as a gift from them. The words blurred together like her vision of them in her tear-filled eyes. She thanked them ardently for allowing her to be a part of their family and for the gift before climbing into the carriage with a touch too much haste to escape the pain of parting. Despite their warmth, she couldn't help wondering if they were glad to see her leaving. The responsibility of a ward could be a nuisance and they would be starting their own family soon. However, when she watched them as the carriage rolled away, they looked solemn, like the gray clouds behind the manor, and Sunai wiped at her face as though brushing away tears.

Perhaps they would miss her a little.

As soon as they were off the manor grounds, Kashi rode up beside the carriage window she sat gazing out. "Would you prefer to ride, Lady?"

"Please call me Mira, like you used to."

He lowered his gaze for a moment, appearing uncomfortable with her request, but he acquiesced. "Would you prefer to ride, Mira?"

She smiled, warmed by the sound of her name coming from between his lips again. "Yes, you know I would."

"Hold up!"

The escort slowed to a stop at his order and he dismounted to help her down from the carriage. She certainly didn't need the assistance, but rather than object, she took advantage of his offered hand, feeling a warm thrill at his careful touch. Her heart raced when his fingers touched the small of her back as though to steady her when she stepped up to the mare. He also offered her an assist into the saddle before returning to his own mount, aware that skirts, even split for riding, could be a little more cumbersome to mount in. He remained every bit the gentleman through the process, distant yet polite. Even so, she struggled with a foolish desire to climb back into the carriage so they could do it all over again and she could have a legitimate reason for him to touch her.

I do daydream far too much. She forced a smile and nodded to indicate her readiness to move on.

"Move out," he ordered.

As they resumed their journey, one more unexpectedly joined the escort. A gargoyle appeared overhead and proceeded to pace its flight to the speed of the escort. When she looked up, it looked down and she wasn't at all surprised to see bright golden eyes gazing at her. Her instincts told her with no uncertainty that it was the same beast that had joined her on the tower that morning.

"That's odd."

She startled, too absorbed in the creature above them to have noticed Kashi moving his mount over beside her, his hand resting on the crossbow attached to his saddle.

"They rarely leave the manor grounds in the daytime," he commented, his voice tight with unease. "Apparently even the gargoyles wish to see you off."

"That one joined me on the tower this morning," she commented, now more interested in his nearness than in the creature sailing overhead.

"That's extremely unusual." He started to fiddle with the crossbow.

"Please," she implored quickly. "Leave it be. It isn't harming anyone. I'm sure it will turn back in time."

His hand shifted slightly away from the crossbow. "I don't…" He met her eyes and seemed to lose track of what he meant to say. He glanced away.

She scrambled for something to say, eager to chase away his sudden discomfort. "Remember when we used to race down this road, Kashi?"

A faint grin curved his lips, his eyes flickering with a hint of the bright humor of the mischievous child he had been. It didn't seem so long ago. A glimmer of sunlight peaking through the overcast touched upon his warm-toned skin.

"That little mare wouldn't have a chance against this monster." He patted his gelding's neck, leaving the crossbow alone.

"I don't know," she teased, "she has much less weight to carry."

His roguish smile brought out a darker beauty in his handsome features. For a moment, she thought he might forget himself and challenge her to a race as he would have once, but then the playfulness was shut down by a stern scowl.

"We have had our time to be children, Mira. We both have responsibilities and obligations now. There is no sense in pretending otherwise."

"Don't worry," she snapped. "I wouldn't expect you to sully your dreary warrior reputation."

He narrowed his eyes and, to her distress, the expression somehow served to enhance his allure, giving a dangerous edge to his countenance. She squeezed Aiko's sides and the mare moved up into a trot. With a little quick maneuvering, she worked her way up to the head of the column, leaving him behind. The escort let her go without protest. Amidst the open fields, they could see any approaching danger long before it posed a real threat and there was no reason to expect an attack. Their escort was a formality more than anything.

The gargoyle moved ahead of the column as well, pacing his flight with her. Despite how peculiar the behavior was, its presence had the same comforting effect on her now that it had on the tower, easing away her brief temper.

"What shall your name be?" She queried to herself, watching as the creature rode on the wind currents, keeping their pace without any visible effort. The horned head looked down at her, almost as if it had heard her words. From this angle, it was easy enough to confirm that the beast was male, so at least that narrowed the naming options. "How about Kazue? I've always liked that name. I hoped to bestow it upon a son one day, but you are welcome to it for now."

She gasped as the creature above her spiraled into a dive. Behind her, she heard hooves pounding as Kashi sprinted to join her flanked by two other soldiers with their weapons ready. The gargoyle twisted around several yards above them and rose back up to his previous elevation before leveling out again.

One of the men looked from the gargoyle to Kashi, his crossbow ready in hand. "Captain, perhaps we should shoot it down."

When Kashi started to nod she twisted in her saddle to face the soldier. "You will do no such thing!"

The soldier hesitated, looking again to his captain.

"It is behaving oddly, Lady Yukori," Kashi countered.

Although tone was reassuring, his choice of formal address irritated her. She turned her burning gaze on him. "You will not harm it."

Kashi scowled at her, the muscles in his jaw tightening. When she didn't back down, he relented and turned his scowl on the road ahead. "Very well, let the beast be. For now."

"Yes, Captain." The two soldiers responded in unison.

He held up a hand before the two men could slow down to rejoin the rest of the escort and added, "However, I think at least two guards should ride with Lady Yukori at all times as long as the creature is with us, just to be safe."

She rolled her eyes at him and he gave her a warning look.

He shifted his mount close and said under his breath, "I will indulge you in this, but only if you will indulge me as well."

She met his cold grey eyes for a long moment, wondering if his desire to protect her could suggest a spark of affection, or if it was strictly his sense of duty. His expression waxed impatient, so she nodded.

"Good." His response was curt. He pulled his reins in and his mount dropped back, leaving the other two to ride with her.

She stared forward, not caring if anyone noticed the hurt in her eyes and knowing they probably wouldn't trouble themselves with it if they did. She didn't look up at the gargoyle for the rest of the day, figuring that it would only draw unwanted attention to the creature, but its shadow remained a constant companion.

When evening fell, they stopped at a well-kept tavern in a neighboring village and the gargoyle flew away. She felt a distinct sense of loss at his departure, but it was probably best that he ceased the mysterious behavior before Kashi changed his mind. The thought of seeing the beast brought down made her chest ache.

For someone raised in luxury, the tavern and the surrounding village suffered from an overabundance of drab brownness. Perhaps the dreary world outside the sheltered life she knew would help her appreciate the life waiting for her. A few tired women, aged beyond their years and dressed in drab woolen dresses tended tables in the tavern. Their envious glances and the way they flirted listlessly with the soldiers, expressing more resignation than interest, chased away her appetite.

When she voiced a desire to retire early and dine in her room, Kashi escorted her up the stairs himself. He opened the door for her and scanned the room once before turning to leave. With her heart pounding in her throat and a knot in her stomach, she touched his arm to stall him. He turned back to her and a flicker of something showed in his eyes, something that she didn't quite understand, but it elicited a deep longing within her.

"Kashi, would you dine with me?"

"That wouldn't be proper, my lady. Not under the circumstances."

He didn't have to explain what he meant. If he vanished off to her room for any amount of time, the other men might assume they did more than just dine and, given that they were escorting her to meet the man she would likely marry, the ensuing gossip could be disastrous.

"I understand." He started to turn away again and she blurted, "It's just that… I just miss the way it was before you left."

He frowned. "We were children, Mira."

"Only children can have friends?"

He did turn away from her then, a weary hang in his shoulders. "Good night, my lady. I'll post someone outside your door in case you need anything."

"Good night, Captain" she murmured in return, a hollowness eating away inside her as she watched him walk away down the hall.

Perhaps she should have asked Shakari not to send him along, but Shakari wouldn't have understood such a request. It would be a long arduous journey pretending not to care for him, forcing herself not to reach for him. Perhaps it would become easier once she had Dannesk along to distract her.

The next day, they barely left the dreary village behind before Kazue appeared overhead again. Mira was so pleased to see the gargoyle that she had to work to keep from bouncing in her saddle. As silly as it might be, she didn't feel so lonely with him there.

The large beast made it clear the previous day that it followed her, and not the escort in general, by keeping pace with her always. Today it behaved the same. Wherever she rode amidst the stretched-out escort, the gargoyle mirrored her position in the bright blue sky above. She couldn't help smirking when the guards began rubbing their necks grown sore from trying to keep a constant eye on Kazue.

They traveled well into that night before reaching the next stopping point and she couldn't see well enough in the dark to know when the gargoyle left them, but she was certain he had. The next morning, she fretted that he might not join them again, worrying over it enough that she barely noticed when Kashi moved his mount up alongside her. Then the sound of the beast's leathery wings beating a slow drum rhythm through the air reached them and the now familiar gargoyle flew into his place above.

"Good morning, Kazue," she greeted.

"You named it?" Kashi's brows rose, pinching

together in an expression of disbelief.

She blushed and fussed with the mare's soot black mane. "Well, yes. It seemed only proper that he should have a name if he is going to be traveling with us."

To her great pleasure, he responded to this information not with the anticipated ridicule, but with a fond smile and small shake of his head. "You always did like collecting creatures. You recall the wild hare you tried to adopt."

She grinned, a warmth spreading through her in response to his friendlier mood. "I do believe it ended up in a stew."

"Which you adamantly refused to eat." Kashi chuckled. "This is by far the most unusual creature you've taken in yet."

"I'm not sure who took who in." She glanced up at the large predator.

"It certainly seems that he is taken with you." He followed her gaze up, frowning.

She shrugged. What was wrong with her that she could capture the devotion of such a beast, but not that of the man she adored? She longed to speak with him more, but the frustration that accompanied the thought made it hard to think of anything to say that wouldn't sound petulant. They continued in silence.

In the late afternoon, they came over a rise in the rolling landscape that offered a view of the pastoral Yukori manor in the distance. The trees and fields burned by the fire were gone. Younger, healthy trees grew now, bright with emerald foliage and the land grew rich with grassy fields and flourishing crops, the soil revitalized by the very fire that destroyed the old fields.

She increased the pace, eager to see her old home again and be distracted from Kashi's confusing presence, but as they drew near, she spotted many gargoyles flying above and around the manor house.

She slowed her pace again. Were they territorial? If so, Kazue might find himself in a tricky situation soon. Since she could do nothing to stop him, she settled for watching, waiting for a reaction from the local flock as they approached the manor grounds, aware that Kashi watched her in turn, perhaps wondering at her variable speed and the death grip she had on Aiko's reins.

A rider emerged from the gates and galloped toward them. She recognized him, even from this distance, and kicked Aiko faster to meet him. The gargoyle kept pace as she galloped toward the oncoming rider. They both skidded their mounts to a halt as they converged, narrowly avoiding a collision, a reckless game reminiscent of their childhood. Kazue slowed and proceeded to circle above them, his wing strokes long and leisurely.

Dannesk kept glancing anxiously up at the beast while he greeted her. "Mira. I've been waiting for you. How long has it been since you've been back here?"

She reached out to take his hand and squeezed it, leaning in to lay an awkward kiss on his cheek as their horses pranced from the excitement of the brief run. "Not since the wedding." She looked past him at the manor. You could no longer tell the older portion from the new with the remodels and updates done. The rebuilt stables stood on the other side.

"I see you brought a bit of memorabilia from the Arkesh manor?" He raised his eyebrows and pointed a finger at the gargoyle still circling above them.

She smiled. "He's been following me. I don't know why, but he doesn't seem to mean any harm. I've been calling him Kazue."

Dannesk chuckled and adjusted his collar, giving the predator another nervous glance. "An odd pet, Sister, but at least the cook won't be stewing this one up for dinner. Hopefully Lord Barik isn't the jealous kind."

"Very funny." She gave him a playful shove and the horses danced apart. "The courtyard garden is blooming beautifully."

He offered a wry smile. "Ina has made it her personal duty to retrain the gardeners. At least it gives her something to do while she's with child."

Kashi trotted up to join them. He looked so very handsome on the big, dark bay gelding, sitting comfortable in the saddle like an extension of the animal. Her cheeks warmed and she glanced down at the reins in her hands, worried her face might betray her inappropriate affections.

"Kashi. It's great to have you along."

"Danni." He returned the greeting with a little more restraint, but they shook hands with exuberance as if they hadn't seen one another only a short time ago.

"Shall we?" Dannesk gestured towards the manor house. "Ina has had a grand meal prepared."

"Sounds delightful," Kashi replied.

Mira fell back behind as the two men led the way to the manor house. It occurred to her now that having Dannesk along wasn't going to make things better. Indeed, she already felt even more alone as he and Kashi chatted ahead of her, finding a common bond in their gender, if nothing else. Her protectors, reunited to see her off to her future with as little regard for her desires now as they had in their youth.

While the two men chatted, she watched Kazue approach the manor, her palms growing moist with sweat. She held her breath when he flew into the midst of the other sky dancers. The others closed in around him and her heart began to race, but they merely circled, each local beast brushing wings once with the newcomer before they returned to usual business. She exhaled a shaky breath and followed the others to the manor entrance.

After a wearying supper that Mira spent trying to hide her sorrow and be properly formal without being unfriendly, the two men retired to a sitting room to drink and talk and Ina retired to her rooms, her pregnancy fatiguing her. Left to her own resources, Mira went up to the highest tower and sat on the wall to watch the gargoyles, humoring the faint hope that Kazue might come join her.

Absurd as she thought the notion was, the gargoyle didn't let her down. He lit gracefully on the tower and regarded her, striking gold eyes glowing in the light of a bright moon. His snout was somewhere between that of a cats and a dogs in length. Large canines glinted like stars in the pale light as his mouth hung open, panting from the effort of his flight. A small horn spiraled up behind each eye, set just in front of fine pointed ears.

"You aren't so ugly as I once thought, you know," she remarked. The creature might not understand what she said, but it was nice to speak anyway, to pretend someone cared what she had to say.

The large predator took a few steps toward her and she tensed, eyes drawn back to those tapered canines. They curved back at an angle perfect for tearing into flesh. Seeming to sense her apprehension, the gargoyle drew back the most forward paw and sat. Its gold eyes regarded her, brimming with an intelligence she hadn't expected to find in such a creature.

Intrigued, she spoke again in a more welcoming tone to see how it would respond. "I don't know why you followed me, Kazue, but I have been glad of your presence."

Apparently encouraged by her tone, the creature rose and stepped forward again. She couldn't stop herself from tensing once more and half-rose from her seat. He immediately stopped and lay down this time, curling under the blanket of his wings and resting his head on his paws.

"I'm sorry. I know you seem nice enough, but you are a predator and more than large enough to overpower me. I don't know what to expect from you. There is no precedent for this type of behavior among your kind. You understand my anxiety, I'm sure."

The bright eyes blinked, serene and patient.

She smiled, then glanced out over the wall and breathed deep of the cool evening air. "Ah, Kazue, what have I done? I have daydreamed my young life away and now I have nothing to show for it. I'll be married off to a stranger and waste away as a proper lady, forever a decoration in the shadow of my husband. I have been a fool."

A strange noise came from the creature behind her and she glanced back in alarm. At first, she thought it was growling. Then she noticed that its eyes had drifted closed and its expression exuded contentment. It was purring. The realization brought a moment of wonder, followed seconds later by the sting of jealousy.

"I'm glad you're having such a good time," she huffed.

The gargoyle opened his eyes and lifted his head. The hint of sadness in that remarkable gaze twisted guilt in her chest. Perhaps it was ludicrous, but she felt as though he understood her sorrow in that moment, that somehow, he experienced something similar.

"I'm sorry, my friend. I suppose I could benefit from a good sleep. I shall hope to see you tomorrow, Kazue."

The creature's head inclined as if it nodded in response to her words and her nerves danced at the implications. She felt the golden-eyed gaze following her when she left the tower.

•

"How has the trip gone so far?"

Kashi glanced up from his drink. He met Dannesk's eyes for a moment and wished that it was Sunai who sat across from him. She would never judge him for these feelings and he could relieve much of his current tension by confiding in her. Mira's brother, on the other hand, would not find his woes at all amusing.

He settled for a dismissive shrug. "It's been rather uneventful, other than that gargoyle."

"Yes," Dannesk scowled into his empty drink. He set it down on the polished dark wood table between them and refilled it from the decanter there. "It is rather odd. I've never seen one of those beasts give someone a first glance, let alone take a fancy to someone enough to follow them across the countryside. Do you think it's dangerous?"

"It's a predator almost as big as a horse; of course it's dangerous," Kashi replied. "Still, this one hasn't acted aggressively toward any of us and Mira seems to take pleasure in its presence."

Dannesk chuckled and ran a finger around the brim of his glass. "Sometimes I wish she would grow up more. Other times I think it would be a terrible shame if she ever did."

A shame indeed. Kashi nodded solemn agreement. He remembered the expression of childlike delight on her face that morning when she had greeted the gargoyle as vividly as he remembered the wounded look in her eyes when he cut her down for daydreaming on the tower at Arkesh manor. If only there were some way to stop thinking about her. Maybe time and distance would solve that for him, though it hadn't during his four years at the academy in Beikang. Perhaps it would change once she was married.

"So, the rest of us are settling down," Dannesk said, changing the subject, at least in his perception. "What are your plans?"

Kashi bit down on a surge of sour resentment. It was so easy for the rest of them. Their lives had been laid out neatly before them practically from birth. For the bastard son of a lord, it would never be so neat and tidy. And yet…

Mira does not seem so happy with her lot. He had expected her to be happier about her potential betrothed. It was an excellent match politically. But this was Mira. She had never shown much interest in a life as the lady of a manor. Perhaps he had wanted her to be happy about the match so he could stop looking for something more in the glances she gave him. He took a deep breath and stared into the fire.

"After this, I will probably go back to Beikang." He admired his own ability to sound civil despite the raging of his emotions.

"Back to the military then?"

Kashi nodded. "There's been unrest in the northern provinces. An opportunity to prove myself, perhaps."

"It's a good plan." Dannesk rubbed his chin and stared into his drink. "If you continue to perform as you have been, you might even end up with lands of your own eventually."

Kashi held his silence. Part of him wanted to resent Shakari for being the sole inheritor of Arkesh manor and lands, but such was the law. His half-brother had no more control over their father's extramarital activities than his mother had obviously had. As the bastard son, he would pay for those transgressions. Now that age had taken the mind of old Lord Arkesh, he rarely even recognized his own children anymore. There was no one for Kashi to direct his anger at and no way to have the life, or the lady, he wanted. If he ever did receive lands in recognition of his service, it would be long after she was married and settled with a family of her own.

He glanced up at Dannesk as the other man leaned over to refill his glass for him.

"You seem distant tonight, wrapped in some unreachable melancholy," Dannesk commented as he leaned back in his chair again and smacked the decanter down on the table a little harder than necessary.

Kashi shook his head. "I'm well. Tired perhaps. All this travel can be draining."

Dannesk smiled and nodded, sympathetic. "That it can be and we are leaving early on the morrow. Perhaps we should call it a night."

Kashi smiled wryly into his full glass. What was Mira doing now? Was she asleep in a soft bed wrapped in some comforting dream? "I think it will be a night regardless of what we call it."

Dannesk shook his head and chuckled as Kashi downed the drink in one swallow and set the glass on the table. "Sleep well, Captain," he said as he stood to leave.

"Likewise, Lord Yukori."

Dannesk inclined his head respectfully before walking out.

Kashi didn't go to the room they had lent him right away, but sat gazing into the fire for a while, letting the alcohol sooth his tension. It also enhanced the inappropriate urge to go in search of Mira. He kept that urge locked up tight. The flickering flames offered no answers, but they at least offered comfort and warmth.

After a time, a serving boy came in to put the fire out. He stopped in the doorway.

"Apologies, my Lord. I did not realize anyone was still here."

Kashi rose and the boy stepped to one side so he could exit into the hallway. "It's Captain, not Lord, and I was just leaving."

"Sorry, Captain." The boy stared at the floor as he passed.

"No harm done," he added in a gentler tone to assuage a twist of guilt for intimidating the boy.

The boy only nodded.

Kashi shook his head and wandered toward his room. He turned down one hallway then stepped quickly back into the shadows of a doorway when he spotted Mira coming through the door from the room under the tower. The sorrowful expression and slump in her shoulders made his heart ache. He wanted to reach out and comfort her, but it wouldn't be proper, so he watched her from the silent shadows as she walked down the hall and disappeared into her room.

This would be a long journey.

In the morning, Mira's evening encounter with the gargoyle was still at the fore of her thoughts. She left her chambers early and stole away, padding barefoot through the wood-floored halls to her great aunt Gemma's chambers. The old woman would be awake. She liked to watch the morning coming in through her bedroom window. Assuming, of course, that she hadn't changed much since Mira's last visit.

When she arrived at the familiar door, Mira knocked gently, a much smaller hand knocking on the heavy old door in her memories. How many times had she snuck to Gemma's rooms at dawn in her early childhood, before the fire forced their grandmother to send them away?

"Do I hear a young woman at my door?"

Mira grinned and tried to make her voice deep. "No, you hear a young man."

"By lord and by land, I believe I hear my Mira. Come in child. Do not make me wait to see you. At my age, I might pass before you enter."

She giggled and went inside, pausing to click the door closed behind her.

Gemma sat in a plush ivory chair in the small sitting area by her windows. Her wrinkled face crinkling even more when she smiled at Mira, her green eyes almost hidden in folds of pale, parchment skin. Mira walked over and knelt before her, taking her old, gnarled hands and placing a kiss on each. Gemma withdrew one hand from Mira's gentle grasp and touched her cheek, her lips pulling back in a broad smile that revealed how few teeth she still possessed. Her old hands trembled so much more than they had the last time Mira saw her.

"Darling Mira. I see you so seldom now. You have grown so much. The little girl I knew has become such a beautiful woman."

"You are too kind, Gemma."

"Sit child. I will ring for more tea." The old woman took hold of the bell that sat on the table and rang it with shocking force, creating a harsh clanging as Mira sat in the chair across from her. A moment later, a stick of a girl appeared from a servant's door in the corner of the room wearing a shift and apron that hung loose off her small frame. Her curtsy was as awkward as a new-born foals first steps. New to the position and clearly not the one the clothing was intended for.

"Bring an extra cup and more tea, my dear."

"Yes, my lady." The young girl fumbled through another curtsy and hurried from the room.

Gemma spoke as Mira watched the girl disappear. "My previous servant had a sick son to tend to. Lord Yukori sent her home with a full year's pay at my request to tend to him. This young girl has much to learn, but she is sweet and new clothes are being made for her."

It reassured her that her brother would do something for a mere servant. Even if it was at Gemma's behest, it was a kind thing to do.

"What troubles you Mira? Is it Lord Valin that worries you?"

Mira stared at the old woman, a bemused smile twitching the corners of her mouth up. "How is it that you always know my thoughts before I do, Gemma? If you must know, yes, this meeting and likely marriage troubles me, but it was inevitable, wasn't it?"

"Yes child, I suppose it was. Though, smart as you are, I always thought you might go to the city and rise into politics. Some ladies have done such, you know."

Mira heaved a great sigh. "I would have liked to. But I didn't really come to speak of that."

"What then?"

"Can't I just come to see you?"

Gemma smiled, no less sly and attentive for her advanced age. "Yes, my dear, but you have something on your mind."

She thought about denying it, but that perceptive gleam in Gemma's eyes promised a battle if she tried. Looking out the window into the faint glow of predawn, Mira spotted several dark forms dipping down into the courtyard, the gargoyles beginning their morning flight. Was this how she developed the habit of watching them? Did Gemma watch them too?

She relented to Gemma's insistent look with a fond smile and a nod. "Yes, Gemma, I do have something on my mind."

The serving girl returned then and poured them both a warm cup of tea. When she was gone again, Mira met the old woman's eyes.

"What do you know of gargoyles?"

"Ah. Is that what it is? I heard one followed you here. Very strange behavior indeed." Gemma nodded sagely. "The legends say that mages of old always had gargoyles around them as much as a warrior always has his sword at hand."

"Yes. But those are legends and I am no mage."

"Perhaps, but you have many great mages far back in your family history."

Mira frowned. "Says who?"

"Your grandmother, and her mother before her, and on back for many generations."

"Ah, I see." She smiled indulgently.

Gemma, not one to be patronized, frowned crossly. "You would call us all liars then?"

"No, I would call you a bunch of dear little women with big imaginations and too much time to daydream." *Traits that really do seem to run in the family.*

Mira waited for her to say something, but the bent old woman stared out the window and sipped at her tea. Her lips moved now and then as though she spoke, but no sound came out. Mira sipped at her own slightly over-steeped tea and waited. Gemma's eyes began to droop and her hands sank slowly to her lap, the tea tipping precariously. Mira stood up and gently took the teacup from her. Gemma's eyes opened, vivid green like her own, and regarded Mira with a fuzzy confusion. Then her eyes brightened, the fog clearing, and she smiled again.

"Oh yes. Mira. We were speaking of gargoyles." Mira sat back down and nodded, setting Gemma's teacup on the tile mosaic in the round table between them, depicting a young woman sitting demurely in a blooming meadow. "They are magical creatures. Very solitary. They like the high roofs of the manor houses to perch upon, but they conduct their business, hunting and mating, where human eyes cannot see them. We know very little about them. You must never touch one." She added the last as though just remembering something vital.

Mira perked up at this. "Why mustn't you touch them?"

It was Gemma who smiled indulgently now. "Because they are magical, Child."

"But what would happen?"

Gemma shrugged her frail shoulders. "How would I know? I haven't touched one now have I?"

"Then how do you know it's bad? Has anyone ever done it?"

Gemma stared at her for a long time and Mira had the strange feeling she was holding something back. "Other than the mages of old, I don't know of anyone that has, but that doesn't make it a good idea, Mira."

There was a knock on the door, two soft taps in quick succession followed by two slow hard raps. Mira grinned and Gemma nodded to her conspiratorially.

"By lord and by land, could that be my Danni?" Mira did a fair emulation of Gemma's voice, but Dannesk opened the door and chuckled, regarding her with no surprise.

"Mira, I thought I might find you here. Good morning, Gemma." He crossed the room and bent down to give Gemma a kiss on the cheek. The old woman flushed with delight and placed her hand over the hand he set on the arm of her chair, giving it a gentle squeeze. "Mira, Ina would like us to break fast together before we depart. Would you care to join us, Gemma?"

"No. At my age such excitement might put an end to me."

Dannesk shook his head and rolled his eyes to the ceiling.

Mira grinned, then she rose from her chair and knelt before Gemma again. "Are you sure you won't join us? Your company would be such a treat."

Gemma placed a dry hand on her cheek, soft and light as a butterfly wing, and smiled at her fondly. "No, it is too hard for me to wander around the manor these days. Go child. Go with my love."

Sudden tears stung Mira's eyes. This could be her last goodbye with her great aunt. "Thank you, Gemma." She reached up and hugged the old woman. Gemma kissed her on the cheek.

"Remember what I said," Gemma reminded her as they parted. She waved them away then and Mira could see the shine of tears in the woman's eyes.

Dannesk offered her his arm and she wrapped hers into it, resting her hand on his forearm as he led her from the room. He said nothing and she appreciated the silence. She focused on keeping her breathing slow and steady. On keeping her thoughts away from the fact that she was leaving behind everything she loved and the painful realization that she might not see Gemma again.

She wiped a tear away discreetly and tried not to be angry with her brother for following through with his side of their agreement.

By the time they arrived in the dining hall she had composed herself and managed to find a greeting smile for Ina. A moment after she had taken her seat, Kashi joined them. He scanned the table, noting that the only other set place was next to her, something she had also noticed. He hesitated for a moment, meeting her eyes apprehensively.

Was it so awful to be near her?

He donned his new stern expression then and took the seat. Her pulse raced at his nearness even as her chest ached from his hesitation. His shoulder was inches from hers, his hand so close to her own. She could feel the warmth of his body. Or was that merely the heat of a flush rising in her neck and face. She could only hope it wasn't as obvious as it felt. She looked down at the empty plate and tried to think of something else. The gargoyle. Her pending engagement. Gemma.

Suddenly she was blinking back tears and all she wanted was for Kashi to put an arm around her shoulders and hold her close.

A lot of help that was.

"Captain Marikashi. Lady Mira." Ina nodded to each of them in turn. "It is good that you could both be here. If we only had Shakari it would be like old times, though you weren't so serious back then," she added with a sideways glance for Kashi who shifted uneasily in his seat, his gaze falling to his plate as Mira's had only moments before. "I wish I could ride with you, but such a journey would not be safe for the baby."

"Of course not," Mira stated, jumping in to refocus her thoughts. "I too wish you could come with us. I hope that, if I stay at the Barik manor, I will be able to return to meet the new family member."

"Lord Valin seems a good man, I don't think he would deny such a simple request," Ina replied warmly.

"Enough of this talk, let us eat," Dannesk interjected. "We need to get on the road soon."

"Yes, of course. Sorry, my dear. It seems that I tend to run nostalgic when I am with child." Ina smiled to her two guests. "Please, eat."

•

Mira hadn't expected the flood of tears from Ina when they departed that morning. Certainly, they had been good friends in their youth, but all of that was so long ago now. The emotional parting left her drained and short-tempered, not at all ready for another long day on the road.

They traveled as they had before, only this time Kashi and Dannesk rode together, discussing weapons, warfare, and politics. Experience taught Mira that her thoughts rarely received welcome in such conversations even when they were relevant, so she rode behind them, a short distance in front of the rest of the escort. Kazue once again mirrored her position, her only companion now that the two men had each other's company to occupy them.

They rode this way for four days, Kazue always vanishing when they stopped for the night. The terrain gradually changed. Rolling farmland and pasture gave way to forest now and sometimes the trees grew so thickly around the road that the foliage blocked out her view of the gargoyle. At those moments, she felt so alone that she wanted to weep. Then the trees would thin and Kazue would still be there, somehow still perfectly paced with her. It was disconcerting how his being there affected her moods, as if his very being had become linked with hers. Even when she tried not to think of the strange creature, his presence lurked on the edge of her conscience, like a shadow in her mind.

When they didn't reach the next village before dark, Kashi made the call to stop at a small manor to avoid camping. He apparently thought Mira unequal to the hardship, which she found offensive, though she held her tongue. The lord and lady of the residence warmly welcomed them. They offered guest rooms to her and Dannesk. The rest of the escort, including Kashi, was offered space in the stables with the horses.

She lay awake long into the evening in the comfortable—if small—room, inexplicably restless, wondering where Kazue stayed at night. Here in the dense forest, he could hide almost anywhere. Perhaps he hunted at night. She hadn't seen him depart to hunt during the day, so it made sense that he must eat at night. If that were true though, when did he find time to sleep?

Unable to rest, she donned one of her travel dresses and rose, sneaking carefully through the small manor so as not to wake anyone. She had to sneak past two servant boys sleeping near the stove to get to the side door off the kitchen. Wrapped in threadbare blankets, the soot smeared youths didn't stir from their slumber when she tiptoed past and cautiously opened the door. It creaked and her heart jumped. One of the boys moaned in his sleep. When they showed no other signs of waking, she slipped out and eased the door shut behind her.

Once outside, she breathed deep of the cool night air, brisk and invigorating. She considered, for a moment, going to get Aiko to go for a night ride. Then she remembered that the soldiers and Kashi slept in the stable. The idea dissolved and instead she made her way carefully around the back of the manor toward the rose garden she had seen through the windows earlier. The trees had been cleared around the garden to allow for adequate sunlight. She walked there among the blooming roses in the moonlight and caressed the petals of the prettiest blooms, leaning down to breathe in their fragrance.

After an uncertain amount of time, she found herself standing at the back edge of the garden. The path tapered off to nothing where it met the edge of the forest.

Feeling almost as if she walked in a dream, barely in touch with her conscious mind, she followed the path to its end and beyond, entering the dark woods. She could see the trees as little more than tall, shadowed sentinels in the deep dark, but she continued to walk with purpose, weaving through them until she came upon a small, moonlit clearing. Kazue rested in the center of the clearing. When she emerged from the trees, the gargoyle opened his eyes. The moon reflected off those golden depths as he rose, giving them a surreal glow and making him appear every bit the magical creature Gemma claimed he was.

She paused, not sure what to do or why she had come here. How had she known where to find him?

The gargoyle stretched his massive, leathery wings and she drew in a breath, awed by how magnificent he looked. How could she have ever thought such a majestic creature ugly?

"Kazue," she whispered.

The gargoyle sat, regarding her with his serene gaze.

I must be dreaming, I would never go out into the night like this, alone. She walked toward him.

While sitting, his head rose a little higher than Aiko's did. Mira stopped a few feet from him and he cocked his head to one side, his eyes seeming to search her soul. Slowly, she knelt and held her hand out to him. Kazue regarded her, his manner so very regal, her pose of deference so very right. Then he stood and her heart sped up, racing with fear and excitement, her pulse pounding in her ears. The creature stepped toward her, stopping with his black nose only inches from her hand.

Without warning, the massive wings flared out and Kazue let out a powerful, startling roar that shook her to her bones. She cringed and pulled her hand back, panic surging through her system with dizzying force. Now she would die for her temerity, daring to approach the predator alone far from help. But Kazue folded his wings then and sat again. He bowed his head to her, his golden eyes closing. Her breath came in small gasps as she tried to compose herself, the fear in her blood as intoxicating as any strong wine.

When Kazue remained seated there, his head bowed and eyes closed, for a minute or more, she rose and dared to reach for him again. This time her fingers tentatively touched his brow. When nothing happened, she ran her fingers down between his eyes to his nose along skin dry and surprisingly smooth, almost like silk. She touched his brow again, caressing gently between his small horns this time, enjoying the feel of his silken skin, then she drew her hand away. Kazue opened his golden eyes and lifted his head to look at her.

"I don't understand. Why have you followed me?" She was surprised to find that tears ran down her cheeks. She did nothing to check them as she met that riveting golden-eyed gaze.

Kazue stood, his expression solemn and full of a wisdom she couldn't understand. He stepped up close, putting his face inches from hers. She was keenly aware of the tapered canines, but she didn't fear them. He sniffed her face, then his rough pink tongue darted out and licked a tear from her cheek. She sucked in a breath in surprise. The gargoyle turned and walked a few feet away then before jumping into the air, leaving her standing in the clearing alone.

A few seconds passed, frozen in time, then she heard the sounds of something crashing through the trees behind her. Startled, she spun around in time to see Kashi and three other soldiers break out into the clearing. The surprise on Kashi's face when he saw her almost made her want to laugh, but, after the encounter, she was just a little too bewildered to do so.

"What are you doing out here?"

The demand in his tone angered her. "I wanted some fresh air," she snapped.

"It was foolish to come out her alone. There could be dangerous animals out here, or dangerous men for that matter. We heard some animal cry out a moment ago."

"Yes. I heard it too," she replied, wiping the tears from her face before he got close enough to see them in the dark.

"Well?" He frowned at her and she scowled back.

"Well, what?"

Another soldier approached. "Captain, should we keep looking?"

Kashi nodded to the man. "Yes, check another ten yards out. Report to me if you find anything. Otherwise, return to the stable when you're done. I will escort the Lady Mira back to the manor house."

"I can find my way..." Kashi's cut her off with an angry look and she realized she shouldn't push, especially given that he was only worried for her safety. *I am precious cargo after all.*

She shoved aside the thought and forced a respectful tone, hoping to deflect his temper. "Thank you, my lord."

When the others left the clearing, he grabbed her wrist in a viselike grip and started to pull her back towards the manor. She twisted and wrenched her hand away. He spun around, his expression unreadable in the dark. When he started to reach for her again, she took a quick step back.

"You will not drag me back there like some misbehaving child."

"Isn't it appropriate?" He snapped in return.

He would never understand what brought her out here. She doubted he would even listen if she tried to explain. Would he never let her be an adult? He stood glaring down at her, so handsome in the dark, so splendidly gorgeous in his anger. So frustrating. "When will you see me for what I am?"

"And what is that?"

The anger in his glare cut into her and she closed her eyes to it, trying to fight back the rush of sorrow. The rising flood wouldn't be stopped, so she grabbed up her skirts and bolted past him. He called after her, but she didn't stop running until she was back at the kitchen entrance. She managed to choke back her sobs long enough to sneak back to her borrowed room without encountering anyone, though she heard sounds of movement around the house. Once safely back in the room, she threw herself face down on the bed. Grabbing a pillow, she wept into it to muffle the sound until she had cried herself dry, then she drifted off into a fitful sleep, dreaming of golden eyes.

The next day, Mira felt mysteriously refreshed, despite her nocturnal outing and the incident with Kashi. She expected to receive a lecture from Dannesk about her evening adventures. To her surprise, however, he said nothing and it became clear, as the day wore on, that Kashi hadn't mentioned it to him. He must have ordered his warriors not to bring it up either, or Dannesk would have known and she knew him well enough to know he wouldn't hold his tongue if he did.

Kazue flew overhead as always, but he felt closer somehow, as if he strode along next to Aiko rather than gliding along far above them. The fingers that touched him and the place where he licked her cheek tingled at times when she couldn't see him through the trees. The strange sensation ate away at her loneliness. She felt like she was a part of something more than just Mira Yukori, a lonely young woman on her way to meet her suitor. She started to hum to herself, her spirits soaring with the gargoyle.

"What has you so cheerful today?"

She glanced over and met her brother's eyes. He had slowed his mount enough that he rode beside her now.

"I'm simply enjoying the fresh forest air," she replied, finding that it was at least partly true.

"You seem to be enjoying the forest air a lot lately,"

Kashi grumbled. His night had clearly not left him refreshed.

She met his beautiful grey eyes with a steady gaze, bolstered by something that was both a part of her and apart from her. "And what is wrong with that, Captain?"

"Nothing." He shrugged, though the slight narrowing of his eyes belied the gesture. "Hopefully, you will enjoy the Barik air as much."

She winced inwardly at the sting of his words, but she'd grown tired of letting him get to her. She dredged up a sweet smile, though it made her feel nauseous. "I am sure I will, Captain."

Kashi drew back a fraction. If she didn't know better, she might believe her words hurt him. She shrugged and turned away.

Dannesk shook his head at them. "Why do I feel like I just witnessed a sword fight? When did you two grow so hostile toward each other?"

"Things change" Kashi turned to stare stonily ahead.

Dannesk shook his head at the other man then turned back to Mira. "Mira, we will arrive at Barik manor tomorrow. It would be more proper if you—"

"Arrived in the carriage," she cut him off. "Yes. I understand. I'll ride in the carriage tomorrow like a proper lady."

Dannesk's eyes widened. "Hm. This fresh air is bolstering your temper, dear sister." She narrowed her eyes in mock offense and he grinned. "On a more serious note, what do we do about your pet? I'm not sure he will be welcome."

"Kazue?" She couldn't see the gargoyle above the trees at that moment, but the faint tingle in her fingertips assured her of his presence. "I have no control over him, Danni."

Dannesk frowned. "I suppose not. I guess we shall see what happens."

"It will be fine," she assured him.

•

Dannesk looked apprehensive the next morning when they prepared to leave their campsite, which she had born without complaint, finding a certain freedom in sleeping out in the trees. She knew he expected her to argue over riding in the carriage, even though she had agreed to it the day before. She bid him good morning, pointedly ignoring Kashi, and climbed into the carriage without another word. Dannesk stared after her for a long moment, until one of the warriors handed him the reins to his mount. She watched out the window as he shook his head, looking puzzled, and mounted up. Aiko, they tied to the back of the carriage and started the last short stretch of their long journey.

When Kazue joined them, he did not fly above the carriage, but off to the side weaving through the trees where Mira could see him from her seat beside the window. She smiled a silent greeting to the gargoyle.

They moved back into open farmlands and hills shortly after starting the day and continued through much of the same all morning. Kazue rose up out of sight, taking advantage of the open sky. Not long after noon, they came in sight of the manor house of the Barik holding. It rose like a mountain from the landscape, easily the largest manor she had seen, with five substantial towers and several wings sprawling out from the massive central building. A sudden wash of apprehension gave her the intense and ridiculous desire to leap from the carriage and run away.

Kazue dove down into her line of sight, then he spun and shot back up into the sky. She poked her head out the window, her gaze now following his flight. He dove again, spiraling down, and let out a high-pitched cry nothing like the roar she had heard in the woods. The gargoyle then flew ahead, joining the throng that played on the currents around the manor house. Just as they had at Yukori manor, these gargoyles performed their strange greeting ritual. Then they started to dart at Kazue. At first, she thought they meant to attack him, but as it went on, it started to look more like a dance. Kazue rose high into the air and dove back down repeatedly while the gargoyles of Barik manor took turns darting out and spiraling around him.

Most of the escort watched the display with alarm that morphed to fascination. After a short period of this dancing each gargoyle, after spiraling once more around Kazue, flew up and perched on a tower or rooftop until only Kazue still flew. Then the golden-eyed beast joined the group on one of the closer towers and the gargoyles simply sat watching them as they entered the main courtyard. Even she felt a touch of apprehension at their sudden attention. Kazue she'd grown used to, a whole flock acting out of character was something else.

A group of people, mostly staff it appeared, stood lined up in front of the manor entrance. They all showed hints of uneasiness after the display, wringing their hands and darting quick glances from the man who stood before them watching the carriage roll in to the gargoyles perched above, but they held their places.

The man waiting for them was lean and tall, his neatly trimmed blond hair framing a narrow, but not unattractive, face. His dark blue eyes held a glimmer of sour humor, enhanced by the tight, bitter line of his lips. He wore dark blue pants and a snugly fitted vest and jacket with tails dipping down in the back. Both the vest and jacket were embroidered tastefully in black and the fine ivory shirt he wore beneath had a hint of a shine to it. In a complete package, he made a striking figure, but he stirred nothing more than sadness in Mira.

A groom took Dannesk's horse as he dismounted. Kashi dismounted and stood respectfully at his right shoulder, his face a stern mask.

"Lord Barik," Dannesk greeted the man with his typical exuberant handshake and fondness swelled in her for her brother.

"Lord Yukori," Valin returned the greeting with a smile, but Mira, watching discreetly from the shadows of the carriage, noted that the smile did not reach his eyes.

"This is Captain Marikashi. Lord Arkesh sent him and six of his men to bolster the escort to honor her time as his family's ward."

"Captain Marikashi," Lord Valin greeted with a respectful nod. Kashi returned the gesture with an abbreviated bow. "I thank you for helping ensure the Lady Yukori's safe arrival."

"It was my Lord Arkesh's pleasure," Kashi replied, his tone devoid of emotion.

A sting of sorrow met his dispassionate reply, though she knew the response had been appropriate.

Dannesk approached the carriage. She waited patiently until the door opened, then grabbed her skirts in one hand and took his offered hand with the other. She had donned an emerald gown with pale gold accents that she knew lit her green eyes on fire. Her mahogany hair she pulled up on the sides and wrapped into an emerald studded clip, with choice locks curling down along the side of her face. One of the few styles she could do without the assistance of a lady's maid that had a flattering effect on the shape of her face, bringing out her cheekbones. If she had to play the part of the bride-to-be, she saw no reason not to play it well.

The success of her efforts that morning lit approval in Lord Valin's eyes. The bitter line of his lips and the sour humor in his eyes both faded and, for an instant, he became truly handsome. The change only saddened her more, but she presented her most charming smile for him. Valin smiled in return and the expression reflected faintly in his eyes this time.

"This is the Lady Mira Yukori," Dannesk introduced, leading her by the hand to Lord Valin and passing her hand gently and gracefully over to him.

"My lord." She offered a respectful curtsy.

Valin held her hand in a light, almost tentative grip, his skin cold and dry. He bowed over her hand somewhat stiffly and brushed the back of it with a brief kiss. His lips were also cold.

"My lady, it is my pleasure to welcome you."

She rose from the curtsy. He kept her hand for a moment longer. The sour humor returned to his eyes.

"It seems the whole manor has turned out to greet you." He swept his other arm to indicate not the staff behind him, but the gargoyles still perched upon the outcrops of the manor.

He released her hand then and Mira let it sink to her side as she looked up at the rows of gargoyles. She found it surprisingly easy to spot Kazue among them, his horns swept back just so, his gold eyes glinting in the sunlight as he watched her.

She smiled.

"They please you?" Valin asked in a low voice.

She brought her gaze back to the men around her. Dannesk shifted his weight beside her, his gaze dropping to the ground to hide his discomfort. Kashi looked faintly amused, if anything, which she found a touch disconcerting.

She looked into the hard blue eyes she was fated to become accustomed to. Lies were not the way to start any relationship. "Yes, Lord Valin, they do please me."

Valin searched her face with his eyes, looking for something. She couldn't guess what he hoped to find in her, so she gazed back at him calmly, offering nothing.

A light breeze played with the loose locks of her hair, bringing with it the faintly salty musk of sweaty horses and an undercurrent of rich summer grass. A wind chime hanging from an iron post by one corner of the building, discolored with age, chimed, its sonorous tone creating a solemn music in contrast to the bright afternoon. The fingers that touched Kazue tingled and she battled the urge to look up at him again.

Finally, Valin gave up and looked away, his gaze coming to rest on her brother. "Please come inside. There are refreshments waiting. I am sure your long journey has been exhausting."

"That would be most appreciated." Dannesk replied, though he hesitated. "If it is no inconvenience to you, I would have Captain Marikashi join us. He represents the interests of Lord and Lady Arkesh."

Valin narrowed his eyes a fraction as he turned to regard Kashi, but his manner remained polite. "Of course. Do join us, Captain."

Valin offered his arm and she rested her hand upon it. As he led her into the manor, she stole another quick glance up at Kazue and the gargoyle stood and stretched his broad leathery wings. She worried for a moment that he would shriek again, or roar as he had in the woods, but he launched from the parapet and coasted over the courtyard. The other gargoyles followed, launching from their perches and taking to the air to dance upon the currents as they did at dusk and dawn. The muscles in Valin's arm tightened, the only evidence that their peculiar behavior bothered him.

She turned her attention to the manor house as they passed through the double doors into the interior. The rooms they walked through were spacious with heavy furniture sitting in the shadows of those dark, cold spaces. Everything about the place felt cold and disused, though meticulously tidy. It smelled of the oils used to care for the wood and the familiar hint of smoke from many candles and fireplaces. The faintest stench of illness snuck up beneath the other aromas.

The staff that dispersed throughout the grounds and the building watched them pass, their sideways glances distant and wary. Valin didn't appear to notice them. He led his guests to a large sitting room with an arrangement of maroon chairs and couches to sit upon and a table laden with choice delicacies and wine. One of the chairs held in its aged embrace a very old man with thinning grey hair and yellowish skin, the source of the sick smell that overpowered the food, killing what little appetite her nerves hadn't already done away with. His narrow face and hard blue eyes were a mirror image of Valin only elderly and frail.

"This is my father, Lord Ander Barik."

Valin introduced him with an unmistakable ire in his tone that unsettled Mira. She curtsied gracefully when Valin introduced her, but the old man waved his skeletal hand at each of them as one might try to wave away an annoying fly. They took seats around the table and accepted goblets of wine from the serving boy who Valin then abruptly dismissed. No longer hungry, Mira took one of the small cakes from the table and nibbled at it for the sake of appearances. As delicious as it was, she could barely force the tiny bites down.

"The last I had heard you were quite ill, Lord Barik," Dannesk stated carefully. "It is good to see you are up and around."

Valin looked uncomfortable and Mira could understand given the fierce look that his father flashed him.

"Yes. I am not quite ready to be stripped of my life or my title." The strained wheeze as he spoke added little conviction to his words.

Valin shifted in his seat. "Father..."

"Be quiet, Valin." Anger ignited a cold burn in Valin's eyes before he looked away, but he held his peace. "You see, Lord Yukori, I had intended a joining of my manor with that of Lord Johnis. As such, this insurrection comes as something of a surprise to me, but I will acknowledge the effort you put in to bringing your sister here. I would like to propose a trial period of sorts. I will allow your sister to remain here as my ward for three months, during which time I will determine if she is fit to be the next Lady Barik. If so, she will wed Valin at the end of the trial period. Otherwise, she will return, unharmed, to your care."

Rage flowed into Dannesk's eyes, his face reddening as Ander spoke. She touched his arm discreetly, reminding him to control his temper. Ander followed the movement with disapproving eyes and her own anger began to rise.

Dannesk took a deep breath. "This is highly irregular, Lord Ander. Not to mention, insulting to my sister and to our family name."

Pride rose in her at the self-control he managed. The slight edge to his voice said he wanted to explode, but only someone familiar with his temper would catch it. She heard the soft sound of Valin grinding his teeth though no one else appeared to notice it.

This wasn't at all what she expected—what any of them expected—in coming here. She had dreaded leaving what she loved behind to become a bride to a complete stranger. Now they wanted her to be the ward of a temperamental old man who thought her unworthy of his name. Prove herself? What exactly did he expect her to prove? She glanced at Dannesk and saw the torment in his face. Barik held great prestige as one of the wealthiest families in the region. It would be hard to find a better match to improve their family's standing, but to accept such an absurd proposal...

"This is what I offer. It is the only arrangement I will agree to, Lord Yukori, and I am still lord of this manor,"

Ander stated, turning away to cough weakly into his hand while Dannesk sputtered in a rather unbecoming way.

Refuse.

But to refuse the offer would destroy all negotiations and make a waste of their journey. It would be a most valuable alliance and she knew her brother well enough to know he wouldn't let it slip from his fingers without a fight. As much as he cared for her, he had a duty to make their name as strong as it could be.

She glanced at Kashi. He met her eyes and gave a slight shake of his head, his expression grim. With a sinking in her gut, she turned back to her brother, awaiting his decision.

"Your answer, Lord Yukori," Ander prompted.

She caught her breath when Kashi spoke into the lingering silence. "Perhaps, the esteemed Lord Ander would allow a compromise."

All eyes turned to Kashi, even the narrowed, cynical eyes of the elder Barik.

"What do you propose, Captain?"

"If someone were to stay here with Lady Mira— a chaperone to ensure that her virtue and position are not compromised—Lord Yukori might find this to be a more acceptable proposition."

"It seems a reasonable compromise, father," Valin interjected, his eyes never leaving Kashi. "You cannot expect them to turn her over without any sort of protection on their investment."

Ander looked thoughtful. "That seems a reasonable request. Lord Dannesk, what say you to this amendment?"

"Perhaps," Dannesk released the words hesitantly, as if it hurt to speak them. "Though it would need to be someone I truly trusted."

"I will do it," Kashi stated, his gray eyes still holding Valin's hostage.

Alarm pierced through Mira. Whatever Kashi had in mind, she could not imagine spending all her waking hours with him and not doing something to betray her feelings. It would be disastrous if Valin, or worse yet, Ander, discovered how she felt about the captain. The idea was utter madness.

"I don't know if that's such a good idea," Dannesk began.

Valin cut him off with a casual wave of his hand, tearing his gaze away from Kashi to look intently at Dannesk. "On the contrary, I think it is brilliant. Captain Marikashi appears to be a capable man. Neither you nor I would need to worry about the Lady Mira's safety while she is here, and, as you stated, he represents the interests of Lord and Lady Arkesh, whose ward she has been until now. It seems most appropriate that he should continue that role."

"What about your plans to return to Beikang?" Dannesk countered.

Kashi shrugged, avoiding Mira's eyes when she tried to catch his gaze. "I am not expected back until fall."

Dannesk seemed unable to speak. He looked at Mira and she shrugged helplessly, unable to think of anything to say. When she looked at Kashi again, he finally met her gaze, his jaw set with grim determination. She longed to know what he was thinking, but now wasn't the time to ask.

Finally, Dannesk exhaled, deflating. "I would trust you with my life, Captain Marikashi. I know I can trust you with my sister's. You, my dear sister," he paused, smiling fondly even as he shook his head at her. "You are proving to be quite a handful, but I suppose that is Lord Ander's problem for a time."

Ander chuckled, though there was no humor in the

sound. "No, Lord Dannesk, for now she seems to be Captain Marikashi's problem."

Lord Ander vanished to his rooms after they agreed upon the details of the arrangement. He paused several times on his way from the room to catch his breath. His illness had made him very weak and the discussion had apparently taken a heavy toll. Valin said very little the rest of the evening. He presented them with a grand feast, which Ander did not attend, then had his servants show them to their rooms for the night.

In the morning, Dannesk departed reluctantly and, although she tried to be strong, she could not stop the tears that ran down her cheeks. Kashi, who had already taken up his place as her silent shadow, said nothing. After Dannesk left, Valin showed them around the manor, though they spoke very little. Dannesk's departure left a hole inside her and Valin was even more distant today than he had been when they first arrived. Perhaps his father's treatment of him the day before still burned his pride.

Though it expanded the lonely hollow within her, the lack of conversation suited. She took careful note of where the tower accesses were located as they toured the vast halls. They gave Kashi a room across from hers, which made her uncomfortable. It also made her worry that sneaking out to the towers wouldn't be as easy as she had hoped, but on the fourth night, after a lonely day spent perusing the gardens and the library with Kashi gazing on in stony silence, she tried anyway.

Valin remained absent most of the time, so she had taken the first few days to get to know the servants of the manor and their routines. She knew when and where they slept and when and where they roamed when awake. She memorized the hallways between her room, the nearest tower access, and every possible hazard between the two. With a candle in hand, for she felt confident enough in her gathered information to take one, she snuck quietly from her room to the tower access, practicing excuses in her head along the way in the event that someone did catch her.

Once safely on the tower with no sign of having alerted anyone to her activities, she sat precariously perched on one merlon and gazed out into the moonlit night. The moon, while only a sliver, seemed bright and close in the dark sky.

The sound of vast wings behind her alerted her to Kazue's arrival. The gusts created by his landing lifted her hair and sent a chill through her. She hadn't been alone in the gargoyles presence since the night in the forest. She needed the comfort that he brought her tonight.

She turned and hopped down from the merlon. Kazue walked up within a few feet of her before sitting and watched her with his brilliant eyes reflecting the silver moonlight. She knelt as she had in the clearing and reached a hand out to him. Kazue's thin lips curved, almost as if smiling. He stood and stepped toward her to push his head into her hand. Giddy warmth filled her and she smiled, delighted.

"I don't understand you, but I am so very glad you're here." She started to cry as she finished speaking and the gargoyle pressed closer.

Yearning for comfort, she wrapped her arms around the large creature's neck and wept upon his silken skin. Kazue sat patiently, folding his wings around her, and let her cry.

Mira woke slowly, the cold hardness of the stone breaking through her sleep. She became aware that she lay curled against the side of something large and warm. What her sleep muddled mind had first taken for a blanket was a large, leathery wing. A confusing mixture of alarm and contentment turned to quick clarity. She had fallen asleep on the tower curled up against Kazue.

"Mira!" Kashi's voice rang out, tight with panic.

Kazue lifted his wing, freeing her to rise and letting in the crisp cold of early morning. As soon as she moved clear of him, Kazue rose and spun away from Kashi, leaping into the air and out over the courtyard. Kashi ran to her and grabbed her hands, holding them out as he looked her over frantically.

"I am fine, Kashi," she protested, pulling her hands back when he released them.

"I thought that beast had…" His voice trailed away. Careful fingers brushed her hair back then he put a warm hand against her cheek.

Her thoughts spiraled into oblivion when she saw the fear in his eyes, fading before a vast relief as he realized she was unharmed. His was the look of someone who thought they had lost someone important. Elation spread through her chest.

He met her eyes then and drew away suddenly.

"What were you doing?" he snapped, his voice and manner becoming stern and distant again.

She closed her eyes for a second, fighting a wave of hurt and frustration. She began to brush out her wrinkled skirts with rough, angry strokes of her hands. "I came up for some air and fell asleep."

"With that thing? It could have killed you."

She narrowed her eyes at him. "If it meant to it would have done so long before now and you know it." Taking a deep breath too cool her temper, she met his gray eyes. "Does anyone else know I'm not in my rooms?"

"No," he replied, his expression sobering. "I thought it best not to raise alarm. I was relatively certain of where I would find you."

"Good." She couldn't imagine either Ander or Valin being tolerant of such peculiar nocturnal activities.

"Promise me you won't do this again."

She glanced out the direction Kazue had gone and shook her head. "I will not promise. I have one comfort in this place. Though it may be an unconventional one, I will not give it up."

"Only one?"

Her frustration and misery charged back in mercilessly at the touch of hurt in his tone. "Yes one. You're leaving."

Not waiting for his response, she hurried to the ladder and climbed down. She probably smelled horrible after sleeping against the gargoyle, though she hadn't noticed the creature smelling all that bad now that she thought about it. In fact, it had an almost pleasant odor, like a horse only with a sweeter undertone, like warmed honey. Her body was stiff and achy from the hard surface though. She thought she might avoid sleeping on the tower in the future just for the sake of her poor muscles.

Kashi followed her to the door of her room and stood still waiting there when she reemerged after freshening up and changing into a clean gown. She nodded to him curtly and started down the hallway. He made no gesture in response, but simply fell in a few steps behind on her right. They broke fast in tense silence. When he wasn't frowning at her, she watched him sadly. Why did he have to wait until now to give some indication that he still cared for her? He could hardly have chosen a more inconvenient time. However, nothing he had done really betrayed any deep feelings. It was probably just fear that the investment he protected might have suffered damage.

Still, the feel of his hand against her face seemed burned into her skin. She touched the cheek and sighed.

He scowled at her.

She gave him a snide look, then she turned her chair to face away from him. Her mind drifted back to her conversation with Gemma. The old woman had told her she must never touch a gargoyle. Well, she had gone far beyond simply touching one, but she could feel no ill effects from the contact, just the innocent tingle that she sometimes felt in her fingertips and the cheek he had licked. Now that she thought about it, she also felt a tickle on the back of her neck now when she thought of him.

A sound drew her attention and she turned to see Valin standing in the doorway. He hadn't joined them during a meal since the morning Dannesk left.

"What a pair of sour faces. You two fit in well around here." He shook his head as he strode into the room.

She blushed and conjured up a smile for him. "Good morning, Lord Valin."

"Lord," Kashi greeted, giving a sharp nod.

Valin nodded once in turn. "Captain," he greeted with equal shortness, then he turned to Mira and pulled a soft smile. "My lady."

"Mira is fine." She offered him the seat next to her with a small wave of her hand.

"It is not fine," Kashi remarked sharply.

She flushed with rage and stood, ready to lash out at him, but Valin touched her arm and she stopped herself. They were bickering like disenchanted lovers. No good would come of that behavior. Without a word, she dropped back down into her seat and glared at the reflection of a candle in the glossy tabletop. Valin sat next to her and arranged some food on his plate before turning a stony gaze on Kashi.

"Captain Marikashi, I think I missed the part where it was decided that your purpose here was to antagonize Lady Mira."

She couldn't hold in a smirk of bitter satisfaction as Kashi tightened his hands briefly into fist, struggling with his temper. His expression changed swiftly from furious to vaguely humiliated before settling into a familiar indifference.

"You are right, Lord Valin. I apologize for my conduct."

"It is not I you should apologize to," Valin returned.

Lord Barik was winning points, with her at least.

"I'm sorry, my lady" Kashi undermined the sincerity of the words with his bland tone.

She bit down upon the urge to reach across the table and dump his water in his lap. Instead, she settled for staring at her half-eaten food, longing for the serenity she had found on the tower with Kazue not so many hours ago. Valin picked at his plate and a faint curious smile played at the corners of his mouth. After a bit, he cleared his throat and looked at her.

"I'm sad to say that father has taken a turn for the worse again," he stated, his tone anything but sorrowful.

"Oh, that's too bad." She cringed, realizing how flippant she had sounded.

Valin merely chuckled. "Yes, that's about how I feel about it. Would you care to go for a ride? I can show you more of our lands. I could even have the cook pack food for a picnic. Enough for three," he added, when Kashi looked up at them.

She brightened at the prospect. She hadn't taken Aiko out since their arrival. The mare would be eager to get out and stretch her legs. "I would enjoy that, my lord."

After finishing the meal with a renewed appetite, she changed into a split riding skirt. Sidesaddle never appealed to her and she avoided it outside of the most formal occasions. If all went well, she would see how good a rider Lord Valin was. It would be nice if they at least had a fondness for riding in common.

She pointedly ignored Kashi as he followed her down to the stable. Valin waited for them there and his mount, a lean roan mare, stood saddled along with both Aiko and Kashi's gelding. They mounted wordlessly. Valin led the way out of the courtyard and away from the manor, his mare jigging sideways with boundless energy. When they had passed beyond the main structure and the extensive stables, he stopped and turned to face them.

"Care to speed up a bit?"

"Certainly," she replied, Aiko starting to dance about in response to her anticipation.

"I'll let you set the pace then, Lady Mira."

Valin swept his hand to direct her onward. She grinned and let Aiko go, squeezing her sides firmly. The little mare surged forward and the other two horses lunged after her. In moments, they pelted down the road at an intoxicating pace, all three horses in a row vying for the lead. A few others on the road, mostly workers from the manor, moved off to the side when they heard the horses pounding down on them like the roll of thunder.

She glanced over at Valin. He grinned like a fool, his eyes shining with tears caused by the wind they created. He looked freer and happier than she had seen him any other time since her arrival. His father's presence hung like a stone around his neck. Without it, he changed to a different man.

Glancing to her other side, she caught Kashi looking at her. His smile stripped away the seriousness that he wore like armor, making him look as young as he was for a moment, younger perhaps. She smiled back, trying to hide the sudden aching in her chest. Leaning lower, she urged Aiko faster, then held on as the fleet little horse pulled on some hidden reserve and began to surge ahead. The tall, lean mare Valin rode pulled ahead a few moments later, then he began to slow her and they followed his example, bringing the horses down gradually to a walk.

As the sound of the horses pounding hooves diminished, another sound caught their attention. Valin's hand dropped to his dagger as he pulled in his mount and looked up. She moved Aiko in close and touched his hand. When he looked at her, she shook her head. He looked askance at Kashi and she followed his gaze.

"The beast follows her," Kashi stated simply.

"But why? What does it want?" Valin looked bothered as he turned his mare and frowned at the creature that now circled above them.

"He doesn't mean any harm," she said, pleading with her eyes and her soft tone.

Again, Valin looked to Kashi for verification and she wanted to push him off his horse for refusing to accept her words.

Kashi met her eyes for a few seconds, looking as though he had to swallow something bitter. "It really does seem to be harmless, at least as far as Lady Mira is concerned."

She smiled her gratitude at his dubious defense of Kazue. It was more than she had hoped for after their encounter that morning. Valin watched the gargoyle for a long moment, turning his mount to follow his flight, then he released his dagger hilt and gave her a long unreadable look.

"Very well. Come. The meadow over the rise backs up to a lake. It's a beautiful spot to stop for a bit, though it really does lose much of its romantic appeal with you along, Captain." He gave them both a crooked smile then and urged his mare forward.

Kashi cut Mira off before she could follow and leaned toward her, his grey eyes fired with intensity. "If I am wrong about that beast and something happens to you, I will chop it into a thousand pieces and hang myself from the highest tower in reprisal for my error."

Not meaning to, she laughed and he drew back, clearly offended. "I'm sorry, but, by lord and by land Kashi, I hope it never comes to that. Such drama." She accidently snorted, which only made her laugh all the harder, doubling over in her saddle.

Kashi exhaled with a faint growl and turned away to ride after Valin.

Her humor waned after a moment and she looked up at the creature that circled above her. What if he followed her everywhere? Trips into the nearby town could be a little awkward, not that she was likely to do many of those. What if she were called to court? As ward or wife to Lord Barik, that wasn't so unlikely.

With a troubled frown, she urged Aiko after the other two.

A beautiful meadow stretched out just over the rise as Valin had said. Carpeted with thick green grass and patches of clover. A dense stand of maples and other less familiar trees, heavy with summer foliage, wrapped around two sides of the meadow leading up to a lake. A small stream ran across one edge of the meadow into the lake, adding its sleepy, serene murmuring to the music of birdsong coming from the trees.

They let the horses graze and spread out a selection of food the manor's cooking staff had prepared on a blanket. Just as they settled onto it, Kazue landed by the edge of the stream. The horses, accustomed to the presence of gargoyles at the manor, showed little interest in him, but both Kashi and Valin shifted their positions to make their weapons more accessible and keep an eye on the large predator.

For her part, Mira was surprised that he joined them. Aside from that morning's incident on the tower, he had kept his distance when other people were around.

"Welcome Kazue," she called softly to the gargoyle. An ear twitched on the horned head and he gave her a brief glance as though returning the greeting.

"She named it?" Valin asked incredulously.

"She names everything," Kashi answered.

They sat in silence for a time, all three watching Kazue as he drank from the stream and then circled three times before lying down. He rested his head on his paws and watched Mira with his golden eyes, not acknowledging her companions in any way.

Valin shifted again and cleared his throat. "I understand that you two grew up together," he remarked, his gaze still riveted upon the gargoyle.

"Mostly," Kashi said, adding, "and what a trial that was."

She looked at him, prepared to express proper outrage at his words, but he smiled and winked at her.

"I'm not the difficult one," she retorted. Plucking a grape from the bundle on the blanket, she threw it at him.

Kashi brought up a hand, snatching the flung fruit from the air, and popped it into his mouth. "Thanks."

She rolled her eyes theatrically, though inside she overflowed with delight at the friendly banter. It was so very reminiscent of the way they had been before he left for the academy. Valin was regarding them both with a distinct look of envy after the brief show of comfortable familiarity, but she only cared that Kashi appeared to have mostly abandoned his stern emotional armor back at the manor.

"Hopefully, she'll not be such a trial as a wife." The hint of strain in Valin's voice caught her attention, forcing her to recognize that edge of jealousy.

Kashi's expression turned more serious then and she longed to kick Valin for ruining the mood, but he couldn't understand what that brief levity between them meant to her. Better that he didn't, she supposed.

"I wouldn't count on that," Kashi stated, regarding her thoughtfully now.

"That isn't nice, Kashi." She found it all too easy to sound as though she'd been hurt by his words.

Kashi gave Valin a sympathetic, disarming smile. "Any woman who arrives at your gate in the company of a gargoyle is likely to be a challenge at best."

She met his eyes, disconcerted by the hint of remorse she saw in them when he glanced her way. His gaze quickly moved on to Kazue, who continued to watch her.

She choked down her longing and smiled tolerance at them both. "You know too little about gargoyles to judge such things."

With that statement, she rose and walked down toward the lake past where Kazue lay. She could sense the tension increasing in her companions when the gargoyle rose and joined her, walking the rest of the way to the edge of the lake by her side like an enormous dog. She knelt at the water's edge and looked at her reflection, wavering on the ripples caused by a gentle breeze. Kazue sat next to her, his reflection joining hers in the lazy lapping of the water. She reached a hand up to rest it on the soft skin of his shoulder and exhaled, trying to release the sorrow in her chest.

"I have never heard of such a thing," Valin remarked, a mix of awe and unease tightening his voice.

"Nor have I," Kashi replied. "If anyone were ever going to befriend one of the beasts though, it somehow doesn't surprise me that she would be the one."

They lowered their voices then, but somehow, she could still hear them despite the distance. Perhaps the acoustics of the meadow carried them to her. She sat quiet on her heels and listened, trailing the fingers of her other hand in the cool water.

"Lord Valin?"

An edge of serious tension in Kashi's voice captured her full attention and she had to fight a twinge of guilt at eavesdropping. Kazue's muscles shifted under her hand, his presence warm and comforting.

"Yes, Captain." Valin sounded cautious, equally aware of the change in Kashi's tone now that she had left them.

"You would not mistreat her?" It was voiced as a question, but with a hint of warning in the tone.

"Why the concern?"

The evasive reply made her cringe. Kashi appreciated directness. He had little tolerance for chasing answers, especially with a question such as that.

"That isn't your concern," Kashi growled.

"Actually," Valin countered, "I think it is. But to answer your question, no, I would not ever mistreat her."

"You give your word?"

Valin's voice opened up to a bottomless sorrow when he replied. "I do."

A single tear ran down her cheek. She watched it in the reflection until it dripped from her chin and fell into the lake. It created a tiny ring of ripples in the reflection. She met her own gaze in the reflection and started. The eyes staring back at her were bright gold. She jumped back from the reflection in alarm. Kazue didn't react to her panic. His calm gaze moved to follow her patiently. Behind her, Kashi and Valin had both risen, but they were hesitant to approach with Kazue so close.

"What's wrong, Mira?"

"Nothing, Kashi." She placed a hand to her chest, feeling the frantic beat of her heart. "I was startled by a bee."

Both men chuckled.

"You certainly startled us," Valin replied.

"Women," Kashi said with apparent exasperation and Valin laughed his agreement.

She avoided looking at them, afraid they might see what she had seen in the water. Slowly, she returned to the spot next to Kazue and knelt again. Steeling herself, she looked into the water. Her eyes looked back, now a brilliant green. The same color they had always been. She exhaled her relief and looked into the eyes of Kazue's reflection. Gold, molten and rich, looked back at her. Perhaps the reflections had mixed in the water somehow.

Why me? There was no answer in those gold depths no matter how long she stared into them, not one that she could understand at least.

Frustrated, she stirred the water with her fingers, destroying the reflections, then she returned to the blanket and sat across from Valin and Kashi. Kazue returned to his prior resting place to watch her.

"So, what does a gargoyle feel like?" Valin asked.

She glanced up suspiciously, wondering if he teased, but his expression held genuine interest. "Like silk, actually." She smiled at a butterfly that landed on her knee. "At least Kazue's skin is amazingly soft to the touch. I can't speak for any other gargoyles."

"Really?" Kashi cocked his head and raised one disbelieving brow at the big predator. "They don't look soft."

"Yes, Kashi, really. I didn't expect it either." She didn't want to talk about the gargoyle now. The whole thing confused her and made her feel almost unbearably different from them.

Valin pressed on though, apparently fascinated by the subject.

"So how did this happen?"

She glanced at Kazue, his gold eyes watching steadily, unblinking. Turning back, she found both men watching expectantly. "I don't know. He looked at me one day when I was watching the gargoyles from the tower at Arkesh and he has been following me since I left." She fiddled with a grape stem. "Can we go back now? I'm tired."

"Are you all right, Mira?"

She couldn't bear the concern in Kashi's voice, not now. "Yes, I just…" She met his eyes, wondering if he would betray her secret. "I didn't sleep well."

Kashi said nothing, though he narrowed his eyes a touch. He might know where she slept last night, though he did not know how soundly she had actually slept there.

"It is the new residence, my lady. You'll get used to it in time. Help me pick up and we shall head back."

She smiled weary thanks at Valin as they rose. They rode back to the manor in silence with Kazue's cooling shadow hanging over them, his wing beats slow and dispirited. He did not play on the air currents as he usually did, and his lack of animation only served to deepen her melancholy. Valin, his mood also subdued now, bid her rest well when they returned to the manor, disappearing into its cavernous depths. Kashi followed her up to the door of her room.

"Mira." He spoke as she opened the door to her chamber. She paused, tempted to ignore him. After a few seconds, she made herself turn back. "Perhaps you should reconsider spending time with that creature. You seem troubled."

"It is you that troubles me, Kashi, not Kazue. I find your presence… confusing. Please, let me be for a while."

At any other time, such candor might have shocked her into embarrassment, but she turned away from him now, without the energy to care what he thought of her words, and closed the door firmly on him.

Kashi stared at the closed door, probably the least substantial of the barriers standing between them. He touched the ornate scrollwork handle that her hand had warmed only a moment ago. She had all but admitted her affection for him. Not that he ever really doubted that she had some liking for him, but to have it rise so close to the surface, beautiful and untouchable, caused a longing within him too painful to brush aside. He would be doing her a disservice if he let anything come of it. With a great force of will, he took his hand from the handle and turned down the long, lonely hall.

He didn't much feel like retiring to his rooms yet and he doubted that Mira was in any danger of coming to harm in her room. At that moment, he posed the biggest threat to her virtue. He thought of the gargoyle and their conversation in the meadow. She had been right, he knew too little about gargoyles to make judgements. To be honest, he could not think of anyone who did know much of anything about them. Someone had to know something about the beasts.

With a new sense of purpose, he made his way down to the manor's library on the ground floor.

The library, one of the finest collections he had seen outside of Beikang, waited unoccupied. A few moments after his arrival, a serving boy scuttled in and Kashi requested a fire to warm the room and a drink to warm himself. Once the fire burned, giving warmth and welcome to the big empty room, and strong drink warmed him on the inside, he began searching the towering shelves in earnest. He had no clue where one might find information on the peculiar creatures. On a whim, he picked up a book on lore and began to flip through the pages.

"I would not have taken you for a scholar, Captain."

He continued to flip through the pages of the book. "They teach more than combat at the academy, Lord Valin, you should know that."

He caught the other man's shrug out of the corner of his eye. Valin picked up a volume and flipped to a random page. He seemed to be involved in the book for a moment, so Kashi waited patiently for him to express the real purpose of his visit. He didn't believe Valin had coincidentally wandered down here at this exact time out of a desire to do some reading of his own.

"She is a rather remarkable woman, isn't she?"

"Who?" Kashi skimmed a page, pretending distraction.

"Don't play daft, Captain. The Lady Mira."

He chuckled. "Remarkable? That is one way to describe her I suppose."

"Oh?" Valin closed the book and raised his brow at Kashi, who flipped through several more pages, though he had stopped even trying to read them. "How would you describe her?"

Kashi turned to face him now, lowering the book. "If you are looking for an evaluation of your bride-to-be, Lord Valin, you have come to the wrong place. You will have to discover who she is on your own. If there is something else you wish to ask or say, please do me the honor of getting to the point."

"Why did you stay?"

Kashi opened his mouth to reply and Valin held up a hand to stall him.

"I want the real reason. Any one of the Arkesh soldiers could have acted as her guardian, and it might have been more appropriate. This is rather a low assignment for someone of your rank. A waste of your skills, I would think. You must have a more personal interest."

He closed the book and returned it to the shelf. "It should come as no surprise that she is dear to me, Lord Valin. She was practically raised as my sister. I would not see her hurt and, to put it lightly, your father's welcome wasn't especially reassuring."

"I can't argue that." He dusted off the cover of the book he had taken down before putting it back on the shelf as well. "And yet, I sense there is more to it than that. I am rarely wrong about such things."

Kashi felt the lash of his temper trying to rise and forced it down. "The Lady Mira is an extraordinary woman, Lord Valin. If you can see that much, you will convince your father of it and marry her. If not, you are a fool. What, other than that, matters here?"

Valin hesitated before his demanding gaze. He seemed at a loss for something to say. They both knew that Kashi's wishes played no part in Mira's future. It was Valin who currently had the most control over that.

Kashi nodded, picked up his drink, and finished it in a gulp. He set the cup firmly back on the table. "Very well then. Good evening to you, Lord Valin." He turned sharp on the ball of his foot and left the room, his original purpose abandoned.

•

In the morning, Kashi took time to clean up and prepare for the day before crossing the hallway to knock gently on Mira's door. She was usually up and around by now. It wasn't Mira, however, who answered, but rather the ladies' maid Barik had provided for her.

"I'm sorry, Captain Marikashi, but Lady Mira is not feeling well and will be staying in her chambers today."

He tried to peer around the woman into the room. She shifted her stance to block his view, doing so remarkably well for a woman of such slight build.

"Is there anything I can do for her?"

"Thank you, Captain, but I have seen to her needs and will continue to do so."

"Perhaps I could ask her."

The woman said nothing, nor did she move out of his way.

He stood there for a moment longer and the woman held his gaze, her manner somehow subservient and authoritative. In his experience, only a woman could master the art of being both at once. "Please pass along my well wishes. If she does need anything, don't hesitate to call on me."

"For certain." the woman vanished back into the room, shutting the door in his face.

As he turned away, he saw Valin heading up the hallway toward him. The other man stopped a few feet away and looked askance at the closed door.

"Apparently, Lady Mira is not feeling well and will be staying in her rooms today," Kashi informed him.

"Ah, so we are being snubbed."

He glanced at the door then back at Valin, feeling a welcome spark of camaraderie for the man. "It would seem that way."

"Well, perhaps you would care to spar with me then?"

Kashi grinned, the spark becoming a small flame. "If you're up for it."

He followed Valin to the practice grounds nestled between the manor's west wing and the stables. The morning was overcast and cool, which made it a perfect time for practice. They both donned minimal armor in an attempt to avoid dire injury and grabbed blunted steel swords from the rack. Given his certainty that they each harbored some jealousy toward the other where Mira was concerned, the steel blades posed a risk, but neither gave the wooden swords more than a passing glance. They were both in the mood to take the chance.

The practice field was a large dirt arena with a rough wood rail around it that sported damage from innumerable sword strikes. As soon as they faced one another, Valin charged him. Kashi hadn't risen to the rank of captain by letting overzealous opponents catch him by surprise. He parried the attack and spun Valin off, allowing the other man's momentum to carry him past. Valin had anticipated the move though, and used Kashi's spin-off to twist himself around and parry the return attack. The intensity in Valin' eyes confirmed his suspicion that the other man held a grudge against him and he did not have to ask why.

They fought with passion and Kashi narrowly avoided numerous strikes that would have left him hurting for several days. He had no choice but to mirror the other man's intensity to keep him at bay. His own resentment threatened to take control of the fight. Valin would wed the woman he loved, and that didn't exactly endear him to the man.

Valin charged him again as he had the first time, but this time he made a quick last-minute dodge to evade Kashi's block, a move that might have succeeded… against a novice. He was far from a novice. He started to move into the block Valin expected then he twisted out at the last second and swung around, striking the other man hard across the ribs. Valin grunted in pain and staggered, but he caught himself and came back at Kashi again. The pain seemed to focus him rather than building upon his reckless anger and a reluctant respect for the other man took root in Kashi.

They exchanged a volley of attacks, then Valin dropped into a more defensive stance. Kashi suspected that he was either tiring or trying to lull him into thinking so. He decided to give it a chance and came at him with a series of more powerful, aggressive strikes. A painful blow to the upper arm corrected the mistake and Kashi fell back again. He grinned then, exhilarated by the fight, and noticed that Valin wore a similar grin, oblivious to the sweat dripping down his face.

They fought a while longer, both beginning to show signs of fatigue, then Valin stepped back into a defensive posture and signaled a stop. Kashi set his blunted blade point in the dirt and leaned on the weapon, breathing hard. Valin mirrored his posture, though whether the imitation was intentional or not, he couldn't tell.

"You don't have to fight me for her," Kashi stated as he started to catch his breath.

"On the contrary, Captain," Valin answered, breathing just as hard, "as long as you are here, I am afraid I do. Arrangements may have been made for her hand, but her heart is another matter. She sees nothing but you. Well, you and that beast."

Kashi glanced toward the looming manor that hid her away from him, not sure how to respond to the observation. If it were untrue, he would not hesitate to say as much, but he couldn't say for certain either way.

"At least I don't have to defeat you at the sword for her. It seems you have me outclassed in that."

He grinned, turning back to Valin. "I think," he said, rubbing his aching arm, "that you underestimate yourself."

"Come," Valin made a half-hearted sweep across the dirt with his sword, leaving a faint line in its wake. "Join me for a drink."

Kashi hesitated for a minute. Part of him wanted to despise this man for getting to have what he so desperately wanted, but he found that there wasn't much left to feed that hatred. Valin seemed a decent man and he fought well, which won him Kashi's respect if nothing else. More importantly, he'd given his word that he wouldn't mistreat her.

"With pleasure," he said finally and followed Valin back to the weapon room to discard the swords and armor.

•

For the next few days, Mira stayed in her chambers, requesting that her meals be brought there. It was the only way she could think of to avoid Kashi, for he would never dare come into her private chambers against her will. The third evening of her self-imposed isolation, Valin sent a servant to invite her company for supper. She reluctantly accepted, staying in her room until the time came to go down to the dining room with Kashi as her silent, brooding shadow.

Valin looked quite pleased to see them both, but his smile disintegrated the moment his father, apparently feeling better again, joined them. The unpleasant man ordered a place setting added and Valin retreated into glowering silence.

"I understand you have been pouting in your rooms, child," Ander remarked over the meal.

She kept her eyes on her plate so the old lord would not see the hatred in them. "I have not been feeling well, my Lord," she replied with forced civility.

"You should find yourself a healthy bride." Ander chuckled, looking at Valin to see his reaction.

A loud screech stung her ears as Valin shoved his chair away from the table and stood. He met Mira's eyes for a quick moment then strode brusquely from the room. She despised him then; despised him for not defending her and for leaving her there to face his father alone, or as good as alone. Kashi could say nothing without the risk of Ander having him removed from the manor, which would do her no good.

She pulled her napkin from her lap, wiped her mouth delicately, and set it on the table next to her plate. "Please excuse me, my Lord, I haven't much appetite this evening."

"Go then. It is more pleasant without you."

She said nothing, wary of her own anger as Kashi rose to accompany her. She stopped at the doorway. Turning back, she glared daggers at the old man, but spoke in her most polite tone.

"Be well, Lord Ander."

The bitter old man didn't look up, he just waved her away with a careless hand. She spun on one foot and left. That night, she snuck up on the tower and sat with Kazue for a long time. The gargoyle curled up on the cold stones and rested his head on her thigh. She found the creature's presence immensely calming. Her anger, her sadness, all of it faded away as she sat there. Such a glorious serenity that she did not doubt came entirely from Kazue. Did he absorb her angst or did his serenity simply overpower it?

Perhaps it didn't matter. All that mattered was that he remained for her, even though she had shunned him with the others during her self-imposed isolation. She swore to him that she would not do so again.

Kashi read over the missive that had arrived that morning again and looked up at Valin. The other man shifted, his face a tortured mask of distress. Kashi couldn't help wondering if it was the assault on the kingdom that upset the man so much or just his father's refusal to let him go to the front lines.

Ander Barik finally recovered from his coughing fit. "You are needed here. There are things to do in preparation for my passing. You have a duty to this family."

The slight narrowing of Valin's eyes said that passing couldn't possibly come quickly enough.

"Do you hear me, Valin."

Valin didn't look at the older man. "Everyone in the manor hears you, Father." He snapped. "I will fulfill my duty to the family. Now, if you will excuse us."

Not waiting for a response, Valin left the room and Kashi followed.

For Kashi's part, this made his own inevitable departure less complicated. He had to go now. Nothing could change that.

"You will keep her safe." He voiced it as a command rather than a question as he matched the other man's fast angry strides.

Valin stopped and turned to face him. "I swear it."

Kashi met his eyes and, satisfied with what he saw, he returned the nod. "I'll gather my things. I will be leaving within the hour."

Valin scowled. "I wish I were going with you. My father is a fool."

"He is indeed, but then we would have to figure out what to do with Mira. I would not leave her here alone with him."

"Neither would I," Valin agreed. "I'll have the kitchen staff put food together for your journey."

"Thank you," Kashi replied with genuine appreciation.

The Lord Valin might harbor a misplaced jealousy toward him, given that he could never pose a true threat for Mira's hand, but he didn't seem a bad man. Kashi could not decline the summons, but Mira would be safe so long as Valin remained here.

He folded the missive and headed to his room where he pulled his things together quickly and stuffed them in the saddlebags he had left lying in a corner of the room since his arrival. When that task was complete, he slung the bags over his shoulder and left the room. Only one rather daunting task remained before he could leave. It might be better to leave and have Valin tell her after he was gone, but he couldn't do that to her, or to himself. He might not ever see her again and certainly not before she was wed to Valin.

With a burning sense of dread, he crossed the hall and knocked on her door. When no one answered, he glanced up and down the hall for any observers, then opened the door and stepped inside. The chamber waited empty, as he thought it might. Leave it to Mira to go missing when he had so little time to seek her out. He walked back into the hall and stood there considering what he knew about her and where she might be and began his search in the most likely place.

•

That morning, Mira had returned to her rooms to break fast and declare herself unwell again, then she snuck back up on the tower. Kazue joined her there for a time, then rose and left her, flying off into the distance when the sound of hoofbeats pounded into courtyard far below. She stood and went to lean on the parapet, watching the distant horizon where he had vanished. Perhaps he had gone to hunt, but she wished he had not left. After a few minutes, she went back down into the manor and made her way to an unfurnished chamber she had discovered that looked out over the courtyard to see who had arrived. A strange horse stood before the manor, slick with sweat, its sides heaving. Someone had brought it food and water. The unfamiliar animal, clearly driven hard, made her uneasy. An urgent message must accompany such a visitor.

"Mira."

She didn't turn. Kashi's tone caused dread to sweep through her like some beast, catching its talons in her throat.

"Mira, Hishae has broken the peace treaty. The queen is calling in military from all the holdings. Shakari will have already gone with his troops. The messenger said the Yukori troops have also gone, though your brother received a stay of service for now because of Ina's pregnancy. My name specifically is called out in the missive to Arkesh. I am a captain in her army. I must go." The words came fast. His voice apologetically soft and yet charged with a sense of urgency. "Valin will look after you."

Dread wrapped bands of cold around her heart, slowly squeezing in. "Isn't Valin going?"

"Lord Ander is requiring that he stay to deal with the transition of the manor."

"If he would only have the good grace to pass on." She gripped the windowsill tight, the wood solid and strong under her hands as she stared out at the weary horse, resenting it for the message it carried. "I love you, Kashi," she blurted, still not turning to face him. That she made the confession aloud shocked her, but it was too late to stop it now. "I have always loved you."

"I believe that."

She did turn now. She wanted to be angry with him, but something in his eyes crushed her anger. He held the missive in his hand, a missive she despised without needing to read it.

"What kind of answer is that?"

"The one I will give you."

He moved closer and bitter tears stung her eyes, but they did not fall. She searched his grey eyes, digging for his true feelings and was shocked to find her sorrow, her longing, mirrored there. Raising her hand, she curled her fingers around the back of his neck and pulled him to her. He didn't resist. He returned her kiss, wrapping his arms tight around her. For an exquisite moment, the rest of the world vanished and a glorious burning infused her body and mind. When they parted, she turned her back on him, afraid she wouldn't be able to keep control of her emotions while looking into his eyes.

"I will not say goodbye, nor will I see you off," she stated, swallowing back tears.

His strong hand took her shoulder and turned her around to face him again. She looked down, ashamed of the tears that had begun to fall, but he placed his hand under her chin and lifted her face up to him. Her tears fell freely now. He kissed her again, long and sweet, the salt of her tears flavoring their lips. Then he pulled her into his embrace and held her against him for several minutes while she wept. Then, without a word, he backed away and left the room.

She longed to go after him and beg him to stay. Clinging to what dignity she had, she walked instead to the window and watched. After a time, a groom brought his horse around and his saddlebags were fastened in place behind the saddle. A few moments later, he strode from the manor, leapt into the saddle, and galloped away without a backward glance.

The floor creaked behind her as someone else entered the room.

"Your beloved is gone."

She hastily wiped away her tears and glared around at Lord Ander, angry with him for encroaching upon her misery. The last person she wished to see right then.

"Is this where you usually go when you sneak about my manor at night?"

She ignored the question, lifting her chin in defiance of him. "I like you better when you're bedridden."

"That is something you and my son have in common then."

She didn't respond. Instead, she turned her gaze back out the window and stared off toward the horizon where Kashi had disappeared.

"You do love the captain, don't you?" Ander pressed as he moved around the perimeter of the room, watching her from the deeper shadows like a thief assessing a target.

"Does it matter, my lord?"

Slinking over, he joined her in front of the windows. "You have changed since you arrived here."

"I don't know what you mean." She met his eyes, beady glints in the shadows of his gaunt face. It irritated her that he would not let her be.

He moved closer still, stopping few feet away from her and she could easily see the yellowish discoloration of his skin from his illness in the light from one window.

"You seem more confident." He peered into her eyes and his narrowed. "And those strange little flecks of gold in your eyes, so bright in the right lighting. I don't remember those."

She fought down a surge of alarm as she recalled the reflection she had seen in the river, struggling to keep her expression calm. "My eyes are as they have always been, my lord. Eyes do not change. Please excuse me."

She curtsied stiffly to him and turned to try to leave the room in a composed fashion, though her heart raced wildly now. Valin stood in the doorway. There was no need to ask how much he had heard, the raw pain in his expression was answer enough. Her heart felt as if it shattered in her chest when he turned away without speaking and headed back down the hall, his footsteps heavy. Fighting back a sob, she lifted her skirts and ran from the room, darting around Valin in the hallway and not stopping until she reached the solitude of her room.

Once in her chambers, she ran to a mirror and stared into her eyes. Ander spoke the truth. When she angled toward the sunlight, her green eyes shone with tiny flecks of gold that hadn't been there before. Fear overcame misery and she backed away from the mirror in horror. She tripped and fell back against the bed, striking her shoulder on the wood frame. Motivated by fresh pain, she scrambled to her feet and bolted from her rooms, running back up to the tower.

Kazue waited there, sitting patient as ever.

She ran up to the great beast.

"What is this?" She screamed at him, gesturing to her eyes with her hands. Did he even understand her?

The gargoyle regarded her serenely with his brilliant gold eyes and calmness begin to flow through her. She turned away from him.

"No! I don't want to be calm!"

After a moment, his soft face nudged her hand. There was no point in screaming at the poor creature. He couldn't offer her any answers. Even if he had the answers, he couldn't give them to her in any way she would understand. She dropped to her knees and hid her face in her hands, weeping in frustration and fear and longing.

"This is madness," she sobbed.

Kazue sat beside her and wrapped one massive wing around her shoulders. Eventually the tears ran dry. Fear and frustration faded away with them, but the longing remained, stronger now than ever.

Kashi drove his gelding hard away from the manor. What he wanted more than anything was to go back and convince Mira to run away with him, but he could never turn his back on Shakari or on his duty to the kingdom. He should never have kissed her. He had not initiated it, at least not the first time. The second kiss he took full responsibility for, but it was the first that haunted him as he rode away, leaving her farther behind with each long stride. Such gentle passion, such longing filled that kiss. It took everything he had to walk away when he did. Whatever battles waited ahead of him, he couldn't imagine any being as hard as the one he had just fought with himself.

The worst thing was that now he felt as though he was deserting her. The notion was foolish. She had everything she needed, all the security and prestige she could hope for with Valin. Her tears riddled him with guilt, even though she knew as well as he did that they could never be together. Barik was a good match and when the elder Barik died, she would have a fine life with Valin.

The thought of her happy with Valin stung like the bite of an arrow in his chest.

He camped for a short time that night then rode hard the next day with thoughts of her still tormenting him. The only thing he might have done differently would have been to deny her that first kiss that opened the door for him. Letting it happen only served to get her under his skin more than ever. The pain in her eyes and her tears tormented him endlessly as he rode. There was nothing he could do to change their fates, was there?

He shook his head and focused on the road. His thoughts, he knew, should be on the conflict with the Hishae provinces, not on some woman he could never have. There were upsetting rumors coming out of the Northern provinces, rumors of magic and dark powers from legends centuries old. That deserved attention. Attention he found it hard to give.

More than one man told him that love could addle the mind. He never realized until this moment how completely true that was.

In the late afternoon, the gelding started to falter, losing strength. Even such a strong, steady mount could not keep up the harsh pace he'd set indefinitely. He turned in at the small manor they had stayed in on the way to Barik. After he showed the royal missive, they traded him a fresh mount for the weary gelding. It hurt to leave such a fine companion behind, but the new mount was fresh and ready to run. He would trade horses again at Yukori manor, which meant he could afford to push the horse a little harder than he normally might have. He didn't accept the offer of a night's lodging, though he gratefully took the food they offered before continuing as far as he could before stopping to camp again when the dark prevented safe travel at speed.

By morning of the fifth day after leaving Barik, he rode the exhausted horse hard into the Yukori courtyard. The guards greeted him and saw that someone came to take the horse as Kashi, feeling about as tired as he imagined the horse did, staggered into the manor. A servant ushered him into the front receiving room to await the lord or lady of the house. Weary from the hard ride, he sprawled in one of the plush chairs and promptly fell asleep.

"Kashi."

Mira's voice echoed in his mind and a fresh pang of loss stabbed through him when he opened his eyes to find Ina smiling down at him.

"Would you care to join us for supper?"

He sat up, suddenly fully awake. "What time is it?"

"Time for supper." She smiled indulgently, an expression that brought their shared father to mind.

"I should have been back on the road hours ago." He rubbed his eyes and got to his feet.

"The kingdom can do without you for little longer, Kashi." Her firm tone demanded compliance. "You clearly needed the rest."

"Ina," he breathed her name with a mixture of fondness and frustration, "it will take long enough to get there without wasting time on such luxuries."

Her expression turned sour. "You will make worse time if we refuse to provide you provisions and a fresh horse. You can waste one evening on your sister and brother-in-law."

He almost relented to the bitter desire to point out that she was only his half-sister, but her look of fond tolerance steered him away from inflammatory comments. He searched his mind for an argument that would convince her to let him continue on his way, but nothing came.

"You win, Ina. You usually do."

She smiled triumphantly, her face glowing with instant pleasure. "Good, go clean up. You smell like horse sweat. Join us in the dining room when you are done."

He did as ordered. There was no point arguing with Ina after she made up her mind about something. When he entered the dining room, Dannesk and Ina were already seated, waiting for him. The food smelled marvelous and after four days of travel rations, it made his mouth water and his stomach growl.

"Marikashi!" Dannesk greeted him with genuine enthusiasm. "Come, have a seat."

"Dannesk," he greeted with a sedate nod, then he nodded to Ina and she nodded back wearing a self-satisfied smirk.

A grudging gratitude emerged towards his half-sister for demanding that he stay as he sat before a plate already loaded with fine food. They ate in relative silence and Kashi suspected this courtesy was for his benefit. He had nearly finished the last leg of duck when Dannesk asked the question he had been dreading.

"How is Mira?"

Kashi met his eyes, trying not to think of the taste of her lips, salted with tears. "She was well when I left." That wasn't entirely honest, but it would do no good to go into such details. "I would not have left her there alone if I didn't have to, but I believe Valin will watch over her."

Dannesk eyed him shrewdly. "Do you?"

Kashi recalled with uncomfortable clarity the tears welling in her eyes and running down her soft passion-flushed cheeks. He gave himself a mental slap and refocused on the man before him. "Yes, I do. I think he is honorable and she will be safe there."

"Valin is not serving then?"

"No, his father insisted that he stay on to work out some issues with the manor before he passes on. If it had not been for that, I might have brought Mira back here with me. I would not leave her with only Lord Ander for company." Ina raised her eyebrows at his defiant tone, but he pretended not to notice.

"I imagine that would have destroyed the marriage agreement, but I wouldn't have held it against you.

Ander Barik is an insufferable man. I wish him upon no one."

"He can't be that bad," Ina interjected.

Dannesk reached over to place his hand on top of hers on the table and gave it a squeeze. "You're always willing to see good in everyone," he said, offering a fond smile.

Powerful resentment caught Kashi by surprise as he watched them. He looked down, pretending interest in a stray bit of meat he had missed while he struggled with the insistent emotion. After a few seconds, he placed his napkin on the table and stood.

"I hate to be impolite, but I am still exhausted."

Ina and Dannesk rose as well.

"Of course, Kashi." Ina's brow furrowed with worry, though she kept her concerns to herself. "Please, help yourself to one of the guest rooms."

"Thank you for the wonderful meal. I am afraid I will have to leave very early—"

"A fresh horse and provisions will be ready for you if you leave before sunrise," Ina assured him. He had held up his side of the bargain, now she would hold up hers.

He nodded and they walked him from the room. Ina gave him a firm hug and he thought he saw a hint of tears in her eyes before she turned away.

Dannesk gripped his hand firmly. "If things go poorly, I may end up joining you soon."

"We will hope, for both our sakes, that they don't."

Dannesk smiled, though worry cast a cloud over the expression. "Yes. Watch out for yourself."

Kashi glanced once more at Ina, who would no longer look at him and nodded. "I will."

They bid him good night and Kashi started toward one of the guest rooms, eager to lose himself in sleep on a soft bed, but a young serving girl intercepted him. She wrung her hands nervously as she stepped into his path from a dark doorway.

"Captain…" her voice wavered.

"Yes?"

"My Lady Gemma would like you to attend her."

That was odd. He sank down on one knee to look the girl in the eyes. "Me? Captain Marikashi?"

The girl looked so nervous he feared she might faint, but he held her gaze until she muttered a tiny yes.

"Very well then, lead on."

The girl led the way up to a room in the east wing of the manor and knocked softly on the door.

"Bring the captain in, child," a frail voice called from within the room.

The girl opened the door and stepped aside. Kashi entered and met the striking green eyes that peered out at him from a wrinkled old face. Eyes so much like Mira's that it took his breath away for a second. The door closed behind him and the old woman gestured to the chair across from her.

"Lady Gemma," he greeted, sinking into the offered chair.

"My darling Mira was the last one to sit there before you."

He glanced down at the arm of the chair where his hand rested and imagined her hand there. After a moment, he looked up to find Gemma watching him with a sly smile. Then her expression turned cold and serious.

"I don't thank you for taking her to Barik." Her sharp tone matched her expression.

He recoiled a touch, surprised by the statement as well as the anger in her voice. "It wasn't my choice, my lady."

Her slight shoulders lifted in a shrug, the anger sliding off like a discarded shawl. "How was she when you left?"

"Well enough. She seemed to be adjusting," he answered warily.

"What about her eyes?"

He almost asked where she was going with that odd question, then he paused and thought back on the last time he had seen Mira. He had noticed something odd about her eyes, when the light struck them right before she had kissed him, but the kiss had pushed it from his mind.

"They seemed... different somehow."

The old woman leaned forward intently. The clarity in those green eyes made her questions even more disturbing. "In what way?"

He shook his head, trying to remember.

"A hint of gold in them, perhaps?" She prompted.

He nodded. "That was it. There were flecks of gold in them that I hadn't noticed before."

She leaned back and closed her eyes.

"What's this about?" He asked when she did not move for a time.

The old woman opened her eyes and he was struck again by how like Mira's eyes they were.

"She has touched the gargoyle."

His brow crinkled with confusion. "Yes, many times."

She shook her head gravely at him. "You don't understand, child."

He could not remember the last time someone had called him child. He frowned at her. "Perhaps if you explained, I would."

"Gargoyles are magic creatures. Their magic can be shared with a human through physical contact, a willing bond. Mira is absorbing its magic."

He resisted the temptation to touch her skin and see if she might be with fever. "Are you feeling well, Lady Gemma?"

If ever a look could have killed him, he didn't doubt that this would be the one. She glared at him fiercely and clutched the arms of the chair. For a moment, he thought she might rise and come at him, but then she sighed, shook her head, and looked out the window into the darkness, her figure shrinking down into the chair.

"The young are such fools," she murmured, then she looked at him again. "There are powers at work that you simply don't understand. Powers long ago dismissed as mere legend."

Her earnest tone and the lucidity in her eyes made him uneasy again. "Gemma, is Mira in danger?"

She stared at him for a long time and he met her gaze firmly, needing to know the answer. He caressed the fabric of the chair arm with his fingertips, thinking again of Mira's hand resting there.

She frowned. "We are all in danger, Captain."

"In what way? I want to understand what you're trying to tell me."

"Leave me please. I am tired."

Though he wanted to press her, she truly looked exhausted and he could not do so in good conscience. Reluctantly, he allowed her to send him away. A short time later, he found himself standing outside of the room where Mira had slept on their way through the first time. He longed to have her there where he could open the door just a crack and look in to see that she was all right. He told himself that he did not believe Gemma's talk of magic, the ravings of a woman well past her prime, but it left him ill at ease. Her eyes *had* been different when he looked into them, before she kissed him. The thought gave him a chill though he tried to tell himself the memory had been altered by Gemma's words. He simply didn't believe himself.

•

It took Kashi a little over two days to reach Arkesh manor. After Ina waylaid him at Yukori manor, he was somewhat reluctant to stop and see Sunai, but knowing he could change horses again had allowed him to continue the breakneck pace he set. The guards admitted him through the gates without question and he left his sweat soaked mount with a stable boy.

Sunai greeted him warmly in the manor, though she stopped short of hugging him, instead waving a hand under her wrinkled nose.

"You smell like a sweaty horse, Kashi," she remarked flatly. "You can't have gotten the missive that long ago. You must have traveled fast to get here so soon."

"Very. I can't stay. I just need a fresh mount and to replenish my packs," he stated, dismissing her comments.

She narrowed her eyes at him and he feared he might have to argue with her over leaving right away as he had with Ina.

"Running from something?"

The response puzzled him. "I've been summoned to the front lines."

"I am sure they will save some fighting for you, Kashi." Her sharp, angry reply left him confused.

"What exactly would I be running from?"

"Love."

Now he narrowed his eyes, anger surging through him in a refreshing wave. "Perhaps you failed to notice, but the woman I love is going to be marrying a man far more appropriate to her station. You know I wish things could have been different."

"Did you break her heart again, when you left?"

"Again!"

"Yes again." She stepped closer. Getting into his face. Her ferocity might have almost been endearing if it hadn't been directed at him. "You broke her heart every day after your return from the academy with your callous indifference."

"What choice did I have?" he demanded. "Whether I ran away or walked, I had to leave her eventually." He spun and started toward the door.

"Kashi, wait!"

He stopped reluctantly and turned to face her when she didn't say anything. Tears streamed down her soft cheeks.

"I'm sorry, Kashi. I know you love each other and it just doesn't seem fair that you cannot be together."

He walked back to her and placed a hand on her cheek, wiping away a tear with his thumb. "This is about Shakari, isn't it?"

Sunai fell against him and started to weep. He wrapped his arms around her and held her while she cried. She had confided her anxiety about not having gotten with child yet before he left for Barik and now Shakari was gone to help deal with the conflict in Hishae. If something happened to him, she would lose not just the man he loved, but everything else as well. With no Arkesh heir and no possibility of one on the way, the manor could be taken from her.

"I'll watch over him for you, Sunai. I'll see him home safe," he said when she quieted some.

She stepped back from him, fussily wiping at the dampness under her eyes. "I know you will." She stood silent for a moment and he could see that she fought back another wave of tears. She finally emerged victorious. "Come, we must get you some provisions and a new horse. I am wasting your time."

He stopped her for a moment with a hand on her arm and she slowly met his eyes. "You are never a waste of my time."

She smiled tremulously and nodded. "Thank you, Kashi."

Within the hour, he had a new horse, a young mare built for speed, waiting in the courtyard with full saddlebags strapped on her back. He had nothing left to say to Sunai, so he hugged her, squeezed her hand, and once more promised to watch over Shakari. He left the courtyard at a gallop and wondered where he would get his next mount. He had several days travel ahead of him and, with no definite plan on where to obtain a replacement, he would have to conserve this one more than he had the others. With Sunai's plight to drive him, he thought less of his own sadness at leaving Mira. Instead, he fretted over whether he would be able to make good on his promise to bring his half-brother home safe.

For most of the following week, Mira avoided Valin and his father, finding it easy to do so in the massive manor. Ander seemed to have taken another turn for the worse, for she did not see him when she dared wander the commonly used halls of the manor. Most every day she went up and spent time with Kazue. Despite her fear and her confusion, she couldn't be angry at the gargoyle. Whatever happened because of her contact with him, she could not believe he meant her any harm. He was her one source of peace.

This day she sat back against one of the tower's stone parapets and Kazue rested his head on her leg. She placed her hand on his shoulder, where the massive muscles that controlled his wings gave his back a hump. His physical presence radiated calmness that she could see herself becoming addicted to, if she wasn't already.

The muscles twitched slightly under her hand as Kazue drifted off to sleep. The gargoyle seemed as comforted by her presence as she was by his, but perhaps she only projected that. The relationship still felt so strange, so unprecedented, that it almost made her feel freakish. At the same time she felt so completely welcome and wanted in the gargoyles presence that she could not bring herself to turn away from him.

She exhaled softly.

Kazue opened one eye and shifted his head to watch Valin as he climbed up carefully through the trapdoor. She met the young lord's eyes, a touch of the sadness she had been hiding from returning with his arrival.

He hesitated near the top, staring at the large predator resting with her. "May I join you?"

She gestured to the hard surface beside her. "Find yourself a comfortable bit of stone to lean on," she replied with a wry smile.

Valin smiled faintly in return and started to approach with marked caution. "I would not have found you if you hadn't left the lower door cracked today. You're quite skilled at avoiding people, even in their own home." He stopped again a few feet away. "Does Kazue mind?"

She stroked the gargoyle's head between his back-swept horns. "If he does, he will undoubtedly leave. You are in no danger."

To her relief, the gargoyle remained when Valin lowered himself down a few feet to her right. After a moment, Kazue closed the one eye again, his mouth curving up in that way that made him look as if he were smiling.

"I feared the truth from the moment I first met you," Valin commented vaguely, folding his hands in his lap.

"What truth?"

"That you and Captain Marikashi were in love." His voice caught, betraying stronger emotion than his face showed.

"I don't know that it goes both ways," she replied absently. It occurred to her then that perhaps she should have denied it, though it was probably much too late to try that tactic.

"It does," he replied with certainty.

A familiar, painful longing twisted in her chest in response to his words.

They sat in silence and she stroked Kazue's head while Valin regarded the gargoyle. His eyes sparked with a hint of wonder despite the somber mood. After a short time in silence, he looked away, out over the opposite wall at the deepening blue of the late afternoon sky. Wisps of cloud raced on a wind high above them, part of another world.

"I'm sorry about this, Mira."

"Sorry about what?"

"My father never approved of this match. The only reason I agreed to Dannesk's proposal and brought you all this way was to torment him. I've never defied him, though I have often wanted to. It was a last attempt to prove to myself that I wasn't his pawn. It wasn't fair to you. I was merely being petty and vindictive."

She reached over and took his hand to comfort him. Perhaps some of the comfort Kazue gave her would pass to him. "Petty and vindictive is the example your father gave you. If anyone is to blame, it's him." Valin looked at her and the torment in his eyes made her want to help him. She swallowed hard. "I know I could learn to love you in time."

He smiled bitterly, though she could see his gentler side still lurking shyly behind that emotional armor. "You could learn to love me as a friend or brother, perhaps." He gave her hand a small squeeze before pulling his away. "No, Mira, I think it would be best if I let you go and married the Lady Johnis as father wanted."

She stared at him in alarm, Kazue's head the only thing keeping her from jumping up in panic. "My brother would lock me in a tower for the rest of my life if I came back now!"

Valin chuckled, though she didn't see any humor in the statement. "My little wildflower, he would do no such thing. Those who spend time around you care about you. They can't seem to help it. He may be disappointed, but there are other good alliances to be made with other young lords who will not know where your heart truly lies."

She gazed down at her deserted hand. "But none of them will be Kashi," she said softly, remembering the way his kiss made her feel. It was cruel to lament this way to Valin, but the words were out before she considered that. She braced for his anger, but it didn't come.

"The queen requested him specifically. It is highly possible that he might be granted lands after the conflict is over if he proves himself worthy."

She experienced a brief surge of hope, but stamped it down quickly. "Yes. I'm sure he'll be granted enough land to hold his coffin."

Valin stood and looked down at her with a forced smile. "Come now, little bitter one, it will all work out. I will compose a letter from my father, stating that he insists upon my marriage to the Lady Johnis and will not be swayed. We'll make it all his fault. How does that sound?"

She gazed up at him, an aching of guilt in her chest. "I feel as though I have wronged you."

He shook his head. "We will call it even then. I would be honored if you would dine with me on the west sitting room terrace this evening. Father won't be joining us. He doesn't go outside in the evenings. His health, you know."

She smiled at his conspiratorial wink. "That would be grand."

Once Valin vanished back down the ladder, she smiled down at Kazue. "I suppose you will return to Yukori manor with me, my friend." The gargoyle purred and she laughed softly as it vibrated through her leg. "I'll take that as a yes."

●

A few days later, Mira joined the escort Valin assembled for her in the courtyard of the Barik manor. He first sent off a courier in the direction of the Johnis holding, then he walked over to where she waited. For propriety sake, he had provided a carriage, but for now, it only carried her things. She doubted she would ride in it at all, what with the pleasant weather and having Aiko to ride.

Valin walked up to her and took her hands. "Be safe, Mira."

"I will. I hope the Lady Johnis is worthy of you." She gave him a playful wink.

"I hope she is half of what you are. Your short time here has changed my outlook for the better, my lady. I feel stronger for having known you. You will always be welcome here."

"Thank you, my lord."

There was nothing more to say. Valin gave her a quick, gentle kiss on the cheek before she mounted up on Aiko. She rode away with the escort hoping that she wasn't being a fool again by not fighting to change his mind. It didn't really matter, she supposed, since it had been his decision to send her home. It wasn't fair to expect that he would take her for his wife knowing not only that she loved another, but also who that other was. Some men didn't seem to care about such things. Valin, it appeared, was not one of those men, and she respected him for it, even if it meant her future became again uncertain.

With Kazue overhead, Mira and her unfamiliar escort made good time the first day. The gargoyle kept her from feeling lonely and awkward among the strange men. On the second afternoon, however, she started to feel an inexplicable unease, as of some closing danger, while they rode through the deep woods. The escort, seeming to also sense something, rode closer around her and she could sense Kazue overhead, though she could not see him through the trees. The overcast sky made the woods darker than usual, and she began to feel like something or someone watched them from the myriad shadows. The woods had gone quiet, but not in a peaceful way.

Something whistled through the air and the front two soldiers dropped from their mounts with crossbow bolts protruding from their throats. Mira choked on a scream when Aiko spooked to one side. She gripped the reins, and turned the mare toward the rest of the party, despairing at the apparent good aim of their unseen attackers as the coach driver and footman fell from their seats, both also skewered through the throat. The hidden bowmen continued to attack from somewhere in the trees, powerful crossbows striking devastation upon the escort. Then men surged from the shadows, swords singing from leather sheathes.

Aiko spun in panic and Mira fought to control her, a sense of hopelessness closing in. She couldn't give up, however. If they took her alive, there were things they could do that would be far worse than dying quickly from a crossbow bolt.

As soon as she managed to get the mare pointed at a clear spot between two groups of combatants, she kicked her hard. Aiko lunged forward. They charged down the road, barely drawing free of the combat when someone rushed out in front of them and the mare skidded to a stop, almost throwing Mira over her head. The mare was a pleasure mount, not a warhorse trained to run down an opponent. The man, wearing a haphazard compilation of ragged leather and threadbare wool clothing, grabbed Aiko's reins and leered up at Mira in a way that made her blood run cold.

Time slowed as his other hand, holding a short dagger, rose towards her. A ground-shaking roar made him spin around, dropping her reins. She yanked her foot from the stirrup and kicked him hard in the back, making him stagger forward as Kazue lunged. The bandit crumpled like a doll under the force of the gargoyle's attack and his scream cut short when Kazue tore most of his throat away, nearly beheading him with one bite.

Her stomach turned at the grotesque display of the gargoyle's lethality, but the nausea vanished before a gut-wrenching fear for his life when she spotted one of the archers in a tree training his crossbow on the beast. Panic and hatred flared up and, as she met the archer's cold gaze, his crossbow burst into flames. He cried out, dropping the weapon and toppling from the tree. Kazue took two lunging strides and surged into the air, flying low under the branches of the trees. Terror and confusion diminished with the gargoyle's arrival. Mira kicked Aiko hard again, sending the mare charging after the gargoyle.

They didn't stop their flight when the sounds of the fighting had faded far behind them, but continued their headlong rush down the roadway for some time. Dark started to fall and Mira slowed Aiko so that she could watch the road around them, hoping to find the manor they had stayed in on their way to the Barik holding. Kazue landed and walked alongside the horse, seeming reluctant to stray any further away from her. She appreciated his concern, hoping desperately that he wouldn't take to the air again, at least not until she found a safe refuge for the night.

When she found the manor, a powerful relief left her feeling weak. Her whole body trembled with lingering fear and the horror of what she had seen. All of her things were lost with the carriage and she didn't know if any of the Barik soldiers survived the attack, but it didn't seem likely. Guilt nagged at her for abandoning them, but there had been so many bandits and death at the hands of their ilk rarely went easily for a woman. There wasn't much she could have done for them.

Perhaps the Queen had pulled the road patrols back in preparation for battle with Hishae. If so, then the roads were no longer safe to travel, though she wouldn't have expected them to get to this state so quickly.

She turned Aiko down the road to the manor. As they came within sight of the large building, Kazue slowed, making a deep huffing sound low in his chest. His unease made her nervous, but she continued onward, relief at having found the manor turning gradually to dread. Just inside the quiet little courtyard she came upon the body of the doorman lying sprawled near the open door, his eyes staring blankly into the building, his throat cut. She stopped Aiko and looked up at the manor. When she spotted a body hanging out a broken second floor window, she knew they didn't dare linger.

Afraid the killers might still be around, assuming this atrocity wasn't also the work of the same band that had attacked her escort, she turned Aiko and cantered back out to the road. Kazue took to the air, but he stayed below the trees, keeping close to her. Aiko, however, had run for a long time and could no longer maintain the aggressive pace, so they slowed back to a walk and Mira searched her mind for what to do. Fear screamed through her mind, its white noise the only thing louder than her grumbling stomach. Night had fallen and she had nowhere to go, but she feared stopping out here in the forest.

Kazue landed and made the huffing sound again, but this time he appeared to be trying to get her attention. He took a few steps off the road, then turned back and regarded her expectantly. With no other options, she turned Aiko to follow him into the trees. They didn't go far before he stopped alongside a small creek. Enough grass grew near the water that Aiko could graze for a time so Mira dismounted. She almost took the saddle off, wanting to give the mare a proper rest, but it would slow her best means of escape so she left it on, murmuring an apology to the mare.

Kazue drank from the stream then lay on the ground and she followed his example, drinking her fill before curling up next to him as she had on the tower. The ground, carpeted with a thick layer of moss and needles from the trees, made a passable bed. Kazue blanketed her with his wing and she pressed in close to his warmth. She drifted off wondering how he could always be so warm without any fur.

In the morning, she sat for a time listening to the gurgle of the water and pondering her situation while Kazue went off alone, presumably to hunt. Barik manor was still closer than the Yukori holding, but she would have to go back through the site of the bandit attack to get there. That alone provided enough incentive to continue toward her family home. If she pushed Aiko, they could reach Yukori in three days, maybe less. She couldn't stop at an inn. Any coin she'd had now belonged to the bandits. She had a few jewels she could trade, though doing so would make her look desperate and that would make her appear an easy target. As a woman traveling alone, she would draw enough unwanted attention without even trying.

Kazue landed by the creek, his cheeks puffed comically. He marched over to her and spit out four fat apples by her leg. She picked up the proffered fruits and examined them. A few round holes marred the surfaces where teeth broke the skin and a bit of saliva slicked them, but nothing a rinse in the creek couldn't fix. Although far less than she would have liked for breaking her fast, they were more than she expected given the circumstances.

"Thank you, Kazue." She dipped the apples to the chill creek to rinse them.

The apples, ripe and rich with sweet juices, made for a quick meal followed by a long drink from the creek.

It occurred to her that she should hide her jewelry so she tore off a piece of her skirt with a little assistance from one of Kazue's sharp talons, placed all her jewelry in it, and tied it to her belt. With that taken care of, she offered Aiko the apple cores before climbing into the saddle. They returned to the road, wary now of the possible dangers, and struck out east toward Yukori at a fast trot.

Kazue flew low with them and she worried about what might happen if they encountered other travelers. Fretting over it served no purpose since she couldn't control the gargoyle. Kazue would do as he pleased, including ensuring she didn't starve apparently.

At least he didn't bring me meat. She had no experience building a fire from the available materials, though she knew it could be done.

An image flashed into her weary mind of the archer whose crossbow had burst into flames when she looked at him. How had that happened? Had Kazue done it somehow? Gemma said gargoyles were magical creatures. Perhaps she could ask the old woman more about it when she arrived safely back at Yukori manor.

The thought brought a wistful smile to her cold lips and Aiko moved into a canter, responding to the rise in her mood.

Her pleasant thoughts of home soon faded before remembered images of the Barik men falling to the ground with bolts in their throats, their lives snuffed in an instant. Did any of them have families waiting for their return? And what of the dead at the manor? Who would tend to their bodies? She shuddered in the saddle, and gritted her teeth against an inner chill.

By late afternoon, they had reached the open, rolling farmlands. She liked being able to see for miles around, but the exposure also made her uneasy. There was no way to hide out here. Her stomach growled insistently and she was shaky with hunger, yet the chance of finding the residents slain like those at the manor made her reluctant to ride to any of the distant farmhouses. Kazue brought her another couple of apples earlier and she had wiped the damp away on her split skirts before eating them. She didn't know how long one could live on apples alone, but at least they had much moisture in them to help quench her thirst. Kazue hadn't left her again since they exited the forest. He flew just above when they moved at speed and walked alongside when she let Aiko walk for periods to rest.

As evening drew near, she spotted a rickety wagon approaching. Kazue moved off into the distance, managing to hide himself in the tall grasses more effectively than she would have thought possible. She was both relieved and alarmed by his disappearance, but she forced herself to ride towards the wagon with the pretense of confidence. A grizzled man drove the tired looking nag between the traces and two wary looking youths sat in the back, holding hammers across their laps. They appeared ready to defend themselves.

The old man stopped the horse and let her close the last few yards between them.

"Good sirs," she greeted, hoping they didn't hear the slight tremble in her voice.

"Lady," the old man replied gruffly as the two in the wagon glowered at her.

"I wondered if you might have any food to spare. I have no coin, but I do have items I could trade. I only need..." she trailed off when his eyes narrowed.

"Why are you out here alone?" He peered around as if he expected an attack to come from the thin air.

Her shoulders sank. No show of confidence or desperation would win her much from them, it seemed. She pressed on anyway, daring to try honesty. "Good sir, I rode from Barik manor with an escort. We were attacked by bandits in the wood. I managed to escape during the fighting, but I have only my mare and the clothing on my back to get me home. Please, I will give you all of my jewelry for just a bit of food."

She pulled the pouch from her belt and offered it over to him. He snatched the offered bundle, watching her while his fingers worked at the tie. He looked into it and, after a long moment, nodded slowly.

"You'll be safer without these. They'll buy you a few meals and a bed for the night if you wish. We'll feed your mare too. I am Kripalu. These are my sons, Bhauma and Manuja." The two young men in the back nodded in turn, their wary expressions giving way to guarded civility.

She smiled, the wave of relief making her feel almost too weak to continue. "Thank you, good sir. I cannot tell you what this means to me. I am Mira."

She rode behind the wagon to their home. Kazue remained hidden. No doubt he stayed away to give her this opportunity. She didn't doubt that he would return in the morning when she rode out alone again. Two children, a young boy and a younger girl, greeted them outside a small listing farmhouse. Both carried makeshift weapons around with them. More proof that things really had deteriorated with remarkable speed.

"This is my third son, Tanaya, and my daughter, Induja." The two children nodded and stared at her warily. "Tanaya, take her horse to the paddock and give the poor thing some hay and water."

Mira hesitated at letting the mare out of her sight, but if these people meant her any harm the chance to escape had already passed. She watched the boy lead Aiko away, the mare's feet dragging and her head hung low.

Kripalu summoned her along into the small house.

The warmth of a fire greeted her. The house smelled faintly of mildew and unwashed bodies, but the magnificent aroma of a spiced stew overpowered the less pleasant odors. The aroma made her feel faint after going so long on so little food, but she stayed on her feet through force of will. The strong spicing would hide any spoiling items in the stew, but after eating apples slathered in gargoyle saliva, she didn't think much would fall below her current standards.

The woman who stood chopping vegetables—a hardened, rough creature—still bore faint traces of a younger beauty in the fine bones of her drawn features. She looked up when Kripalu cleared his throat and her tired eyes widened in surprise.

"Josa," Mira heard the slight hint of deference in Kripalu's voice and bit back a smile. "This is Mira. She'll be joining us for the night."

Josa's piercing gaze picked over Mira carefully, the resistance in her eyes growing. Kripalu quickly handed her the pouch of jewelry. She regarded the contents in confusion, then her eyes widened again and she curtsied. "Lady Mira Yukori."

Now Kripalu stared at Mira in open alarm and bowed, gesturing hastily for his children to do the same.

"No, please. Please don't," Mira pleaded. "You needn't treat me any differently than you would treat any guest. Please. I insist."

They rose. The two children grinned and whispered excitedly, oblivious to their parents' distress.

Josa held the pouch out to her. "We cannot take these, m'lady. It wouldn't be proper."

"Please, you can get better use out of them than I can and, as your husband said, I'm safer without them. Bandits attacked my escort. I can't return to Barik and, if I am to reach Yukori in one piece, I'm better off without such trinkets."

Josa turned to her husband, her brow furrowing into tight lines. "By lord and by land, Krip, send Bhauma and Manuja to Yukori. They must send an escort for the lady."

"No. I will not put you or your children at risk. I can reach Yukori alone. All I ask is a little food, a bed, and whatever news you have." Josa didn't look fully convinced. "Please," she pressed.

The woman finally nodded. "Very well, m'lady. We will do as you ask."

"Thank you, and keep the jewelry. It's the least I can do to repay you."

Josa nodded and returned the pouch to Kripalu who tucked it away in a small cupboard. As they ate together, the family gradually relaxed enough to treat her a little less formally. She appreciated the change and tried to be pleasant and polite, despite her monstrous appetite. The evening wore on and they sent the two youngest to bed, though Mira doubted the curious children stayed there. She could almost feel them listening on the other side of the rough-made wood wall.

"You asked for news," Kripalu said solemnly. "What do you know of the war?"

War? Had it already escalated to full on war? "All I know is that Hishae broke peace with the kingdom. I've heard nothing more since."

Josa hung her head and the cold deep inside Mira expanded, a cold that took root within her the day Kashi left.

"Hishae attacked the city of Laki without provocation several weeks ago. Queen Isaye put out a call for troops and began pulling her road patrols back to Beikang that day. Within three days, we started to hear about the bandit attacks. We don't know where they all came from, but it doesn't sound as if the patrols will be back anytime soon. We've been left to fend for ourselves."

"Why? Is the threat from Hishae so great we can't afford to defend our own people against such petty criminals?" She almost did not want to hear the answer, but as someone who suffered the consequences of that decision, she had to know.

"Hishae's army occupies Laki now and, last we heard, the army from Beikang hasn't managed to make any inroads into the city. The first battle was a bloodbath for our side. There are rumors of some flying beasts fighting for Hishae."

Panic spiked. "Gargoyles?"

"No. Some birdlike creatures."

There was some relief in knowing gargoyles weren't fighting for the enemy. That would make traveling with one especially difficult. But Laki was one of the richest cities in the kingdom with its coveted diamond mines. The queen wouldn't stand by and let it fall to Hishae if she could stop it. "But Hishae is an ally? Why did they turn on us? And when did they become so powerful?"

"I only know what I have heard from passing travelers. There are rumors that Hishae's researchers rediscovered some old magic." Kripalu shook his head, sorrow in the drooping of his shoulders. "I only know it's made our lives harder here. Some say Hishae was always a sleeping dragon, resting and growing strong while we sat back with our self-assured delusion of supremacy. I know nothing of war, m'lady. I only know that if it doesn't end quickly, we will be forced to send our sons into the fight."

"We aren't afraid to fight," Manuja boasted.

"Yes." Mira ignored the young man's comment, fearing she might offend if she offered her true opinion of that. "Many I love are already there."

Josa and Kripalu looked down at the empty dishes and Josa stood, making herself busy gathering them up. "Well, we should all probably get some sleep. We don't have much to offer, m'lady, but it's warmer than a bed under the stars if not a great deal softer."

Mira thought of Kazue and doubted that it would be warmer, but she said nothing. Josa set the dishes in a tub and led Mira to a small separated section of the house. A single bed lay on the floor, tucked against the wall, the clothing and other items around the sparely furnished room making it clear who usually slept here.

"I will not take your bed," she stated firmly.

Josa's eyes narrowed and she pressed her chapped lips into a tight line. Her hands curled to fists and rested on her hips as if preparing for a shouting match with one of her children.

"You will do us the honor of taking this bed. It is the best we have to offer and I will have it no other way."

Mira opened her mouth to protest.

"No. This is your bed for tonight."

She gave in. The bed, while only half the size of the one she slept in at Barik and not a fraction as soft, at least provided her with a reasonably safe place to spend the night.

t dawn the next day, Mira declined the offer to share their morning meal. She suspected they would use more food trying to meet her perceived needs than they would typically use for the entire family in one meal. After a brief argument, she accepted a small sack of provisions from Kripalu. When he offered to send his two eldest to escort her, she firmly refused and thanked them for their hospitality. She felt awkward riding away, as if there were something more that she should have said or done, but she could not think what it might have been. Rather than dwell on the subject, she urged Aiko into a fast trot and had barely started down their road when Kazue swooped down from above and returned to his place flying above her.

For a time, she amused herself wondering if the farmer's family saw the gargoyle join her and what they thought of that. Eventually, however, those thoughts lost her interest and she focused on the journey, pushing Aiko as hard as she dared.

They saw few travelers, and of those, none dared come near with Kazue shadowing her. The region almost seemed to have come to a standstill. As evening fell, she considered riding on through the night. They were no more than four or five hours from the Yukori manor at her best estimate and she wanted to be home.

Aiko needed the rest though, and she had startled herself awake several times when she drifted off and nearly slid from the saddle. She found a copse of trees a short distance from the road that offered some seclusion and let Aiko graze.

She slept for a time curled up next to Kazue. When she woke later in the night, the gargoyle left her. She ate some of the food the farmer had given her, a bit of chewy stale bread and tough dried meat, and watched Aiko graze in the dark while she waited for Kazue to return.

A soft, rustling in the underbrush made her nerves dance to life. Kazue would come from the sky, not slink in through the grass and bushes.

She stood, heart racing, and scanned the ground for something to use as a weapon.

Two figures emerged from the trees, their features obscured by shadows in the pale moonlight.

"Who are you?" She tried to sound unafraid, but her voice trembled, undermining the attempted ruse.

"We've been watching you for a while." The man spoke in a soft, sinister hiss, intended to intimidate. It worked. "We saw your pet fly away."

"I have nothing." She took a step toward where Aiko stood resting now that she had eaten.

One of the men sidestepped quickly around toward the mare and she stopped, not wanting to give up the animal, but knowing she stood no chance against these men. The man still in front of her chuckled.

"You've a nice horse. We'll be takin' her, but we'd hoped for a little hospitality first."

The menace in his voice made the breath catch in her throat. She spun, bolting away from them. Both men sprinted after her and the one who had moved over near Aiko caught hold of her by the back of her travel worn dress. The fabric tore away and she relished a second of exhilarating freedom before stumbling over a branch in the grass. They both fell, his weight landing on top of her. She struggled, fighting him as he turned her over. He backhanded her across the mouth. The copper tang of blood spread on her tongue as her teeth cut into her lip and fury boiled up within her. This couldn't happen now, not so close to her home. It wouldn't happen.

The man grabbed her wrists, then let go with a sharp cry, recoiling back. She scrambled to her feet. They were both too close for her to run away, so she steeled herself to try to fight them off. The man who had grabbed her stared at her with eyes full of fear and anger. He cradled his hands against his chest. The other man looked from his companion to her and back again.

"Why'd you let go of her?"

"The whore cut me," the first man hissed, glaring daggers at her.

She shook her head. She had done no such thing. He held out his hands so the other could see them in the pale moonlight. There was just enough light that she could see dark blood welling from a cut on each palm. Then a faint glint of gold in the darkness drew her eyes to a shadowed shape in the trees.

"Give me the knife, pretty, before I do much worse to you."

The man's angry sneer faded, turning to alarm when she smiled. Following her gaze, he spun around and saw the dark figure standing in the trees behind them.

"Meet Kazue." Loathing, black and bitter, like nothing she ever felt before, dripped from her words like a vile toxin.

Kazue lunged. The first man threw up his hands, but the gargoyles powerful jaws crushed them and continued through with uncanny speed, abruptly cutting off the man's screams. The remaining bandit ran, but he had no chance of outpacing the enraged predator.

She covered her ears and struggled with a surge of nausea when Kazue's jaws closed around the back of the second man's neck. The sickening crunching sound passed through the inadequate barrier and she sank to her knees. Despite her efforts, the contents of her stomach made a forceful evacuation.

Trembling, she crawled away from the sour smelling vomit and spat to get some of the taste out of her mouth. When she was steady again, she stood and walked over to the second man. Kazue stood panting next to him, his jaws painted black with blood in the darkness. Steeling herself against another wave of nausea, she picked up one hand and crouched down to look at it. A fresh split opened his palm as if someone had sliced with a sharp blade.

She dropped the hand and backed away in alarm. She hadn't done that. She couldn't have.

Her hands shook and she wiped them on her skirt, then she wiped at the trickle of blood running from her mouth and finally turned her back on the body.

They returned to the road and she set a hard pace. The sun rose, bright and bleak, upon a familiar landscape. She pushed Aiko even harder then, knowing how close they were to home. When the manor came into sight, she yearned to press faster still, but the mare trembled with each stride, so she slowed instead, not wanting to kill the poor animal. Kazue landed beside her and they continued toward the manor at a measured walk.

Beyond the gates, she could see household staff going about their business as usual, a comforting sight after her visit to the manor in the woods. Things weren't entirely unchanged however. Most of the workers carried weapons at their belts and loaded crossbows rested in the windows of the gate towers, certainly with skilled bowmen waiting in the shadows to use them.

She almost urged Aiko to a trot, impatient to enter, when the gates opened and two figures came riding hard toward her. Yukori soldiers in full livery. She wasn't as pleased to see them as she knew she should be. Unease settled in as they drew near, their solemn expressions hinting at a deeper unrest within those waiting walls.

At the last moment, Kazue took to the sky and the two soldiers reined in their mounts, their eyes widening in recognition.

"Lady Yukori. Your arrival is something of a surprise. May we escort you in?"

They were a little late to be of much use, but she nodded. They probably burned with curiosity at her disheveled state and lack of escort. Let them burn. "Thank you, please lead on. I think we could pick up the pace a touch."

The soldiers nodded and fell in on either side of her. Kazue flew ahead, the other gargoyles paying him no mind this time, and perched on the manor, looking down on her with his bright watchful eyes as they rode into the courtyard. She left Aiko with a stable boy, giving explicit instructions on how the mare should be cared for after the long trek. The poor animal had earned that much consideration at the least for her efforts. That done, she strode swiftly up to the door. It flew open and Ina burst out like a quail from the bushes, wrapping her arms around Mira and clutching her tightly. Startled, she returned the frantic embrace and found it unexpectedly wonderful to stand for a moment in the arms of a friend after her traumatic journey, even if the other woman's huge belly did make it a little awkward.

Finally, Ina stepped back. Silent tears ran down her cheeks. She looked Mira over and a vague alarm twisted her lovely features.

"By lord and by land, Mira, what has happened to you?"

"The escort Valin sent with me was beset by bandits. I don't know that any of them survived, but I managed to escape. I was attacked again by two men less than a day's hard ride from here. They..." She couldn't quite decide what to say about that so she finally muttered, "They tore my dress."

"Were you..."

"No!" Mira saw where the question was going by the horrified look on Ina's face. She shuddered. "They didn't get what they were after, though it was a near thing."

"I'm so glad you're here, whatever the reason. Danni's been hurt. Oh, Mira." Ina clearly struggled to maintain her composure, but she finally lost control and crumpled to the ground, sobbing.

Panic burst through Mira. She wanted to run into the manor and find her brother to see that he was all right. Instead, she knelt and took hold of Ina's shoulders, looking the woman in the eyes. "Ina, what's happened?"

Ina continued to sob.

Mira looked up at the pallid doorman. "Where is my brother?"

"I can show you to him, my lady."

She nodded and pulled Ina to her feet. "Come, Ina, we will go see him."

Ina continued to weep as Mira guided her down the halls behind the doorman. He led them to a previously unused bedchamber on the ground floor and knocked softly on the door. After a short delay, a woman emerged. Dark blood stained her shift and apron and Mira's panic grew to a dizzying intensity. The dusky-haired woman frowned at Ina.

"She should be in bed. Take her to her room," she demanded of the doorman. "I will speak with this woman alone."

The doorman gently took Ina's shoulders and guided her away. She offered no resistance. When they were gone, Mira focused on the woman before her. "I am Mira, Dannesk's sister."

"I figured as much. You have some of the same features. He is resting. I am Yuuki. I assist doctor Daichiro in town."

"What happened?"

Yuuki glanced after Ina. "Did she tell you anything?"

"No. She just started sobbing, and if someone doesn't tell me something soon, I'm likely to get violent."

Yuuki nodded, unruffled. "Sit with me." She indicated chairs that had been set in the hallway near the room.

Swallowing frustration, Mira sat.

Yuuki sat next to her and folder her hands in her lap. "First, are you all right? There's dried blood on your chin and bruise on your cheek. Did you fall?"

"Oh. No, I'm fine. It isn't anything to be concerned over." As she spoke, she moistened a finger with her tongue and rubbed at her chin.

After a moment, Yuuki nodded satisfaction. "Better. Lord Dannesk rode out to one of the residences in the holding this morning. There was apparently an incident there with some bandits, so he took a unit of soldiers to check into it. When they returned, your brother and several of his men had been badly wounded."

"How badly?"

Yuuki exhaled, her sympathetic look further expanding the dreadful cold inside Mira. "He was shot through the abdomen with a crossbow bolt. There's very little we can do for him."

"No!" Mira snapped to her feet and started toward the door.

Yuuki grabbed her arm to stop her. "You must not upset him. He's barely holding on as it is and upsetting him could increase the blood loss."

Mira stared longingly at the door. "Can't I see him?"

"Yes," Yuuki replied. "Clean yourself up and hide that bruise with some powder. If you go in there looking like this you are sure to upset him."

Mira nodded and bolted down the hall to Ina and Dannesk's chambers. Once there, she found Ina's vanity. The woman in the mirror gazed back at her with green eyes heavily streaked through with gold. She could do nothing about that, but the mussed hair and the bruise she could make pretty. Ina entered the room and dug a dress out of her wardrobe for Mira to change into. It might be a little tight in places given the differences in their figures, but it would be better than the tattered thing she wore now.

When she was done, Ina followed her silently back to where Dannesk was being tended. Yuuki nodded approvingly at Mira, though she gave Ina a severe look before letting them in.

A man stood over the bed, checking Dannesk's pulse at his throat. He glanced at Mira and Ina when they entered, but said nothing. Mira approached the bed. Dannesk lay there, ghostly pale, his brow furrowed and damp with sweat. Bandages soaked in dark blood wrapped his abdomen. Mira sat next to him and took his hand in her own. She glanced askance at the doctor. The man regarded her sternly, then he finally nodded. Ina went around and sat on Dannesk's other side, taking that hand in her trembling one.

"Danni," Mira whispered, fighting the painful tightening in her throat.

His eyelids fluttered and opened. Mira winced when he turned his head and a soft moan whispered through lips drained of color. Several seconds passed before his eyes finally focused on her. His smile was weak. She brushed his hair away from his forehead, tears stinging her eyes.

"I… I'm glad Valin let you come." The words were slow, as if each one required a struggle, and an invisible dagger twisted in her chest. She bit back the tears and forced a smile.

"I wanted to see you, Danni. I thought you might want to ride back to Barik manor with me for the wedding." Such an awful lie, but it made him smile.

"I would… would have liked that." His eyes closed and he moaned again, seeming unaware of the sound.

"Don't go, Danni" Despite her efforts, the tears began to fall and she clutched his hand tighter.

"I…" He fell silent for a long moment, his face twisting into a grimace and his hand tightening on hers almost painfully. "I didn't want to."

The hand she held went limp and his face relaxed into neutrality. With a growing sense of horror, she stared at his suddenly peaceful countenance. The doctor placed a hand on his throat and shook his head.

"No!" Ina's shriek of agony cut the sudden silence. She dropped to her knees next to the bed and clutched Dannesk's hand. The doctor took hold of her shoulders and squeezed them.

"I am so sorry, Lady Ina, but you must calm yourself. You don't want to harm the baby."

Mira stood. Calmly, she reached up and brushed closed her brother's eyes. A ghastly emptiness filled her as she left the room. Yuuki met her gaze and her expression twisted in heartfelt sympathy. Mira turned and walked down the hall. She left the manor and crossed the courtyard. In the garden, she walked to a bench that stared back at the manor and sat there. For a long time, she sat there alone, then Kazue came and stood before her, regarding her with his intelligent gold eyes. She dropped her head into her hands then and wept. Kazue shifted close and wrapped one silky soft wing around her.

CHAPTER THIRTEEN

I should never have kissed her.

The mare staggered mid-stride, jarring him from his thoughts and almost from the saddle. The animal had missed many strides of late, her exhaustion beginning to show through. He couldn't push her much farther, but he still felt the intense need to—*to run away*—to get to the capital as quickly as possible. He also tried to avoid slowing due to an increase in less reputable looking travelers along the roadway, rough looking men carrying crude weapons, most traveling in groups of three or more. They sneered at him when they saw him, but chose to leave him be, perhaps because of his speed and the weapons he carried which he made no effort to hide. One well-aimed bow could change that quickly though, so he stayed on his guard. Hours and days long since began to blur together since he'd taken to resting at odd times in case any of those he saw hoped to follow and catch him unaware.

In a few places, he saw the results of their attacks, a burning farmhouse in the distance one day, a family lying slain by the road near an overturned wagon a few days later, their belongings ransacked and their draft beast taken. The mother, left lying naked in her own blood, had evidently fared the worst.

How quickly bandits moved in on the heels of conflict, growing bold and aggressive now that road patrols returned to the capital. Was the situation so dire that the queen felt it worth the risk of letting such rabble run the roads to terrorize her people?

The mare stumbled several times in a row and he relented, letting her slow to a fatigued trot. Yamoto Stable, a few days outside of the capital, catered to military and upper-class patrons. They specialized in breeding and training warhorses, though they also put out some of the finest hunters and carriage horses money could buy. He could get another horse there, but he wouldn't be able to trade straight across for it. Any horse he got there would cost him a fair bit in addition to his rundown mount, but it would be coin well spent on a mount he could take into battle.

He become more conscientious of his pace once he made the decision, giving the mare breaks to rest and eat so as not to push her beyond recovery before he arrived at the stable.

Eventually, the vast pastures and training fields came into view. The stables, larger by far than the manor house that oversaw it all, loomed in the distance, buildings that housed the finest horseflesh in the kingdom. He eased the mare along at a long, casual trot up to the main gates. Six men stood guard, two on either side of the ornate ironwork gates and one on each gate tower alongside wielding crossbows, a sign of the rapidly changing state of things.

A seventh man, bristling with weaponry, stepped out of the near tower upon his approach, his dark eyes narrowed suspiciously. "State your business!"

"I am in need of a new horse." He patted the neck of the weary mare. She snorted once and stomped a hoof as if to object to his belated kindness.

The gate guard eyed the mare critically, then turned his skeptical gaze up to Kashi. "We don't sell just any horses to any man, good Sir."

He shifted his jacket back to show the rank branded into the scabbard at his hip. "It's Captain, actually, Captain Marikashi Arkesh."

The introduction opened the guard's expression into a welcoming smile. "Excuse me, Captain. I imagine you'll require horse more appropriate to the needs of a soldier. Open the gates!"

He nodded his appreciation as the gates opened to admit him. Swinging from the saddle, he led the mare through. Being a mare, she at least had some breeding value to barter with and Arkesh never dealt in lesser stock, though she didn't look like much to the untrained eye right then, her coat matted with drying sweat and her head hanging low. The guard escorted him to the main residence, a sizeable structure with numerous expansions added on as the family business gained prestige. It was now large enough that it even attracted a small population of gargoyles. Their presence drove Mira back to the forefront of his mind as he watched them playing on the wind currents around the buildings in the early dusk.

When they entered the courtyard of the main residence, a young boy of perhaps eight years intercepted them, eyeing Kashi and the mare with a salesman's severe scrutiny, out of place on one so young. The guard bowed to the youth.

"Master Akimo, Captain Marikashi Arkesh is in need of a warhorse. Would you escort him and his offering to Master Takumora?"

The boy scowled at Kashi. "The mare looks a little used up."

"I rode her from the Arkesh manor to here in three days, she should be."

The boy looked more thoughtful now. He walked up to the mare and moved around her, picking up her feet and feeling her muscles for cramping. Coming back around to the front, he stared at her for a moment longer then nodded.

"Might be worth something." The boy turned and started to walk away. "Follow me, Captain Marikashi."

There were four large stables on the grounds set at the four corners of the main residence with arenas and paddocks consuming the space between. He followed the boy to the easternmost of those stables. A trainer worked with a young horse in the closest arena and several stable hands moved horses about the property, stepping out of the way to let the unfamiliar horse pass safely.

Just outside of the stable, the boy turned to Kashi. "Wait here, Captain Marikashi."

He nodded and the boy vanished into the large building. He re-emerged a few moments later with a man in tow whose stocky, muscular build and rough features put Kashi in mind of a blacksmith. The man smiled at him warmly, his eyes sparkling in anticipation of a deal to be bartered.

"Captain Marikashi Arkesh, it is my pleasure to welcome you. I am Master Takumora Yamoto." He bowed slightly then offered a hand.

Kashi shook it firmly, noting the strength in his grip and the roughness of many calluses. This man worked hard at his business rather than simply overseeing the work of those in his service.

"Master Takumora, I have heard only the best things of your horses."

Takumora nodded. "That is because there are no better." He gave Kashi a long, appraising look, then he turned to the mare. "What do you bring me, Captain?"

"He rode this mare from Arkesh to here in just three days. She'd be a great broodmare for the hunters," the boy piped up suddenly.

Takumora scowled at the youth, though Kashi could see fondness in his eyes. "Akimo," he chided firmly, "that is not the manner of a businessman. You undermine your bargaining strength with such enthusiasm."

"Sorry, Papa." The boy hung his head.

"Go find Kiedo. I would have him try this mare."

"Yes, Papa!" The boy grinned, his shame already forgotten, spun on one foot, and darted off toward another stable.

"She has been driven hard, Master Takumora," Kashi cautioned, concerned for the mare.

"We will not push her, Captain Marikashi, but we must try the mare before we can determine her worth. Has she been bred?"

Kashi stepped away from the mare to allow the man to inspect her. "She has been bred once. She bore a healthy filly with no complications." This mare had, in fact, been the dam of Mira's little mare, Aiko, so he knew she could produce good offspring.

Takumora grunted in response as he inspected her legs and feet. He moved back and circled around her to check her confirmation, then he came up to her head to check her teeth. A slender whip of a man arrived following young Akimo. Takumora spoke with him for a moment and then turned to Kashi.

"This is Master Kiedo, one of my top trainers. May he use your equipment, Captain Marikashi?"

Kashi nodded and pulled off his packs before handing the reins to Kiedo who led the mare into the nearest arena where the man training the young horse had already moved out of the way, anticipating their need. Kashi watched quietly as Kiedo worked with the mare for several minutes. She responded well to his directions, as Kashi had known she would, even worn down as she was. The Arkesh stables weren't as grand as this, but they boasted two fine trainers who kept the animals nicely tuned.

Kiedo brought the mare back out and returned her to Kashi.

"Master Takumora," Kiedo bowed slightly when he addressed the stable owner, "the mare is strong and responsive. She seems to possess an even temper and a willingness to please. She was a touch slow on some of her reactions, though that could be due to exhaustion rather than gaps in training. I would want more time with her to determine what she is most suited for, but she has many fine qualities that would be beneficial to your breeding program."

"See Papa, a good broodmare." The boy puffed up proudly.

"Thank you, Master Kiedo."

Kiedo bowed again and took leave of them. Takumora ruffled the boy's hair absently.

"If it is acceptable to you, Captain Marikashi, I will have Akimo tend to the mare while I show you what mounts I have available for you."

Kashi nodded. "I think that would be appreciated." He let the boy take the reins from him.

"Akimo, clean the captain's equipment when you are done."

"Yes, Papa." The boy led the mare away, talking softly to the animal.

Kashi needed to hurry, but a man like Takumora would run this his way or not at all, so he didn't object to the cleaning of his equipment. It certainly needed the attention.

"Come, Captain Marikashi, I assume you seek a war horse."

"Yes, Master Takumora. I would see what you have available."

"I think I have just the horse for a man of your station." Takumora smiled faintly as he turned and headed towards the southernmost of the stables.

As he followed the stable owner, Kashi did a mental inventory of what he had available for bargaining. He had the mare, and a fair amount of coin. If necessary, he also had a ceremonial military dagger that was of some value, though he would prefer not to part with all of his assets.

They entered one of the large stable blocks. Spacious stalls lined both sides of the wide aisle. Most were occupied, though a few were empty. Kashi eyed the horses as he followed Takumora. Several of the animals looked like good candidates for what he wanted, but Takumora led him to the last set of stalls and grinned broadly at him as he gestured to the stall on the right.

Kashi looked into the stall and saw a big, blood bay stallion with a black mane and tail and four black socks. His nose and the tips of his ears also darkened down to black and he bore a white crescent on his forehead. The stallion was well-muscled and, to Kashi's surprise, quite friendly. The big horse stuck his head over the front of the stall and lipped gently at the hand Kashi presented to him. Kashi scratched the stallion's head in return under his long forelock, noting the way the animal lowered his head for him.

"I think this might be more than I was planning on."

Takumora chuckled. "Try him, Captain. He is primed for combat. He is young and strong. I would make a good deal for you if you prove him in combat and agree to send him back to cover some of my mares within the next year."

"Isn't that a risky proposition for you? If something happens to me or to the horse, you would lose out."

"Perhaps, but I will not give you such a deal that it would hurt me. You are a captain in the Queen's army. The men will notice you and thereby, your mount. It is good advertising. I have a fine stock of warhorses coming up and I need customers."

Kashi eyed the stallion thoughtfully. He was impressive and beautiful. Mira would adore him. She always had a soft spot for the darker bays.

"All right, I'll give him a try."

A short while later, Kashi was sitting in Takumora's receiving room bartering for the stallion. He had run the stallion through a series of exercises he learned in the academy and he could find no fault in the training. In fact, it was almost as if the horse knew more than he did. The stallion had been so sensitive to every movement that he barely knew what he wanted the horse to do before the animal was doing it. He was flawless.

Takumora required first breeding rights on the stallion within a year or as soon as he was able to return if the conflict with Hishae ran longer than that. After that, Kashi would be free to use the stallion to improve Arkesh stock if he so wished. He was handing over the ceremonial dagger, the mare, and a large portion of the coin he had with him in exchange for the stallion. It was more than he should be giving and more horse than he probably needed, but one ride had hooked him. Takumora was a smart man and read his clients a little too well.

Takumora left the room to write up an agreement with an apology that his study was being redesigned and not currently fit for receiving guests. In his absence, a young woman entered the room bearing a tray of small cakes and a decanter of wine. She set these on the table and poured him a glass of wine, then curtsied gracefully. Her dark blond hair was bound partly up in a fancy clip, the rest hanging in ringlets around her face. She wore a well-fitted, pale green gown that enhanced her shape rather boldly.

"Captain, is there anything else I can bring you?"

Kashi looked up at her, his eyes catching unintentionally on the soft curve of her breasts before moving up to her face. Unease made him long to leave as she batted her lashes and gave a slight, sultry pout when he shook his head.

"This is fine, thank you." Kashi picked up the glass and tasted the wine, noting that she continued to watch him, rather than leaving.

"I'm Kaichi Yamoto. Takumora's eldest daughter."

"It is a pleasure to meet you, lady," Kashi said politely, hoping Takumora would return quickly.

Her eyes continued to watch him intently. They were green, like Mira's, but not as dark and missing the sparkle of playfulness that he adored. Her face was soft and a touch rounder than Mira's, though quite lovely in a different way. For a moment, Kashi met her eyes, trying to see her without comparing her to Mira, but he could not. Mira's face, her eyes and the tears falling from them, rose to the front of his mind and he looked away.

"I'm seventeen," she offered, and he could hear a hopeful tremor in her voice.

Kashi shifted in his chair, wondering how he was supposed to respond to that. She clearly wanted to let him know that she was old enough to marry. Knowing that the daughter of a wealthy man like Takumora Yamoto was not only an appropriate match, but actually a very good one for a man of his standing, did not make him any more comfortable. If she was seventeen, it was past time that she should be married or at least entertaining suitors. He could not help wondering if Takumora had sent her in for that very reason.

The door opened then, saving him from coming up with a response. Takumora entered the room and smiled fondly at his daughter, then turned to Kashi with a broad grin.

"I see you have met my Kaichi. She is lovely, isn't she?"

"Yes," Kashi replied, hoping their business would be concluded before wedding proposals joined the negotiations, "she is very lovely."

"Sit, Kaichi. The captain and I are just concluding our bargain."

Kaichi attempted a shy smile as she sat in the chair next to Kashi, though it looked more predatory to him. Takumora set a small inkpot and quill on the table, then handed him the contract and Kashi read it over carefully, making sure there was no mention of marriage in it, before he agreed to the terms. Once he had signed the agreement, he handed it back to Takumora and the stable owner shook his hand vigorously.

"Stay and sup with us, Captain," Takumora invited as they stood.

Kashi noticed Kaichi's eager look and carefully avoided her eyes. "I would be honored, Master Takumora, but I have been too long in reaching the city already. There is a conflict that must be resolved and I cannot in good conscience postpone my duty to the kingdom any longer."

Takumora nodded solemnly. "You are right, Captain Marikashi. The kingdom must come first. Perhaps, when you bring the stallion for breeding, you would stay with us while he is covering the mares. We would be delighted to have you," Takumora gestured, indicating his daughter as well.

"That sounds pleasant," Kashi replied. "I thank you for your hospitality Master Takumora. Lady Kaichi," he offered with a nod to each.

Kaichi stood and curtsied to him. "Thank you, Captain Marikashi," she said in a voice that dripped sweetness.

Takumora led Kashi out to the courtyard. The stallion was brought around, already prepared with Kashi's freshly cleaned equipment. Kashi shook Takumora's hand again then mounted the powerful animal.

"I will be honored to prove him for you, Master Takumora."

Takumora grinned, "I think you will, Captain. Good luck."

Kashi nodded and urged the stallion up to a trot. They passed through the gates and he let him trot easily for a time to warm up his muscles, then he urged him up to a much faster, extended trot. He was interested to see how the animal did for stamina. His trot was long and smooth, much like Mira's little mare. The two would likely produce an impressive foal, with the stallion's strength and Aiko's stamina.

Thinking of Mira, Kashi thought the stallion should probably have a name. He pondered it for a time as the countryside passed by, then patted the stallions shoulder.

"I will call you Omoide."

CHAPTER FOURTEEN

A day and a half later, the massive wall around the city of Beikang rose up before Kashi. The dark grey stone had a blue cast to it, giving it the look of a moonlight night sky. That was why they called it the City of the Moon. The dark stone and the rich, dark wood that were the most plentiful building materials made up most of the structures in the city. Even the major streets near the palace were paved with a cobble made of the dark stone. Passing through the gates was like riding into a bright night.

Omoide was still moving strong, though Kashi could feel that the stallion needed a break. He dismounted outside the main gate. Passage into and out of the city was being monitored more closely than usual, as he had expected. When he approached the gate, a figure burst from the gatehouse and Kashi dropped a hand instinctively to his sword hilt before recognizing his sergeant.

"Captain Marikashi!"

Kashi grinned, infected by the other man's enthusiasm. "Sergeant Rajasi," he greeted in turn.

Rajasi, his blond hair unkempt as always and a good week's worth of stubble darkening his jaw line, grabbed Kashi's offered hand and pulled him in for a rough embrace. He stepped back then and shook his head at Kashi in mock disapproval.

"You look soft, Captain. Life at home has been too kind to you."

Kashi placed a hand on his hilt. "Care to try me, Sergeant?"

Rajasi laughed. "Do I look like a fool?"

Kashi chuckled in return. "Do I have to answer that?"

Rajasi slapped him on the shoulder. "Good to see you, Captain." He stepped to the side and gave Omoide an appraising look. "That is quite the horse."

"I got him from Takumora Yamoto. We'll see how good he really is when we get to the front lines."

Rajasi turned to face him again. "Well, we best get a move on then or we'll miss all the fun. Much of the main force is already on the front lines. Your troop is ready to move when you are, Captain."

Kashi nodded, feeling the sense of urgency again. Shakari would be with the main force and his promise to Sunai nagged at him. He looked over the stallion thoughtfully. "I just need to give him a short rest then we can get out of the city. Where is the troop?"

"Follow me," Rajasi said and led the way into the city.

Kashi led Omoide and walked along beside Rajasi. He was glad to see the Sergeant. Though the other man was oft a bit too eager to spend time planning pranks rather than focusing on training, Kashi and he had been close friends throughout his time at the Academy.

"So, did you make your peace with your lady friend? Mira was her name, wasn't it?"

Kashi grimaced. "She is to be wed to Valin Barik."

"Hmmm. Sorry to hear that," Rajasi replied with a thoughtful scowl. "I had kind of hoped things would work out somehow."

Kashi forced a shrug, pretending indifference. "I always knew it would end this way."

"Hey!" Rajasi brightened suddenly. "Barik is sending troops. We could always arrange an accident."

"We're on the same side," Kashi scolded, making his tone severe. "Regardless, Ander is holding his son back."

Rajasi sighed. "Well, maybe he'll come later if things aren't resolved quickly."

Kashi said nothing. No matter how much he hated the thought of Mira in Valin's arms, he could not bring himself to humor such a thing even in jesting.

"I see that look." Rajasi chuckled. "It's not a bad idea, is it?"

Kashi rolled his eyes, though he couldn't stop a fond smile from stealing across his face at the other man's ridiculous grin. "You're a terrible man, Sergeant."

"Thanks, Captain."

An hour later, Kashi sat on Omoide's back and watched his troop filing out of the city's east gate. He had trained extensively with these men during his time at the academy and had even led them on a few small campaigns. Once to resolve a land dispute that had grown violent and another time to root out a gang of bandits terrorizing a small village. Both had been tests of his ability to lead, and his troop had excelled both times. Without good men, a good captain could only do so much. Kashi counted himself lucky in the quality of the men he had been given to lead.

The sister city of Laki was a mirror image of Beikang in layout but it was built of a pale stone and wood that, along with the quality diamonds mined there, earned it the name, City of the Sun. The sister palace in Laki had been built as a future wedding present for King Mahesh of Hishae's daughter and Queen Isaye's son, but apparently King Mahesh had changed his mind about the alliance. It was strange that such a strong alliance would vanish overnight, but perhaps Hishae had been wooed by another outlying kingdom. Regardless of the cause, it appeared that conquering Beikang had somehow become more appealing than a marital alliance.

Kashi was confident that his troop could reach Laki in a few days of fast marching and still have reserves for combat if they needed to fight right away. It did not take long to get the troop assembled and on the move. Kashi took up the lead with Rajasi flanking him. Rajasi's gelding took an immediate dislike to Omoide, but the big stallion laid his ears back once in warning and otherwise ignored the other horse.

This side of the city, the terrain consisted of rolling hills, some forested, and some open fields. Kashi moved them along at an easy trot, keeping in mind that some of his troop was on foot and the rolling terrain would wear them down. They stopped for a few hours midday, then again for a few hours during the night. The next morning, Kashi allowed a brief break and again at midday that day, checking regularly to ensure that he was not pushing too hard. His troop seemed as anxious to reach the conflict as he was, so they didn't complain.

By nightfall, they had arrived at the war camp on the west side of the river. Kashi was almost surprised to see that Beikang's forces had not already taken the city back. Somehow, he had found it hard to believe that Hishae had really taken Laki, but the fires of the enemy camp lit the east side of the river, between Beikang's army and the city. With a shake of his head, he dismounted, left Omoide and his troop to Sergeant Rajasi, and followed a soldier to the officer's tent.

"Captain Marikashi."

"Major Tatsuo," Kashi greeted the major with a bow of his head and took in the rest of the group. Shakari was there, along with another captain and two sergeants.

"Captain, I'm glad you arrived." The major's dark eyes zeroed in on him intently. "I have something I would like to show you. Captain Nioku, join us. Captain Shakari, please continue this session, we will return momentarily."

Shakari nodded as Kashi and Captain Nioku, a pale man whose slight build made him easy to underestimate in combat, followed the major from the tent. Major Tatsuo led them toward the picket lines and told them to retrieve their mounts. Kashi found Omoide. His saddle had been removed, but he threw a blanket on the stallions back and swung up. When he and Nioku rejoined Tatsuo, the major lead them to a hill some distance from the camp that had a good view of both camps and much of the city.

"Major Hideo met with me this morning. Captain Shakari was there, but since the two of you were not, I will tell you what transpired at that meeting. I conveyed the Queen's demands that they leave the city, demands Major Hideo laughed at."

Kashi heard the tension of anger in Tatsuo's voice. He was silent for a moment and they waited as their mounts shifted restlessly. The night was cool, the air pleasant, but the smells of the campfires kept them in mind of their purpose.

"Major Hideo has given us until tomorrow at dawn to surrender. He claims that they have a weapon we cannot fight. He says that each day after today, we will be faced with an army we cannot harm, and each night after this night, we will be attacked by the great birds that surround the palace. You can just barely see the creatures he speaks of."

Kashi strained his eyes and could make out the forms flying about the palace. In the dark at this distance, he would have thought them gargoyles. He found himself remembering Gemma's words. The old woman had said that they were all in danger, that there were powers at work they did not understand. Could she somehow have known of this secret weapon of Hideo's.

The major sighed. "If not for the presence of those unnatural birds, I would think him mad. They are huge. As big as any gargoyle, if not bigger, and something about them seems wrong somehow. I am still not completely convinced that he isn't mad. Tomorrow I intend to engage in combat with Hishae's army, unless you can think of any alternative. Surrender is clearly not an option."

"With the river between us, there is no good battleground," Nioku commented.

"Yes, I had considered putting up a white flag to lure them over, but it would not be an honorable act."

"The act of taking Laki was not an honorable act," Kashi commented, his tone bitter.

Major Tatsuo turned his dark eyed gaze on Kashi. "That, Captain Marikashi, is why I like having you here. You always seem to find a way to justify my actions for me."

"A pleasure to be of service, Major," Kashi replied, his ire rising as he considered the occupied city.

They sat in silence for a long moment, then a form swept through the sky a short distance away. At first, he thought it might be one of the birds the major had mentioned. The others seemed to think so as well for they both dropped their hands to their swords. Then it circled and he saw that it was a gargoyle. Kashi found himself wanting to reach out to the creature, as if he could touch Mira through it, but he knew it was a foolish thought and he kept his hand resting at his side. Omoide nickered softly, as if the stallion had recognized a companion. Kashi patted the animal's neck and watched as the gargoyle disappeared over the city.

At dawn, the Beikang troops sat in wait. Major Tatsuo and a contingent of soldiers were assembled on the stretch between the camp and the river, a white flag held up by one of the men on the end of a pike. The rest of the army watched and waited for the signal. Just after sunrise, a similar contingent emerged from the Hishae camp. The man at its head, riding a white stallion, had alarmingly pale skin and eyes, and though he was clearly young, his hair was a brilliant silver that reflected the sun. His unnatural appearance filled Kashi with unease and he found himself thinking of the gold in Mira's eyes. Omoide shifted in response to his sudden discomfort and Kashi placed a soothing hand on the stallion's neck.

The contingent followed the pale man, who he believed to be Major Hideo, across the one bridge that spanned the river. There was no fear in their eyes, and that also made Kashi uneasy. Even if they believed the surrender, there was always some fear when approaching an enemy. Death knew no alliances. Hideo pulled up a few yards from Tatsuo and smiled. There was perhaps a hint of madness in that smile, but what Kashi noted was the confidence in it.

"Major Tatsuo, I see you have gathered more troops in the night. I am not that easily fooled."

Kashi tensed. If the other major was aware of the additional troops, then he knew the surrender could not be sincere. The only question then was why he would dare to cross the river with so few men, unless he knew something they did not.

"Major Hideo, I did not seek to fool you. Look at the white flag as an invitation of sorts," Tatsuo replied, his hand dropping to his sword.

Swords flew from their sheathes and Beikang's warriors charged. Hideo continued to smile as he drew his own sword. The bulk of Hishae's army simply watched from across the river, making no move to rescue their Major. Kashi urged Omoide forward and the stallion charged willingly into the mass of warriors, deftly maneuvering into the fray. Kashi attacked one of Hishae's warriors from behind, but his blade slid across the man's back, leaving no mark. Kashi spun Omoide and attacked repeatedly, but could do no harm to the enemy. His blade made no impression, bouncing away from flesh and armor both while Hishae's small contingent cut their way free, leaving a path of bodies behind, and crossed the bridge again.

Several of Beikang's warriors attempted to follow, but were cut down with a volley of arrows and the captains called the rest back. Kashi had lost sight of Major Tatsuo in the combat, but as Hideo spun his mount to face them, his pale countenance spattered with blood, he held up a grizzly trophy. Major Tatsuo's head stared back at them from Hideo's grasp.

"Who succeeds this man?"

Shakari rode forward. He was the next in rank and Kashi watched him anxiously, remembering his promise to Sunai.

"I do."

"And you are?" Hideo asked, lowering the head.

"Major Shakari," Shakari replied, assuming the title that was now his by right.

Hideo nodded. "Perhaps you will listen better than your predecessor. You know now that my soldiers are invulnerable to your weapons. Tonight, you will begin to lose warriors to my birds. I leave you to reconsider your position."

With that, Hideo tossed the head out into the middle of the bridge and turned back into the camp. Kashi rode up beside Shakari who was staring after the pale man.

"What now?" Shakari asked, his voice low so only Kashi could hear.

One of the Beikang soldiers started out on the bridge to retrieve the major's head, but several arrows let fly, landing in the wood of the bridge between him and the head. With a curse, the soldier retreated.

"We stand our ground and find a weakness," Kashi replied under his breath, hatred flowing like fire through his veins.

Days passed and the world outside seemed to disappear. A messenger was sent the day after Dannesk's passing to inform Sunai. Mira wished him luck, considering the bandits that had almost killed her and those that had killed her brother. The day after that, they buried Dannesk in the family tomb on the hill behind the manor. There was little hope that Sunai would be able to come at this time with Shakari at war and the roads unsafe, assuming the messenger even reached her, so they held a small service.

Ina watched the casket being carried in with some composure, but when the doors were shut, she collapsed in sobs. Mira was cold. She couldn't remember ever being this cold before. Kazue watched the funeral proceedings from atop one of the towers and Mira joined him there when it was through. For once, his warmth, his molten eyes, could not seem to bring her comfort. She sat with him for a long time though, appreciating the warmth of his wing wrapped around her, even if it could not touch the cold within her.

Did Kashi still live, or she should mourn him as well? It was a horrible thought and tears ran down her cheeks slowly, though she would have expected to be out of tears by now.

Kazue stood, taking his wing away and turned to

face her. He put his face up close to hers and licked away a tear. His rough tongue sent her back to that first night she had touched him. She had been going to meet Valin Barik then. It wasn't all that long ago, yet so much had changed. What was she to do now? She was here with only Ina, Gemma, the manor staff, and those soldiers who had not gone to the war front.

Ina.

She thought of the poor, delicate creature who had lost a husband and the father of her unborn child. What was Ina supposed to do?

Mira snapped to her feet and Kazue sat back, watching her as she vanished down into the manor. She went quickly to Dannesk's study and sat at his desk. There she composed a letter and sealed it with the Yukori seal. When that was done, she hunted down a soldier and gave him the letter.

"Take this to Lord Valin Barik. Only Lord Valin, not his father." When the soldier nodded his understanding, she continued. "Ride as fast as you dare and be wary. There will be bandits on the roads."

"Yes, my lady."

"Thank you." She stood and watched him leave, then went in search of Ina.

Ina was in Dannesk's study, sitting behind his desk where Mira had been not long before. She didn't acknowledge Mira when she entered. Mira walked over and stood in front of the desk, placing herself directly in Ina's line of site.

"Yes, Mira," she murmured, still not meeting her eyes.

"You are not safe here, Ina. The manor troops are too depleted and many may choose to move on now that Danni is gone."

Ina did look up at her now, her eyes glassy with a store of unshed tears even now. "What am I to do?'

"I have sent word to Lord Valin. I told him of what befell Danni and let him know that you are with child. I left it up to him as to whether he sends troops to reinforce the manor or a carriage to bring you back there."

"There isn't going to be a wedding, is there?" Ina's eyes dropped to her hands, which were clasped on Dannesk's desk.

Mira had expected a fight. The question disconcerted her. "No."

"Doesn't it bother you that the last thing you did was lie to him?"

The words cut into Mira and she lashed back. "The last thing I did was make him smile. What did you do?"

Ina said nothing and Mira stormed from the room, slamming the door behind her. She paced the halls for a time, then finally settled in a cozy sitting room that Dannesk had always favored. A servant found her there and built a fire in the fireplace at one side of the room, then left her in her silence again. A short while later, Ina stepped into the room and stood by the door, looking uncertain as she regarded Mira. Mira did nothing to acknowledge her, feeling that it was only fair to reciprocate the treatment she had received earlier.

"What about you?"

Mira gazed at the fire. "I suppose I will stay with you, wherever you end up."

Ina entered the room, apparently encouraged by the civil response. She sat in a chair across from Mira and joined her in gazing at the fire. "I can't leave here. It would be too dangerous for the baby and this is where…"

Ina did not need to finish. Neither of them wanted to leave the memories of Dannesk, but sometimes wanting didn't come into the calculations. "We will do what we have to do," Mira replied, her stern tone hiding her own reluctance.

"You sound like Danni," Ina replied wistfully. "We could go to Arkesh—"

"No," Mira cut her off. "That takes us east toward the war. We are better off to go west if we go anywhere."

Another figure appeared in the doorway and they both stood in surprise as Gemma hobbled into the room. Ina walked over to the old woman, her brow furrowed with concern.

"Gemma, are you all right?"

Gemma waved Ina off. "I am fine. I must speak with Mira alone."

Ina looked hurt, but she nodded. "Very well. Perhaps you can talk some sense into her."

Once Ina had left the room, Mira walked over to help Gemma to a chair. Gemma accepted the assistance gracefully and made a show of settling into a chair next to the fire. Mira experienced a surge of fondness for the old woman. She returned to her own chair and watched Gemma, waiting for the old woman to settle. The fondness was tempered by a chill of uncertainty when the old woman turned a fierce, determined gaze upon her.

"Did you touch the gargoyle, child? Judging from the change in your eyes, I would say you have."

Mira nodded. "Yes, Gemma, many times."

"I feared as much." The old woman shook her head, her shoulders sinking under some heavy weight. "Mira, there is ancient magic at work in this war. Hishae has unleashed a dangerous power greater than all of us. Someone in their army has tapped into a magic that can only be fought with other ancient magic."

Mira shook her head, confused. "I don't understand. How can you know this, Gemma?"

"There are many different types of magic in the world. Most of them have been hidden away. Many have gone dormant with time, but they only sleep, child. They can be awoken. There are many things about me that you do not know. Suffice it to say that I too have been touched by magic in my time and that magic has given me the ability to feel when the balance of power is thrown off." Gemma leaned forward and Mira felt in that moment as if she truly did not know the old woman whose eyes burned with such uncharacteristic intensity. "You must stop Hishae."

"What?" Mira sat up in her chair. "Gemma, you are not well."

Gemma sank into her seat then, as though some great weight pressed her down. "When I was younger, I belonged to a secret group that was dedicated to rediscovering the old magics. In the process, many of us were changed by the things we found. You remember the fire that burned here?"

"Of course," Mira replied, not sure she wanted to hear any more, but not wanting to be rude to her great aunt.

She blew out a breath. "That was my doing. I was messing with something I should not have been and it had disastrous results for all of us. I will never be able to forgive myself for what happened then."

Mira shook her head, horror unfolding in her chest. Could anyone forgive such a thing? Could she?

Gemma gazed into the fireplace, seeming lost in some past Mira didn't understand. Then she sighed and looked at Mira again. "I cannot undo the past, but I can look to the future. You have magic in you now, child. It has to be you who stops this."

"Why me? I am no warrior and I have no magic." A powerful despair washed through Mira. Not only had she lost Dannesk, but her own beloved Gemma had admitted to causing the tragedy that had changed all of their lives. As she hung her head under the weight of the sadness, the candles throughout the room winked out.

"I see," Gemma replied, her tone smug in the ensuing darkness. Mira stared around in dumbstruck silence as a bell chimed and a door opened. "Please light our candles, dear."

"Yes, m'ladies," a soft voice said and they waited while the serving girl retrieved a lit candle and went around the room lighting the recently extinguished candles.

When Mira looked at Gemma again, the old woman smiled, though her eyes shimmered with sorrow.

"I had nothing to do with that," Mira insisted.

"Has nothing else strange happened to you lately, child?"

Mira found her thoughts turning to the archer whose crossbow had burst into flames and the cut hands of the man who had tried to assault her. "This is madness," she protested.

"War is madness, child. Love is madness."

Clever old woman.

Mira was silent. Love was madness, and if what Gemma said was true, Kashi was doomed if she did not do something. She felt as if a trap were closing around her and she dropped her head into her hands. "How can I just walk into the middle of a war and have any hope of surviving long enough to do anything?"

"That's more like it," Gemma replied with enthusiasm. "You must learn to be unseen in plain sight."

"That's ridiculous. You have gone mad. No one can do that."

"Most people can't, but you have been touched by a gargoyle. Trust in the gift he has given you."

Mira sneered. "Why did he choose me? I'm no warrior."

"He didn't need a warrior. There must be something in you, Mira, that made you the right one just as there was something in him that made him the one they sent to join with you. He has been chosen too and I'm sure it wasn't something he was planning on any more than you were. Trust in their choice. Gargoyles don't err." Gemma stated the last with certainty.

"Not until now," Mira replied, wincing at how petulant she sounded.

Gemma's expression softened. "Go get some rest, child. These things will make more sense when you aren't so tired."

Mira stood and walked over to take the old woman's hands. She kissed her on the forehead, struggling not to dwell on what the woman's meddling with magic had done to their lives. "I doubt it, Gemma, but we will see."

She started toward the exit that would lead her back to her room, but Gemma coughed intentionally and she glanced back over her shoulder.

"Perhaps some fresh air would help clear your mind before you go to bed."

Mira regarded the old woman suspiciously, recognizing it as an attempt to get her to interact with the gargoyle. "Perhaps." Now that she thought about it, she would like to see Kazue. Maybe something in those molten eyes would help her understand all of this.

She made her way up to the westernmost tower. Kazue was already there, watching the trapdoor. How he could know what tower she was going to was beyond her, but maybe it was part of the magic Gemma claimed he had. Mira smiled at him, wistful for a time when his attention was merely a curiosity and a distraction from what seemed bigger woes. She walked over to where he sat and rested a hand on his head.

Panic gripped her for a second as her mind swam and she collapsed into oblivion.

Mira was flying. The sensation was disorienting and she almost panicked before she realized she was not alone. There was another presence with her, a warm and comforting one. She relaxed, trusting Kazue to keep her safe. She recognized the land they were flying over, though she had not been this way in years. They were over the road going east into Beikang. The city rose on the horizon, a magnificent conglomeration of buildings from the tiny, base dwellings of the poor to the extravagant high peaks of the academies. Mira felt a twinge of resentment as they flew over those buildings. It was at one of those academies that the Kashi she knew and loved had become lost.

They passed over the town quickly and banked north with the turn of the main road. For a time, they flew over open countryside, speckled with farms, tracks of forest, and the occasional grand manor. Then she began to see the glowing of hundreds of fires in the distance. The ground was overrun with myriad tents of all sizes. They flew lower and she could see the people and horses milling around the city of tents and campfires. This was the war front and here, somewhere, was Kashi.

They flew lower still, over an open hilltop where three mounted warriors sat gazing at the distant landscape. Then they dropped down and cut around, sweeping a short distance in front of the riders. Mira saw that Kashi was one of the three. His eyes riveted on her—though she was sure it was not her he saw—and followed their flight for a short time. She noticed that he looked strong and healthy, if a bit tired. The sight of him filled her with pleasure.

After circling the three once, they continued past the camp. Across the river from the first camp lay another vast camp in between the river and the grand city of Laki. Sweeping over this camp, she saw that it was infested with warriors wearing the armor of Hishae. At the far side of the city was the new sister palace. Invading military forces moved in and out of the structure that was supposed to be a symbol of the alliance between the two kingdoms.

As they closed in on the sister palace, Mira noticed

creatures flying around it and perching upon the roofs and towers, but they were not gargoyles. A closer look showed that they were some sort of huge bird with night blue and black feathers. They dropped closer and closer to the creatures and she began to feel a terrible despair and desperation filling her. Several of the beasts were feasting on something draped over the peak of a roof. She could see enough to know that the remains were human. Then one of the birds looked directly at them, its eyes white as snow, and let out a blood-curdling shriek. It launched from the roof and came at them, several others joining the chase.

They banked left and flew as fast as they could, diving and twisting in an effort to evade the birds. The nearest of the creatures drew close and struck with its beak. A searing pain shot through her left hip and they lost altitude, spiraling toward the ground. The birds hung back, perhaps thinking they had won, but, at the last moment, they twisted and swept along close to the ground. The birds shrieked their distress, but it was too late, they were too far away now.

Relief washed over her when they turned back west toward home.

When she woke in the morning, Mira found that she was lying curled under Kazue's wing on the tower. She was stiff from lying on the stone, but plenty warm. Kazue turned his head toward her and licked her face as he might that of a pup. Mira giggled and warded him off with her hands. She stood up and regarded this enigmatic creature with fresh curiosity and she slowly remembered her dream. Kazue regarded her back with his sentient golden gaze. As the details of the dream returned, Mira felt a sense of awe and some fear. She noticed the healing wound on his hip.

"You shared a memory, didn't you?" The gargoyle inclined his head and she sat back down, lightheaded. "This is insane."

She remembered also that Kazue sought out Kashi in the dream and an almost overwhelming gratitude filled her for the chance to see him. He had looked strong and handsome as ever, his grey eyes full of stubborn determination.

"So, we go to the sister palace then." She said, tasting the fear and uncertainty around the words as they struggled forth. "It seems as good a place as any to start. First, I must get my things together and speak with a few people, then we will go. You may wish to find some food before we leave."

Kazue stood with her and lunged into the air. Mira watched him for a moment, remembering what it felt like to fly. When she lost track of him, she turned and climbed down into the manor. She crept about, trying to remain unseen, until she located Ina in the atrium. Once she knew where the other woman was, she went to Ina and Dannesk's chambers and raided her brother's wardrobe.

It did not seem practical to go to war in dresses. Dannesk had been of similar height and weight, though most of his pants were tight in the hips and loose at the waist. His shirts, at least, were of a looser style. She selected out several sets of functional clothing. His shoes were a touch too big, but her soft leather riding boots would be functional enough.

Mira took these items to her room and tossed them on her bed. When that was done, she went down to the stables and retrieved a set of saddlebags. Stopping by the kitchen, she stuffed a sack full of the foods that would last longest and took all of this back to her room. She packed the clothes into the bag, leaving out one set that she would change into when she was ready to leave.

She sat regarding her packs for a long time, considering what else she might need, then she stole down to Dannesk's study. Most of his weaponry was displayed on the walls and shelves of the room and she raided these items as well, taking several daggers with a variety of sheaths that she could affix to her person. She considered the swords for a moment, but she did not know how to wield one and wearing one might seem an invitation to those looking for a fight. From the study, she went about the manor gathering some more items that might be of use, including flint for starting fires, then packed these items into her bags.

Finally satisfied, she left her bags in a corner of her room and went to Gemma's chambers. She didn't knock today. Somehow, she did not feel as if it were necessary. Instead, she marched in and Gemma looked up from her chair next to the window and smiled.

"I am leaving tonight, Gemma. I leave you the burden of explaining to Ina. I have enough to figure out without having to deal with that."

Gemma nodded. "I will take care of it. I knew the gargoyle would convince you."

Mira rolled her eyes and sighed. Gemma motioned for her to sit and she sprawled in the chair, finding that she was wearier from her preparations then she had realized.

"I am going to die, you know." Mira stated in a matter of fact tone. "All because a crazy old woman told me I could stop the war and I was foolish enough to believe her."

"You may think of me what you will, my dear, so long as you follow the path that has been laid out before you. I don't want you to be the one. I wish someone else had been chosen, but wishing doesn't change the truth and everyone will suffer if we try to deny it."

Mira shook her head and gazed at her feet, which were splayed out wide upon the floor in a very unladylike manner. The image of Kashi on the battlefront was still strong in her mind, too strong yet for her to lose her resolve. "What is this magic I must face?"

"I do not know exactly, but it is strong. I can feel it in my bones."

"Ah, an old crazy lady with aching bones."

Gemma narrowed her eyes. "Do you want my help?"

Mira held up her hands in a gesture of surrender and Gemma nodded, after a moment she continued.

"Magic is terribly hard to come by, but once obtained, it is even harder to stop."

Mira sat up. "What does that mean? That whoever has this magic is going to be invincible?"

"No more so than you are," Gemma replied.

"I don't feel very invincible," Mira flopped back in the chair again and Gemma shook her head, her lips pressing into a sympathetic line for a second.

"Trust in the magic. You will discover that you have great power. We learned many things when we were researching the old magic. One of the things we discovered was that the magic held by the gargoyles is some of the strongest ever to exist. Your gargoyle will not let you down."

"Kazue," Mira offered, placing a hand over her tired eyes, "I call him Kazue."

"And I do not think you will let him down."

Mira lifted her hand, saw the adoring smile on Gemma's face, and dropped the hand back over her eyes with a sigh. This was insane, but between her dream and Gemma's conviction, she found that she was starting to believe in the madness. Part of her just wanted to do something other than sit and wait for the war to end. She had not been aware of that more reckless side of her nature until now, but it seemed to like the idea that she might be able to do something to stop the war. Worst case, she would get killed, and she would really be the only one to lose anything if that happened.

"Mira?"

She moved her hand away to look at Gemma. If what the old woman said was true, she had been responsible for the burning of the Yukori lands. She had been responsible for Mira and Dannesk being sent to live at Arkesh. She had been responsible for so much loss. However, if not for Gemma, she might have never met Kashi. Was that part a blessing or a curse?

"I'm thinking I need to look less feminine. Do you think I should cut my hair or will it be enough to bind it back?"

"You are a strong woman, Mira. You should have gone to one of the academies."

Mira did not respond to that, she just waited for Gemma to answer the question.

"I love your beautiful hair," Gemma sounded mournful, "but you might be better off to cut it."

Mira nodded and rose from the chair. "Will you dine with us this evening?"

"Yes." Gemma's tone was definite. "It might be my last chance to do so."

Mira started to leave, but Gemma called her back once more.

"I almost forgot. Please take this, child. It is not much, but it should be enough to serve your needs if you are careful." Gemma held a little pouch full of coins out to her.

Mira took it and bowed her head respectfully. "Thank you."

Without another word, she left the room. The remainder of the day she spent finishing her preparations. She went out to the stable and told one of the hands that she would be going for a ride after the evening meal. He argued that it was not safe, but she reminded him of his station and demanded that Aiko be ready by sunset. It might have been easier to sneak down and saddle the mare herself, but she wanted everything as ready as possible so she would have less time to change her mind. She snuck into the sewing room then and stole away with a set of shears that would make short work of cutting her hair. She wrapped the shears in a travelling hood she had taken from Dannesk's wardrobe and stuffed the bundle in the wardrobe in her room for later.

When all was as ready as she could make it, Mira sent word to the kitchens that she, Ina, and Gemma would be taking their evening meal together, then she took a book from the family collection and found a quiet spot in the atrium to read. It seemed the best way to pass the time without brooding over her coming departure. When time came for the evening meal, she sent a summons to Ina and went to the dining room. A short time later Gemma arrived with a serving girl's assistance. They waited for Ina to arrive.

When Ina entered the room, her eyes darted about warily, like a frightened mouse expecting a cat to pounce. She eyed Mira and Gemma with suspicion as she took her seat. They both smiled welcome, though Mira had to suppress irritation at the woman's attitude. The spot at the head of the table where Dannesk used to sit was oppressive in its emptiness and Ina was obvious in her efforts not to look at it.

"I thought we might try to have a nice meal together," Mira explained to try and get her to relax.

"Have you gotten word from Barik?" Ina's tone was bitter and Mira forced herself to be patient.

"It is much too soon."

"Good," Ina replied before focusing on her food, which she picked at with disinterest.

Mira exhaled and met Gemma's sad eyes.

Ina was so wrapped in her own misery that she had not even noticed the streaking of gold in Mira's eyes. Perhaps that was for the best. The fewer questions, the fewer lies there would have to be between them. Mira felt some guilt at leaving Gemma to deal with Ina alone, but no more than she felt for not telling Ina she was leaving. It was a guilt she would have to learn to live, and possibly die, with.

Ina excused herself from the table having eaten almost nothing of the meal. Mira helped Gemma back to her room and kissed the old woman on the cheek before leaving.

"Goodbye, Gemma."

"Be careful," Gemma said, her eyes glossy with tears.

"I think my plans go against that advice from the start, but I will do my best."

Returning to her room, Mira retrieved the hood and shears and stared in the mirror for a long time. She really knew very little about cutting hair. After a bit, she tied it back with a ribbon and cut at the back of the ribbon. A handful of long mahogany hair came away and what was left fell forward around her face. The change was somewhat shocking. It ended up being shorter in the back, but she thought it looked passable. She tossed the severed portion on the bed. It didn't matter much who found it once she was gone.

That done, she changed into Dannesk's clothes. She had selected his simplest attire in dark browns that would not draw attention. Strangely, she felt naked in the simple pants, without layers of skirts around her legs. The shirt was a problem. It was loose, but her breasts were still unfortunately apparent. Mira pulled the shirt off and wrapped her breasts down with some cloth she had grabbed for the purpose, but had hoped not to have to use. Once that was done, the shirt hung a little more properly. Mira donned a simple jacket and pulled the hood up. She strapped a dagger to her calf and another at her belt. A third she stashed in the saddlebags that she flung over her shoulder. The money that Gemma had given her she tied at her belt and tucked inside the pants.

Before leaving the room, she considered her reflection again. It was not perfect, but from a distance, her gender would be hard to determine. The façade might not hold up to close inspection. Still, it was adequate and the travelling hood would help her hide her identity.

She stole quietly from the manor and out to the stables. The boy from earlier in the day was there and

Aiko was saddled and waiting tied in the aisle. The boy looked alarmed when he saw her so Mira quickly pulled back the hood. He stared at her in confusion for a long moment, then his eyes widened in surprise.

"Lady Mira!"

Mira put a finger to her lips and held out a coin to him. "Tell no one you have seen me."

The boy nodded conspiratorially and took the coin with eager fingers. He even helped her secure the saddlebags and opened the stable doors. Mira gave him a warm smile, then she pulled the hood back up and mounted Aiko. She went slowly through the courtyard to keep Aiko's hooves from making too much noise. At the gate, she paid the guards for their silence as well and hurried past. As soon as she was out on the roadway, she let out the breath she had been holding and urged Aiko into a trot.

Kazue appeared almost instantly, shadowing them. Aiko no longer even turned her head to see him, she had become so used to his presence. Mira smiled a welcome to the gargoyle and urged Aiko a little faster. She wanted to put as much distance as possible between them and the manor before sunrise. If they traveled fast enough, it would take less than two days to reach Arkesh. Mira knew it might be a bad idea to stop there, but she wanted to be sure that they received word of Dannesk's passing. It would also be one night she would not have to worry about lodging.

By morning, she was quite tired. Just before sunrise, she turned out across a field and rode into a small copse. They all needed the rest, so she curled up next to Kazue and slept for a time. They were back on the road again by early afternoon. Kazue refused to get far from her now, so she moved Aiko out at a swift pace and ignored the startled expressions of other travelers as she passed by with a gargoyle flying along above her. Her efforts to travel discreetly were demolished by his presence, but she felt far safer with him there, so she didn't try to change it.

After dark, they stopped off the roadside. She was hungry and Aiko needed the rest. Kazue vanished for almost an hour. When he returned, he brought her half of what appeared to be a rabbit, which she declined as politely as she could. She was not about to eat it raw and she hadn't gathered any fuel for a fire. Kazue relented easily and finished off the creature while Mira looked the other way and chewed at some dried meat.

She dared to take a short nap, then they headed on again in the dark. Mira kept them going throughout the remainder of the night and into the next day. By mid-afternoon, they were within sight of Arkesh manor. She slowed their pace to give Aiko a chance to cool down. Kazue landed and walked along beside them. He did not seem especially tired. Even Aiko wasn't breathing as hard as Mira had expected. She was much encouraged by the fitness of her companions and by the lack of problems they had getting this far.

The manor gates were shut and guarded.

"Who are you?" One of the guards demanded, his eyes riveted on Kazue who was still by her side.

Mira pushed back her hood. "Hello, Daiki."

The guard, Daiki, looked hard at her and his jaw dropped. "Lady Yukori?"

"Yes, I must see Lady Arkesh."

"Lord Arkesh has gone to the war front. Lady Arkesh would welcome you, I am sure, though..." Daiki's voice trailed off as he eyed Kazue and fingered his sword hilt.

"The gargoyle is my escort. Let me in, Daiki." She forced command in her tone.

Daiki looked at her again. "This is irregular, Lady Yukori. What has happened to your hair, and why are you dressed this way?"

"We are at war. Yukori did not have men to spare as an escort, so I came in disguise."

Daiki looked doubtful still, but he opened the latch, pulling in the gate. The other guard watched silently as she rode in. Mira did not recognize him and was glad he hadn't raised a fuss.

"Kovu, watch the gate. I am going to see that someone is available to take Lady Yukori's mount."

"Thank you," Mira said as sweetly as possible, knowing his precaution was as much to keep an eye on her as to help her.

At the door, Mira suffered Daiki to help her down, then he took Aiko to the stables himself after many assurances that she would be fine left on her own. When the doorman answered, he looked as astonished as Daiki had.

"Lady Yukori, please come in. I will have Lady Arkesh summoned to the front sitting room at once."

Mira nodded her gratitude and walked in to the entry. The doorman staggered back from the door with a gasp and Mira turned to see that Kazue had started to follow her in. She smiled affectionately at the gargoyle.

"Kazue, it might be best if you stayed outside."

The gargoyle met her eyes, his reluctance painted clearly in them, but he inclined his head and retreated through the door. The doorman shut the door with haste and Mira gave him a stern look. The man flinched under her chastising gaze and she turned her back on him, showing herself to the front sitting room.

The room was chilly and she did not feel much like sitting, so she paced back and forth in front of the picture windows that looked out on the courtyard. She drew the dagger from her belt and fingered the blade. It was Dannesk's favorite dagger, simple and functional with a well-worn black hilt. Ina would be furious that she had taken it, assuming she came out of her depression enough to notice the things that had gone missing.

"By lord and by land, Mira, is that you?"

When Mira turned, Sunai, who had spread her arms as if to embrace her, met her eyes and her hands went to her mouth as she gasped in surprise. It took her a moment to pull her gaze away from Mira's green and gold eyes, but finally she looked uncertainly down at the dagger Mira still held. Mira hastily sheathed the weapon.

"Sunai," Mira greeted her as if nothing were amiss.

"Mira. Your hair. Your eyes. What has happened to you? Your clothes," she added the last with a slight distasteful crinkling of her nose.

"Did our messenger reach you?" She let her own profound sadness roll out with her words and Sunai's expression turned apprehensive.

"What messenger?"

Mira shook her head and was silent for a moment. She hoped that whatever had happened to the messenger they had sent, it was quick and painless as possible. "Dannesk is dead, Sunai."

"No!" Tears began to streak down Sunai's cheeks faster than Mira would have thought possible and the other woman hung her head, wringing her hands in her skirt.

"He was killed by bandits." Mira gave Sunai several minutes to compose herself before she continued. "I sent word to Lord Barik that Ina has need of more troops or an escort to the Barik manor. I understand Shakari has gone to the war front."

Sunai nodded, more tears streaking down her cheeks silently at the mention of her absent husband. "Kashi is there as well."

"Yes, I know."

"Yes, you would know. Mira, why aren't you at Barik Manor?"

"It's hard to explain. I only stopped in to see that you were okay and make sure you had heard about Danni. Perhaps also to beg a meal and a warm bed for the night. I leave for Beikang in the morning."

The other woman stared at her with a suitably shocked expression. "What madness are you spouting, Mira?"

Mira sighed. "I must go, Sunai. That is why I am dressed this way and why I cut my hair. I have a much better chance if people mistake me for a man."

Sunai shook her head, her eyes full of confusion and suffering. "Come, dine with me Mira and I will talk you out of this madness that has consumed you."

Mira chuckled. "Yes, let us eat and you can try as you will to talk sense into me."

Later, as the evening waned, Mira tried to explain what Gemma had said to Sunai, but she did not understand it well enough herself not to sound like a raving lunatic. Sunai watched her with a look of growing skepticism until Mira finally threw up her hands in frustration and stopped trying to explain.

Sunai smiled indulgently. "Good, then you will stay here for now."

"No." Mira stared into the fire for a few minutes, then she smiled to herself. "Come, Sunai, I have someone I want you to meet."

Sunai was surprisingly patient as Mira led her through the manor halls and finally up to the top of one of the towers. They stepped up into the cool night air and only had to wait a moment before Kazue lit upon the tower. Mira smiled a greeting at the gargoyle. Sunai, however, backed away in alarm until she came up against the parapet. Kazue only gave her a momentary glance before folding in his wings and striding over to Mira who turned to face Sunai, resting a hand on the gargoyles head.

"Sunai, this is Kazue."

"Well," Sunai replied, trying to compose herself by adjusting her skirts, "I see you weren't lying about some things."

"I am not lying about any of it, Sunai. Tell me truly, if my going to the war front would save Shakari and Kashi, would you want me to go?"

Sunai met her eyes with a look of dawning wonder. "You are serious, aren't you?" Mira did not respond and Sunai looked away, troubled. "You are like a sister to me, Mira. I don't…"

"Two lives saved for one life risked," Mira interrupted. "Not only that, but thousands more we don't know might be saved."

Sunai said nothing.

"I leave in the morning. I hope you will break fast with me."

Sunai nodded and turned away, climbing down the ladder into the manor. Mira had gone cold inside again. Rather than seeking solace in Kazue's company, she climbed back down and went to her old chambers. It was hard to say when she might have another chance to sleep in such a comfortable bed. It made sense to take advantage of it. Despite her troubled thoughts, she fell asleep quickly and slept soundly, exhausted by her hard travel from Yukori.

The next morning, they talked of frivolous things and Mira enjoyed the pointless chatter. She had no desire to try to explain things again and Sunai seemed to know it. When she finally went to the courtyard to leave, Sunai followed her with some more food and another small pouch of coins. Mira consolidated the coins with those from Gemma and managed, through no small effort, to stuff the additional foodstuffs into her saddlebags. Finally, Sunai handed her a small bundle wrapped in black silk. Mira unwrapped it curiously and found a beautifully made dagger with a fine mahogany handle and a deceptively delicate looking blade.

"I can't take this." She held it back out to Sunai.

"Kashi had this made for you when he was at the academy."

Mira shook her head, confused. "He gave it to you."

Sunai smiled. "He had it made for you. By the time he returned, he didn't think it was appropriate to give it to you. He confessed as much to me. I think it is time it went to the proper owner."

Mira regarded the beautiful piece with a mixture of delight and sadness. Pulling up her pant leg, she removed the dagger that was strapped to her calf and handed it to Sunai. She then replaced it with the new one. In a strange way, it made her feel as if she were closer to Kashi than she had ever been. Kazue landed in the courtyard when Aiko was brought out and Mira embraced Sunai tightly before climbing into the saddle and leaving her other home behind.

Kashi wiped down his blade, cleaning it for the comfort of the action as much as to have it ready if they were indeed attacked by the birds that night as Hideo claimed they would be. He sat at a fire watching some of the soldiers around him. Taro, a burly man, who had once physically wrestled a horse to the ground in a wager, sat gazing at a square of cloth. A favor from the lady he left behind to be in this battle. It looked black in the dark, but Kashi had seen it in daylight enough times to know it was a rich royal blue, worn thin by the big soldier's attentions. There was a frown etched on Taro's face as he stared at the cloth, so deep in thought Kashi wondered if he would even notice if they were attacked.

There was a sense of darkness to the night that defied the bright twinkling of the stars. A frustration and hopelessness after what they had seen today that pushed even the rowdiest of soldiers into their own silent brooding. Even Rajasi had gone quiet. He stared sullenly into the fire while snapping every small twig within reach into tiny pieces that he tossed into the fire with fingers that trembled ever so slightly.

The other two men at the fire he didn't know as well, but they too looked troubled. One picked at a tear in his shirt through which a bandage could be seen, stained with blood. It wasn't a dire wound and the soldier was no novice, but he looked spooked. A sort of shaken confidence in his wide eyes that made Kashi start to worry about the risk of desertion. Their enemy had been untouchable on the battlefield. That was enough to shake up any soldier.

Kashi scowled, tucking away the cloth he'd been cleaning with.

Was there a point? What could they do against an invulnerable enemy short of throwing themselves at their opponents mercy?

The night sky weighed down on him. The mocking stars shone less brightly. Even they were suppressed by this gloom, this hopelessness.

Rajasi hugged his arms around himself. Taro closed a fist around the cloth. The soldier picking at this shirt snapped to his feet and turned to leave the fire, his companion reaching out as if to stop him. There was a whoosh of air and a massive dark form dropped from the sky, grabbing the wounded soldier's shoulders in huge talons. It rose just as suddenly as it appeared, taking the screaming soldier up with it. More screams rose into the night.

Kashi was on his feet, his blade ready. Searching the night for more of the great birds. The stars had gone dark as if some vast blanket of black hung in the sky above them. The camp fires all guttered out at once. There were more screams.

Taro cried out, but his wasn't a cry of terror so much as one of rage. One of the birds had sunk its talons into his left shoulder, but lost its grip on his right. When it started to let go of the left, Taro grabbed its leg, holding it there. His cry turned to one of pain when the beast whipped at him with massive wings, the talons twisting and tear in his flesh as it fought to get free. Rajasi and Kashi were at his side in an instant, slashing at the wings to try to get closer. Then the beast's beak darted in at Taro, stabbing into his skull between his eyes. Taro went limp and the beast pulled free. Kashi's blade cut through one wing severing it near the shoulder. The beast shrieked, and fell. Rajasi lunged forward, slicing through its neck to end the bloodcurdling noise. The great bird dissolved to dust at their feet.

They left Taro's body to try and go help others, but it was a matter of staggering about in the dark, their direction guided by screams. Then there was silence and the stars came back, glaringly bright. The only sound was the screaming of a soldier who had fallen into the coals of a fire in the darkness.

By morning they had a count of thirty-seven missing and twenty-three dead. There were no wounded other than the burned man and someone who had a hand lopped off by another soldier in the darkness. Rajasi was among the missing.

The head on the bridge continued to taunt them, but all attempts to retrieve it were stopped by a barrage of arrows. Throughout the day, the armies watched one another, though neither made a move. It would be suicidal for Beikang's army to attack when they could do no damage and Hishae's forces needed to do nothing for now but hold their position and let their advantages erode morale. In the late evening, Hideo rode out on the bridge again, stopping behind the head of the late Major Tatsuo. Kashi and Nioku rode to the edge of the bridge with Shakari to face him.

"Major Shakari," Hideo greeted them, though he eyed Kashi and Nioku intently as though trying to memorize them.

"Hideo," Shakari replied, dropping the other man's title to insult him.

Hideo only smiled and eyed Kashi thoughtfully as he spoke, though his words were directed at Shakari. "You cannot fight with swords, so you will attack with words. How quaint." With a nudge of his toe, he turned the white stallion so that he was facing Kashi. "You are Captain Marikashi Arkesh?"

Kashi met the silver eyes with calculated indifference. "I am," he answered, forcing ease into his tone as if being singled out in this way hadn't turned his gut.

"Several of our new guests in the dungeons speak highly of your skill."

A chill of dread swept through Kashi. Was Rajasi in those dungeons?

Hideo turned his pale gaze back to Shakari. "Send a messenger to Queen Isaye. Tell her that we will kill no more of her warriors and harm no more of her people. All she must do is surrender her kingdom. I will even release all the prisoners we have taken. I do hope you can remember all of that, Shakari."

Shakari dropped a hand to his sword hilt and Nioku cleared his throat, nudging his horse a step closer. "I do not wish to become major yet," the captain murmured.

Shakari relaxed his hand, though he left it resting on the hilt. Hideo watched their exchange with a satisfied smirk, then he turned his white stallion and rode back into the camp.

That night, the birds came again and seventeen more of Beikang's warriors vanished, though none died in the attack this time, and Shakari summoned Kashi and Nioku to the officer's tent at dawn.

"Do we send the messenger?"

Kashi hesitated, but Nioku nodded. "We must apprise the Queen of the situation. It is only appropriate that she know of his demand and be allowed to make her own decision."

Kashi nodded as well. "All we can do here is stand our ground until we figure out some way to fight them. I think we should send the messenger and I strongly recommend that no one be allowed to move through the camp at night. We will fit as many as we can into the existing tents and gather supplies to build more cover. We can build small structures to protect the men on watch. We cannot let the birds pick off our warriors while we wait."

Shakari met his eyes for a long moment, then nodded. "Yes, we will pass that information through the ranks. I will send a messenger to Beikang today. We also have this, if we can figure out how to make use of it."

Shakari rolled out a parchment. On it was a map of a series of passages. Kashi looked at it for a moment, then up at Shakari.

"What is this?"

"These are the passages underneath Laki. We don't know who built them originally, but they were mapped for use as an emergency escape from the city when they started building the palace. There might be a way for us to use them to our advantage, if we can get to them."

Kashi pointed to a few spots on the map. "These entrances are outside the city walls."

"Yes, I was going to spend a little time going over it to see if there is some way we might be able to get to them. Our only chance of reaching them unseen is during the night, but then we have the birds to deal with."

There were raised voices from the direction of the river. All three grabbed their weapons and left the tent. A large group of Beikang warriors had gathered alongside the river. At the very edge, several bowmen were gathered shooting arrows across the river at a Hishae warrior who was dancing about and calling insults at them. The arrows bounced harmlessly off the man and Kashi saw fear building in the eyes of many Beikang warriors as they watched.

"Stop this now," Kashi muttered under his breath to Shakari.

Shakari strode out to where the bowmen were. "The next man to waste an arrow over this river gets a place of honor next to the late major."

The last arrow sprung free and the bows were all lowered. A volley of arrows flew from the Hishae side then and landed in the ground around where Shakari stood. Kashi watched with a new respect as Shakari scowled at the enemy bowmen, then turned his back on them.

"Back to the camp," he ordered.

The Beikang soldiers retreated from the edge of the river and Shakari did not follow until the last man had left the bank. Kashi breathed a sigh of relief when Shakari was finally out of range of the enemy arrows. Nioku and Kashi passed down the order to travel in groups at night if they had to move outside of one of the tents and set to work assigning camp and practice duties to anyone not working on structures to try to keep the men busy during the day. The more time they had to consider their situation, the more men they would lose to desertion.

That night, Kashi and Shakari were studying the map again when the sounds of a scuffle outside caught their attention. Shakari started toward the tent flap, but Kashi stopped him with a hand on his arm. He had a promise to keep.

"I'm sure it's just a couple of soldiers blowing off steam. I'll break them up and send them back inside."

Shakari relented. "Be careful."

Kashi moved out of the tent with his sword drawn. The birds were overhead, circling the camp like vultures. He hoped they would not lose more men to the beasts. He could see the fight that had broken out a few tents away. Tensions were running high. He glanced up at the birds again. He had never heard of birds of such size. Their feathers had a blue cast in the moonlight, almost like the stone in the city of Beikang.

"Captain!"

Kashi spun and threw himself to the ground as one of the birds dove through the space he had just occupied. The two men had stopped their fight and were running his way, their dispute forgotten. Until now, the beasts had not displayed an ability to hunt in groups, but this time many birds gathered in this one spot. They dove relentlessly at him, keeping the two men away and leaving him vulnerable to their focused onslaught.

Kashi managed to get to his feet and swung at one with his sword. He was rewarded with a jarring sensation when the blade struck home. There was a strong sense of satisfaction in being able to damage these beasts the way they couldn't damage the Hishae soldiers. The blade dug into bone, becoming wedged there. The creature shrieked and twisted violently, wrenching the weapon from his hand. Kashi lost his footing in the struggle to keep hold of the blade and fell as another of the birds dove at his head. There were cries of alarm as more soldiers emerged from the nearby tents to try and come to his aid. Kashi jumped to his feet once more and was driven back to the ground when one of the birds slammed into him, digging talons into his shoulder. He twisted free, grunting in pain as the talons tore from his flesh. He did not have time to get back to his feet before another of the beasts dove in, taking hold of his leg and lifting him into the air.

Kashi twisted, trying to free himself again, but the movement only caused the beast to dig in deeper, tearing into his thigh. He drew the dagger from his belt and struck at the creature's leg. The bird struck back at him with its beak, its flight faltering. Kashi twisted away from the beak and struck at the leg again, cutting deep into it. The bird shrieked and let go of him. He had not realized how far the bird had traveled with him in what seemed to be mere seconds since he had been taken. He slammed into the roof of a house and rolled off, landing with a painful thud in a street within Laki.

The dagger landed a few feet away. Kashi rolled toward the dagger, sucking air back into his lungs. As he climbed to his hands and knees and reached for the weapon, a boot struck him across the ribs, sending him sprawling. He gasped, his vision blurred with agony, and found himself looking up the blade of a sword. There was only one soldier.

Kashi rolled toward the man and grabbed his legs, pulling him down. The soldier cried out as he fell, but he managed to keep hold of his sword. Kashi grabbed his dagger, rolled away from the soldier and struggled to his feet. The enemy soldier was already getting to his feet, his sword ready. Kashi lunged, spun away from his block, and came around behind him, driving the dagger in between his ribs. He hesitated, surprised that the dagger had gone in, then, as the soldier fell, Kashi grabbed the man's sword and turned to take in his surroundings. Seven more Hishae soldiers approached with their weapons drawn. Kashi faced them, but he could feel the pain of his wounds and loss of blood weakening him.

"Put the weapon down, you might live to fight another day," one of the soldiers said reasonably, sheathing his own sword.

Something dripped down into Kashi's vision and he wiped at his face. His hand came away red with blood. He did not remember striking his head, but apparently, he had at some point. His head spun. He had no chance against them. Fighting hard just to remain upright, he lowered the sword. The man who had spoken stepped forward and took it from him.

"Good choice," he said, then he turned to his comrades. "Bind his hands and take him below."

Rage surged through Kashi as his hands were pulled around behind him and bound. The emotion only worsened his dizziness, and he staggered. The soldier behind him twisted his arms, forcing him to stay upright. The pain of his injuries increased in intensity as they pushed him along the streets. Blood soaked his pants from the wounds in his leg and more ran down into his eye, forcing him to close it.

The soldiers took him through a doorway into the city wall and forced him down a ladder into the underground passages. Dizzy, weak, and unable to use his hands for balance, Kashi tumbled down most of the distance to the floor, landing hard on the injured leg. His surroundings swam about him, but he clung to consciousness, managing to get up to his knees on his own before two of the soldiers lifted him the rest of the way to his feet.

When they finally stopped, turning into a small room with several guards, Kashi was sweating with the effort of remaining conscious. He glared at the guards and one of them met his eyes, smiling with grudging admiration before looking away.

"Throw him in a cell and get someone to tend his wounds. Put him in the back corner so he can't rile the others."

His escort left him with the guards and two of them took him into the adjoining room. The room was lined on both sides with cells, most of which were occupied by missing Beikang soldiers. He peered about, searching for Rajasi. The sergeant wasn't among those he saw, but the blood obscuring his vision made it hard to be certain. There was a doorway at the end leading into another room, but they stopped him and put him in the last cell on the left at the end of the first room.

Kashi lay back on the rough cot and closed his eyes. He could not bring himself to do anything more than that at this point. A short time later, he was woken by the sound of the cell door opening. A man and a woman, both in dusty robes, entered and knelt next to the cot. The woman held a stick in front of his mouth and he thought for a second about refusing it, but his pain was already such that he could barely think past it. Kashi took the stick in his teeth and they began to clean his wounds. It was not long before the stick broke.

CHAPTER EIGHTEEN

The roads were more barren than Mira was used to. The lack of patrols and the numbers of bandits had perhaps driven away much of the usual traffic. That would result in hardship for the farmers and artisans who sold their wares in the cities, which would hurt the shoppers as well. Greater risk meant higher prices and those who couldn't make it to the city to sell their wares wouldn't have coin to spend.

Mira shook her head. There was little point in lamenting the plight of the people when her own situation was made more precarious as well. With less traffic, the bandits had fewer targets. That didn't bode well for someone traveling alone. Although, she was not precisely alone, not with Kazue there.

Her second day on the road, she gave a wide berth to a small band of five rough looking men heading the way she had come. As she went around, urging Aiko a little faster, she was surprised to find that two of the men were wearing the tattered uniforms of Beikang's military. Whether that meant they were soldiers who had deserted or that the uniforms were stolen, she couldn't tell, but it increased her apprehension about what she might find when she reached the front.

The men, for their part, glanced at Aiko with a touch of longing, but they paid Mira little mind. Kazue, on the other hand, the uniformed men watched with fear that bordered on terror. Up to this point, most were wary of the gargoyle, but this was the first time she saw such a complete fear of him. The reaction made her wonder if they were indeed soldiers who had seen the giant birds Hishae brought with them.

The next day, she came upon three more men, one of whom was dressed in a dirty uniform. He too looked at Kazue with fear and a resigned despair. Mira pulled Aiko up and faced them, keeping her hood up and deepening her voice. Kazue landed next to her and all three drew weapons. Mira held up a gloved hand to stay them.

"We mean no harm. I am heading to Beikang and was hoping you might have news of the war."

"War," one of the men snorted derisively. "There is no war. The Queen will give up Beikang soon. You'll go back to the west if you are wise."

Mira was so taken aback she almost forgot to disguise her voice. "What do you mean?"

The man in uniform shook his blond head and grimaced. "Hishae has strange powers fighting this war. They have winged creatures that attack in the night and their warriors are invincible. The army is helpless against them." His gaze turned to Kazue, burning over with mistrust. "Beikang's troops will be decimated a little at a time. The Hishae major Hideo promised nightly attacks from the great birds. The Queen will have no choice but to relinquish the throne and hand over her kingdom."

Horror filled Mira as she listened. Along with it came a stronger belief in what Gemma had told her. Hishae had found an ancient magic and Beikang was dying for it.

"Many men are deserting," he added when she said nothing.

"Deserting their captains," she snapped, intending it to sound judgmental and harsh. His flinch told her she had succeeded, though his two companions only sneered at her.

"There is no hope." The man looked down at the sword in his hand as if the weapon itself had betrayed him.

Mira could feel his regret, but the thought of Kashi there, loosing soldiers to the birds and desertion both, crushed any sympathy she might have offered. "There is always hope, so long as you don't give up."

Without waiting for a response, she turned Aiko away from them and urged her to a trot.

Kazue leapt into the air and took his place above them. If what the soldier said was true, she might be too late. How could she have any hope when an entire army was failing? Magic or no, the odds were stacked against her. Still, if there was any chance that she could do something, she had to try. The dagger Sunai had given her, the one from Kashi, was heavy against her leg and there was a similar heaviness in her heart. She clenched her teeth against the looming despair and focused on the road.

That night she found a secluded spot along the road and camped. Kazue disappeared to hunt and Mira spent the time he was gone trying, hopelessly, to light a fire with the flint she had brought. She had never really tried to light a fire this way. The more she tried the more her frustration grew. When Kazue returned, he dropped the back half of a rabbit beside her. Mira looked at the raw, bloody thing then glared at the fire she had tried to build. The small pile of twigs burst into flames. Mira sprung back from the fire as though she had been attacked.

Unconcerned, Kazue curled up next to the fire and rested his head on his paws. His golden eyes drooped closed. Mira stared at the merrily blazing fire, expecting it to do something more sinister than crackle jovially. When nothing else happened, she tossed some wood on and searched out suitable materials around the trees to set up the haunches of the rabbit over the flames to cook. That done, she proceeded to build another small pile of twigs that she sat next to and regarded with curiosity.

She stared intently at the little pile.

Burn.

With intense focus, Mira pushed away her surroundings until there was nothing outside of herself and that little pile of twigs.

Burn.

The pile burst into flames and she jumped in surprise, then grinned, a giddy pleasure bubbling up inside her.

"Kazue, did you see that?"

The gargoyle opened one golden eye for a moment, then closed it again.

"Well, I thought it was rather impressive," she pouted, brushing dirt over the small fire to put it out.

She went back to the original fire to find her makeshift structure starting to burn. With much difficulty and a few burned fingers, she managed to move the haunches onto a sharpened stick to hold manually over the fire. When that was done, she picked at the meat, forcing herself to eat it. Somehow, it was less appetizing when she had seen how it started. After eating, she sat for a time picking up leaves and twigs and lighting the ends on fire with her thoughts. That was how it appeared to happen anyway, though she wasn't quite sure how it really worked.

After a while, when she had some control over the lighting of fires, she started to try to put them out, remembering the candles that had gone out in the sitting room with Gemma. This was harder. The first few tries resulted in burned fingertips as the item she was burning combusted in her fingers. After that, she managed to avoid incinerating anything else, but efforts to put out the fires continued to bear no fruit.

Eventually, Mira curled up next to Kazue.

"I wish I could ask you how this all works," she murmured as she settled against him.

The gargoyle opened an eye and wrapped his wing over her, then his lips curled in a semblance of a smile as he closed the eye again.

She was awoken at dawn by a low rumbling. It took her a moment to realize the sound was coming from Kazue, who had lifted his head and was gazing intently into the predawn grayness. His low growl vibrated through her. Trusting him, she drew the dagger from her belt and rose. Kazue also stood, baring his teeth. There was a crackling of brush and Mira spotted the figure of a man moving amidst the trees. When he drew near, she tightened her hand on the dagger. Kazue growled a louder warning and the figure stopped, holding up hands in a gesture of peace.

"I mean no harm," the familiar voice declared.

To be cautious, she deepened her own voice when she spoke. "What do you want?"

He moved a little closer and she lifted the dagger in preparation to defend herself, not that she expected she would need to with Kazue there. He stopped again.

"I couldn't stop thinking about what you said yesterday."

"Oh." The remorse in his tone triggered her memory. "You're the soldier we met on the road."

"Yes, well, I thought about what you said and I realized I shouldn't have left the war front. If you're still heading that way, I thought we might have an easier time travelling together."

She could almost make out his features in the gray light now. She was touched that her words had made a difference to him, but without a mount, he would only slow her down.

"I am glad you changed your mind, but I am in quite a hurry. I…"

He stopped moving. "Your voice sounds different suddenly."

Mira's heartbeat quickened. She reached to pull up her hood, but he darted forward catching the wrist that still held the dagger. Kazue swiped out with one paw and knocked his legs out from under him. Still holding her wrist, the man pulled her down with him. Mira dropped the dagger as she hit the ground and he grabbed it, placing it at her throat and swinging around so that she was in between him and Kazue.

Kazue's growl was fierce now, his teeth bared and his claws digging deep runnels in the dirt.

"Call him off," the man demanded.

"I don't control him," she snapped.

She thought of the dagger hilt and fire and he dropped the weapon with a cry of pain. She spun away, plucking the dagger up by the blade in case the hilt was still hot, and hurried over next to Kazue. The man knelt on the ground, staring first at his wounded hand then up at her in surprise.

"What was that?"

"A warning," she replied in a tone that promised more of the same if he didn't behave this time.

"You're a woman."

She touched the dagger hilt tentatively. Finding it cool, she gripped it and glared at him. "That makes it okay for you to attack me?"

He shook his head. "That was stupid."

"I won't argue with you there."

He scowled at her as he got to his feet. "Everyone makes mistakes."

"Some of us make more than others," she countered.

"Woman," he roared, and she stiffened in surprise. "At least I know why you aren't at home with a husband. Who could stand that harpy's tongue?"

Mira wanted to be angry with him, but his words brought forth a powerful sorrow. "The man I would marry is fighting the war you ran away from," she murmured.

The soldier shifted and looked down at his feet as if they might have some advice to offer. "I'm sorry, my lady."

She shook her head. "It doesn't matter. You cannot travel with me. Setting aside your abhorrent manners, you have no horse and you would slow me down."

"I'm Sergeant Rajasi."

Mira stared at him for a long moment, trying to figure out what he was thinking. Did he think that his rank would have an influence on her decision? Finally, she shook her head again. "I am Mira and you still cannot travel with me."

He stared at her and the increasing light made his light blue eyes seem to glow. "Why are you out here?"

She raised her eyebrows at him. "You honestly expect me to sit here and tell you my life story? I really haven't the time."

Rajasi grinned. "No, but I bet it would be interesting."

Mira thought about the last several years. Up until a month or so ago, she had led quite a normal life, even boring perhaps. "Not as much as you might think."

"Let me come along with you. I can act as a last line of defense to protect your mare should you and the gargoyle fall."

His words and his dashing smile made her laugh. "I think I might enjoy your company," she said, a bit more lighthearted now as she sheathed the dagger and walked over to where Aiko waited. "However, I must travel fast. There is some flint over there if you want it. It turns out that I don't have a use for it."

"Have it your way, my lady. I'll catch up when I have a horse."

She laughed again and swung up into the saddle. "Your new determination is refreshing. Good luck, Sergeant."

"Safe travels, Lady Mira." He offered an extravagant bow more suited to a royal audience than a bizarre encounter in the woods.

Mira turned Aiko and headed back to the road with Kazue close behind. She regretted that she could not allow the sergeant to join her. His newly found good humor was refreshing. Hopefully, he would manage to keep his resolve and return to the war front. It must be truly dreadful indeed, if ranking officers were deserting. What if Kashi had deserted? No, he would never turn his back on something he considered his duty. Honor was of great importance to him.

With thoughts of Kashi bolstering her spirits, Mira continued her trek. Over the next few days, camping rapidly lost its appeal. Though it was a good opportunity to try to master some of the magic she could no longer deny having, it was lonely and cold, even with Kazue providing company and warmth. She longed for human companionship, but she skirted the villages whenever she could. The more time she spent in heavier population centers, the more likely someone would notice that she was a woman travelling alone and cause her grief, well-meaning or otherwise.

During her evening practice sessions, she managed to figure out how to put out the fire with her magic. After that, she focused her efforts on what Gemma had told her.

"You must learn to be unseen in plain sight."

With a lot of focus, she managed to make several twigs disappear, though she wasn't sure if they had really disappeared or if she had somehow managed to drop them and lose track of them.

CHAPTER NINETEEN

It was late afternoon of the third day after her encounter with Sergeant Rajasi and Mira was looking for a place to camp when she heard distant screams. Part of her wanted to keep going and ignore it, but she spied smoke rising from a farmhouse some ways off from the main road. With a grimace of determination, she turned Aiko toward the house and kicked her up to a run, trying not to think of how, only a short time ago, she would not have even considered that she might be able to help, let alone gone charging into the fray.

As they reached the source of the screams, Mira spotted three men lighting the fields on fire. Another two men were harrying a family that was backed up against the side of a large barn that a sixth man was attempting to set fire to as well. An older man and woman were standing between the bandits and three young children. Kazue veered off and dove into the men lighting the field. At the screams from those men, the two closing in on the family turned around.

Hatred swelled in Mira for these men who would take advantage of those weaker than them and she lifted her right hand. A whip of white light burst from her palm and struck one of the bandits, laying open his chest in a spray of blood. The man collapsed in a heap. The other man froze, unsure what to do with death closing in from two directions. She sent another whip of light at him. The man tried to run, but the light caught him across the side, severing his arm just above the elbow and laying open his ribcage. He collapsed as well.

The man who had been trying to light the barn slammed into Mira from the side and Aiko went over, throwing them both to the ground. She landed clear of Aiko, but pain shot through her shoulder as she struck the hard dirt. This wasn't a stubbed toe or burnt fingertip. This pain was new and powerful and it took her breath away. As she struggled to orient herself, gasping for air, the bandit who had attacked her surged to on his feet and came at her with his sword drawn. The weapon cut into her arm as she twisted away.

With a cry, she got to her knees, her other hand clutching the wound, and focused on the hilt of the weapon. Flame erupted between the man's fingers. He screamed and tried to drop the weapon, but the heat of her fear and pain had melted it to his hands. As he continued to scream in agony, Kazue appeared from nowhere and lunged up, tearing into the man's throat. He was dead before he hit the ground. Mira spread her power out, stamping out the fires with it before they could do any more damage.

She stood there for a moment, breathing hard, her hand pressed over the bleeding cut on her arm. The sound of weeping made her turn around. When her gaze fell upon the huddled family, they backed up to the barn, staring at her in open terror.

"Are any of you hurt?"

She took a step toward them, the old man held up an arm in front of his face in defense, and the woman pulled her children to her and closed her eyes.

They were afraid of her. Looking around, she spotted the two men who had been torn open by her power, their eyes staring blankly at the sky. The third had been killed by Kazue, but not before his hands were grotesquely melted onto the hilt of his sword by her. Horror welled up in her, accompanied by powerful nausea as she took in the carnage.

They were right to fear her.

She grabbed Aiko's reins with her bloody hand and leapt up, using a small boost of the power that seemed to have fully awakened with the conflict to get herself onto the saddle. She wheeled the mare around and kicked her hard, driving her as fast as she would go away from the destruction.

When she finally slowed, it was to turn off the road toward a stand of trees. Once hidden there, she left Aiko to graze and sat back against a tree, hugging her knees to her and moaning under her breath. Kazue came and curled up next to her, but she ignored him for a long time. When she finally looked at him, his gold eyes watched her with that patient wisdom.

"What? You did this to me." Then Mira noticed that he was bleeding from a cut in his shoulder. "You're hurt." She spoke more gently now, bending close to see the wound.

As she watched, the wound closed itself and disappeared, leaving no trace on his silky skin. She sat back and stared at him in surprise. He regarded her with that endless patience and it slowly dawned on her that he was trying to teach her something.

Mira closed her eyes and focused her thoughts on the cut in her arm. For a moment, the pain of the wound increased, but then it began to itch. Slowly the itching faded until there was only a faint memory of the pain. She opened her eyes and checked her arm through the tear in her shirt. The wound was gone. Closing her eyes again, she focused on the bruising in the shoulder and hip that had struck the ground when Aiko fell. After a moment, that pain was gone as well.

This new revelation only served as a brief distraction from her misery. The memory of the fear in the farmer's eyes, fear caused by her, fear *of* her, was too painful, and she could do nothing with her magic to soothe that kind of pain. She leaned her head back against the tree and closed her eyes. She should eat, but she could not find the desire to do so.

Kazue left for a short while and returned with the flank of what might have been a small deer. The gargoyle purred and nudged her knee with his nose until she relented. She took Dannesk's dagger and cut away a portion of the flank, then cooked it through with a thought, not bothering with a fire. With an effort, she managed to choke down the meal, though it was bland and flavorless.

"What have I become, Kazue? I've killed people. Maybe they weren't good people, but what does that make me?"

The gargoyle's expression was at once both sympathetic and unyielding. She could not hold his gaze. She understood. This was what she was supposed to be. A weapon powerful enough to match the power their enemy had discovered. She also understood what the gargoyle's interest in the matter was. The magic flying beasts unleashed by Hishae were as much a threat to the gargoyles as they were to humankind. What if she failed? Would another gargoyle choose someone else and try again?

Mira sighed. She felt terrifyingly powerful and pitifully insignificant.

"No offense, Kazue, but I wish I had never touched you."

She looked up at the gargoyle and met his eyes. The molten gold seemed to move in those eyes and a calmness filled her. This time, she did not turn away from his offering. The calm chased away her torment and muffled the pain of her experience at the farm. She smiled gratefully and curled up on the ground next to the enigmatic creature. She was not planning to run from her emotions, but for now, she needed to rest or she would be of no use to anyone. The calm Kazue had given her let her drift into peaceful slumber.

•

Mira had a decision to make soon. Working her way around the massive city of Beikang would take more time, but crossing through would be more difficult. She could not do so with Kazue by her side. That would certainly bring the city guards down on them. It was possible she could convince him to stay outside the city while she crossed, but that left her relatively unprotected. In a place bursting with people as Beikang was, she was certain to find herself in trouble. She tried to come up with a way to hide his presence, remembering Gemma's words about being unseen in plain sight, but making him invisible did not change his mass. In a crowded city, it would be hard to keep him from being run into, though he might be able to fly overhead.

As she continued east, pondering the dilemma of what to do when she reached the city, she noticed a significant increase in traffic going west. It was no longer limited to groups of men and the occasional merchant. Now there were entire groups of families laden with personal belongings. It gave her a chance to practice making Kazue invisible as she questioned some of the travelers and learned that Queen Isaye had warned of a possible surrender. Many were evacuating the city in fear of what Hishae might do to the Queen's subjects if she did declare surrender.

The news infused Mira with a renewed sense of hopelessness. As powerful as her magic was, she could not imagine a single woman and one gargoyle stopping an army that had the Queen ready to give up. What information she could get of the actual war front sounded like make-believe. The enemy soldiers were said to be impervious to attack and the massive birds assaulted the troops at night, stealing men away and filling the hearts of the soldiers with fear. She had seen the birds in the memory Kazue had shared with her. If they were real, then the rest must be true as well.

The great city was visible on the horizon a full day before they reached the gates. She made the decision to go through. The activity of people leaving the city would take attention away from a single traveler's passing. Her direction of travel contrasted with that of most people around the city, but the majority would be too distracted with their own concerns to care.

They made camp a short distance from the towering city gates. In the dark before dawn, she made all three of them invisible. At sunrise, they joined the mass of humanity around the gates, which were heavily guarded. The few trying to get in and the large majority heading out were all subject to thorough checks before being allowed to move on. Mira carefully led Aiko through the throng, her nerves on fire as they wove through the crowd. They bumped into a few people, but most of those looked around in confusion for a moment and shrugged it off, preoccupied with their own worries.

Once inside the gates, she found a deserted alley and made herself and Aiko visible again. She could at least replenish some of her food supplies in the city. It might have been a bit safer to remain unseen and steal what she needed, but she could not bring herself to do so at a time when so many were already suffering. She would try to obtain what she needed honestly first.

Mira rode out into one of the main streets and tried to orient herself. The bustle was confusing and denser than was likely to be normal with so many preparing to depart. Some of the shops were sure to be open to take advantage of the crowds. She started to turn Aiko when a hand closed on her wrist. Ready to defend herself if necessary, but wary of using magic in the open, she glanced down to see who had grabbed her. The man looking up into her hood let go of her with an expression of shock.

"Sergeant Rajasi," she deflated in relief, noticing the sweat soaked horse he was leading.

"Your eyes," he breathed in return.

"What about them?"

"They're gold. I've never seen eyes like that."

"All gold?" There was a touch of remorse in her voice for the green eyes she had been rather fond of, but not much surprise. Not anymore.

He drew back, his brow furrowing at the odd question. "Well, yes. Didn't you know?"

She sighed and looked away. "You made good time."

"Yes." There was smugness in his tone. "I told you I would catch up."

"Good, you can do the shopping then."

He coughed meaningfully and she looked back down at him. "What?"

"I haven't any coin, my lady."

Mira scowled a warning at him and hissed, "Don't call me that here."

He glanced around to see if anyone was paying them any mind. "Sorry, my la…my lord."

She rolled her eyes. "I have coin. It will be easier if you buy what we need."

Rajasi grinned up at her. "This means we are traveling together now?"

Mira smiled back despite herself. "Yes, so it would seem."

It proved to be quite easy to have the sergeant do the buying. When he told the shopkeepers he was heading back to the front, he got a look of sympathy and, more often than not, a discount off prices inflated by the war. Mira hung back with the horses and did whatever she could not to draw attention to herself. She longed to see Kazue, but she had not come up with a way to make him visible to only her. There were gargoyles near the castle, but one hovering over choice areas of the city for long periods would draw attention, so she kept him hidden.

It was growing dark when they had finished their shopping. The gates were closed when they got to the other side of the city and Mira regarded them with frustration.

"Well, we could get a room at one of the inns," Rajasi offered her a suggestive wink.

Ignoring his insinuation, she shook her head. "No, I don't want to stay in the city."

"They won't let us through."

"They won't let us, no, but they can't stop us either," Mira dropped a veil of invisibility over both of them and their horses.

"Mira?" Rajasi's voice rose a few octaves with panic.

"I'm here. I can't see you either. When the gate opens, go through quickly. We won't have much time to get clear."

"I guess I have to trust you on this."

Mira flushed with guilt at the lingering fear in Rajasi's voice, not that anyone else could see it. Perhaps there were things she should have explained first. It was too late now, however. Focusing her power, she lifted the portcullis and lowered the drawbridge, muffling the noise with magic. Just as the drawbridge was settling, she heard cries of alarm and kicked Aiko through. She hoped the sergeant had done the same as the mare galloped through the opening and off the end of the drawbridge.

She could hear another set of hooves pounding down the road just behind them. She did not dare slow or lift the invisibility until they were well away. She had to trust that Rajasi would follow the sound of Aiko's flight. The thicker stands of trees in the rolling hills on this side of the city would help them find a good place to stay for the night. She kept Aiko moving until full dark had fallen, listening always for the sound of hooves behind them.

When it was good and dark and there was little chance of being seen by anyone from the city, she lifted the invisibility and slowed Aiko. Rajasi's horse spooked and spun when Aiko appeared in front of it. Rajasi got control of the animal, but it startled again when Kazue landed next to Aiko. Once more, Rajasi managed to calm the horse, though it took a little more effort the second time. Mira could hear his frayed nerves in the tremble of his voice as he soothed the animal. When he had his horse standing still if huffing a bit, he regarded her with a mixture of mistrust and fear.

"You don't have to like what I can do," she stated, "but I intend to try to use these powers to stop this war. You may continue to travel with me if you wish. I leave that to you."

She turned Aiko into the woods. For a moment, she heard only Aiko and Kazue picking their footing through the trees, then the other horse was following again. If she were to be honest with herself, she was relieved. She did not want to deal with the judgment and fear in his eyes, but she was tired of having no one to talk to, at least no one who could talk back.

When they stopped, Rajasi built a small fire. Mira lit it with her magic before he could finish fishing around his packs for the flint. The sergeant said nothing. He sat and stared at the fire for a long time without speaking.

She settled across from him and munched on fresh cheese and bread they had bought earlier in the day.

"So, what are you?" Rajasi asked as he accepted a chunk of bread she offered him.

"Just a woman," Mira replied. "Kazue—" she nodded to the gargoyle, "—has shared with me this power so that I might try to stop Hishae. It isn't something I ever asked for, but now that I have it, how can I do anything else?"

"You're a courageous woman." Rajasi looked long at Kazue, who had rested his big head on Mira's thigh. The gargoyle lifted his head and stared back at the sergeant until the sergeant looked away.

"You have the same eyes. You and the beast."

Mira remembered the image she had seen in the water on her picnic with Kashi and Valin. "I had green eyes before. I was actually quite fond of them, but I guess this is part of the deal."

"I will never look at gargoyles the same way again." There was a hint of awe in his tone.

"Hmmm. Me either," she agreed, stroking the big head that again rested in her lap.

"On to less uncomfortable things. Who is this man you would marry?" Rajasi asked, his apprehension seeming to fade as he ate and gazed into the fire.

Less uncomfortable for you perhaps.

"Captain Marikashi," she murmured after a moment of hesitation, part of her hoping he wouldn't hear the name. She didn't see any way it could hurt for him to know, since she did not expect to survive this.

"By lord and by land," he exclaimed with a laugh. "You're *the* Mira! You're the one he had the dagger made for when he first came to the academy."

She looked at him in surprise, then reached under her pant leg and drew the dagger. She handed it to him over the fire, hilt first.

He accepted it with a respect that bordered on reverence.

"I told him at the time that such a fine piece was wasted on a woman. No offence," he added hastily, glancing at her with a hint of apprehension.

She shrugged the comment off. "You know Kashi well then?"

Rajasi handed the blade back to her, his expression sorrowful. "Kashi is a great leader. He always excelled in everything at the academy. I loved him and hated him for that. I would never have believed I could betray him."

"You're his sergeant? How could you?" She might have stood if Kazue's head hadn't somehow grown much heavier all of a sudden.

Rajasi held up a hand to stay her. "I saw what you did to the bandits at that farm, though I didn't believe you had done it until a few hours ago. I have only shame for what I have done and I would not have told you the truth if I didn't believe you to be more than the monster that family took you for."

Anguish closed in around her head and shoulders like a shroud of stone. The pain of that family's fear washed through her anew. "I killed those men, Sergeant. I've never killed anyone before. Until recently, I had never even seen someone killed."

She met his eyes then. He looked torn for a moment and she thought he might have tried to come hold and comfort her if Kazue hadn't been there. It was probably best that he did not.

"My lady, I have killed men for far less noble reasons than to save a family. Your power scared them, and for good reason, but you did what you had to do to save their lives and probably the lives of many others who would have fallen victim to those men. The power you have is terrifying, but if you hadn't used it, they wouldn't have the luxury of being alive to fear and to judge such things."

Mira nodded, though she found it hard to take his words to heart. "Why did you leave Kashi?"

"Because, like that family, I am afraid of what I don't understand. Those giant birds seem to carry despair with them, like a plague to infect our troops. And we couldn't touch the warriors of Hishae. It was as if they were shielded from our weapons, but they wouldn't attack and destroy us as they should have, given their advantage. They simply waited, deflecting our attacks and killing only Major Tatsuo. The birds came in the night I left and I can still hear men screaming as they stole them away. Perhaps their plan is to wait while the slowly dissolving courage of our men destroys us from within."

He picked up a stick and prodded the fire with it. "In some ways, it was easy to leave. Not all of the men who vanished that night were taken by the birds, but none of those who remain know the difference."

Mira could feel his fear as he spoke and it made her cold, even with the fire and Kazue's warmth. "Why do you return then?"

He smiled wryly. "At first, because you made me feel such guilt I couldn't keep going the way I was. Now that I have seen what you can do, I have a small glimmer of hope. Though I still don't see how you will conquer an entire army of invincible warriors."

She gazed thoughtfully into the fire. "I don't think it is necessary to conquer the army. I think, somewhere at the heart of it, is one individual who has gained control of a great power. If I can stop that one, I think the rest will be easy by comparison."

"How will you find that one?"

Mira grinned. "Well, I have been figuring things out as I go so far. Perhaps it will come to me." She winked at the gargoyle and he responded with a slow blink.

Rajasi laughed. "You're mad, woman, but it sounds like as good a plan as any."

He stretched out on the ground and laid his head on his pack. Mira gazed into the fire for a short time longer, then she laid down against Kazue, who stretched one wing over her. She wondered passingly if Rajasi was cold, but the thought drifted away as sleep claimed her.

The sound of a cell door opening woke Kashi from a restless, feverish slumber. He was not sure how long he had been asleep. It could have been minutes or days, but the wound in his leg burned as if someone slathered it with oil and put fire to it. The other injuries were healing well enough, but it mattered little if the wound in his thigh was infecting. He opened his eyes and saw three Hishae soldiers waiting. He thought he recognized one from the night he had been brought to this cell. The other two were unfamiliar.

"Major Hideo would like to meet with you, Captain Marikashi. Can you walk?"

The soldier's polite manner set off warning bells in his head, but he had little choice in the matter. For now, he would have to play along.

He grimaced as he sat up and his head spun. For a time, he sat on the edge of the little cot bracing himself with his hands and tried to focus.

"Help the captain."

Two of the men entered the cell and helped Kashi to his feet. They had to help him walk as well for the wound in his thigh began to seep blood and a yellowish fluid as soon as he put weight on it. The pain was severe; beyond anything he had ever felt and blackness threatened at the edge of his vision. The third man, an officer judging by the insignias on his uniform, glanced down at the leg and shook his head, then he turned and led the way from the room.

Kashi paid careful attention to the route they took, though he was not sure how much he would remember given his current state. They moved down several hallways then turned in to a simple looking door. Beyond the door, they headed up a staircase. The steps changed from roughhewn stone to finely crafted marble once they moved above the underground tunnels. Rooms they passed up here were furnished with heavy, ornate furniture, the walls and ceilings accented with elaborate stucco sculpture, much of it painted gold. They were inside the palace now. Kashi tried to count the doors they passed, but waves of pain and nausea made it hard to keep track.

They finally stopped before a closed door and the officer knocked.

"Enter," a familiar voice called from within.

Hatred swelled in Kashi, giving him strength as they took him into the room and sat him in a chair on one side of a large desk. There was a crystal on a pedestal within the room that seemed to glow, but he could not focus on it. Instead, he did his best to focus on the man sitting behind the desk, long silver hair framing the despised face. Hideo was holding a dagger in one hand that Kashi recognized as his own.

"Wait outside," he ordered, and the soldiers stepped out, shutting the door.

Humiliation burned through Kashi with the realization that he sat alone in a room with the hated major, far too weakened by his injuries to make a move against him.

Hideo smiled. "You killed one of my men, Captain."

Kashi sneered. "If you want an apology, you'll be waiting a long time."

Hideo ignored the comment. "Apparently, it is necessary to protect them within the walls as well as outside of them. Thank you for that lesson."

Hideo stood then and began to pace behind the desk, fingering the point of the dagger. "You don't look so well, Captain," he commented as though observing the weather.

Another wave of dizziness assaulted Kashi and he laid a hand on the desk to steady himself. The wood under his hand was solid and real, helping to ground him.

"From the men we have captured, I have learned that you are well-respected by the soldiers. I would prefer not to kill those men, Captain. I believe that if someone they held great respect for were to take up arms for Hishae, they would follow that one."

Kashi shook his head and regretted the move. He wanted to respond with a vehement refusal, but he was silenced by his own struggle against his wounded, feverish body. It would do his honor no good to throw up in front of the man.

"If you agree, I will have your wounds tended by the best of my physicians and you will be ensuring the survival of your fellow captives," Hideo offered, his tone gentle with false sympathy.

"Give me arms, Hideo," he rasped, "and I will put your head by Tatsuo's."

Hideo narrowed his eyes. "Is that a definite no?" He chuckled to himself, not waiting for an answer. "Just as well. My physicians have more than enough to do keeping the men we torture alive for as long as we need them."

Before Kashi could make a move, Hideo slammed the dagger down through the hand on the desk and twisted it. Kashi cried out as two knuckles tore away from each other. The pain was blinding, but before he collapsed, he grabbed the dagger, ripping it from his hand, and threw it at Hideo. The aim was true, but the dagger's point struck Hideo's chest and fell away, as ineffective as their weapons had been against his soldiers.

The guards had entered the room at Kashi's cry. They glanced from Hideo to Kashi where he knelt on the floor now, curled over the mangled hand.

Hideo glared at him. "Take him back to the cell. Let him bleed to death in front of his men."

"Yes, Major," the officer replied and the two men drug Kashi from the room, leaving a trail of blood behind.

Back in the cellblock, they threw Kashi into the cell and slammed the door behind him. He crumpled to the floor. The bleeding had to be stopped if he was going to live, but he could not find the strength to move. He could hear the footsteps of the soldiers fading.

"Captain," a voice whispered urgently from the next cell. "Captain!"

Kashi tried to focus. He managed to turn his head and thought he recognized the man behind the bars of the adjacent cell, though he could not pull a name through the haze of pain.

"Captain, put the hand through the bars. I can't do much, but I can bind it."

Kashi closed his eyes for a moment. He heard cloth tearing. Was there a point? If he did not bleed to death, he would likely die of infection, which might be more painful anyway. He opened his eyes again. The other soldier had torn both sleeves from his shirt and was watching him with a bleak determination in his dark eyes. Kashi dredged up the strength and managed to drag himself over by the bars. He met the man's eyes as he passed the hand through and remembered his name.

"Thank you, Shunsuke," he murmured, nearly too weak to form the words.

The other man smiled briefly then turned to the wound. "I am afraid this is going to hurt."

Kashi managed a slight nod and let his head rest on the dirty floor, his hand now in the care of the other soldier. There was a sudden burst of horrible pain and Kashi slipped gratefully into blackness.

•

When morning came, Mira and her companions took to the road again. The sister city of Laki was only a few days ride from Beikang. The two cities had grown up together, Laki, the City of the Sun, out of the brilliant white stone and bleached wood of the mountains that loomed further east and Beikang, the City of the Moon, out of the rich dark wood and darker stone from the forests to the south. They were both beautiful cities in their own right.

Mira had never seen Laki before and, when they topped the rise of a hill at sunset, she was breathless with the beauty of the pale city lit by the setting sun. From this distance, the creatures circling the city could have been gargoyles, though she knew differently. The massive war camp that lay between the river and the city walls could have been a grand tournament in the making. The war camp that lay closer to them, close enough that she took a moment to shroud them in invisibility, was disheveled and almost looked abandoned by comparison. The warriors were likely all within the many tents and rough-built structures that littered the area, probably to hide from the great birds over Laki. The sight of Beikang's camp filled her with sorrow and anger, washing away the beauty of the city.

She watched the Beikang camp for a long time, considering what to do now that she had arrived. She could hear Rajasi shifting in the saddle alongside her. He would probably want to return to his proper station, assuming they would take him. However, she wasn't sure she did not have a better use for him. If he returned, she and Kazue were her only resources. With a third, she might be able to do more, but it would be riskier for him, lacking her power.

"Sergeant," she began, tentative.

"I am yours to command, my lady."

She looked in his direction, startled by the declaration. "Why do you say that?"

"Well," he responded, his tone thoughtful, "if Kashi were to give me an order at this moment, I think it would be to protect you. Since I can't take you to safety, it seems that the next best option is simply to stay with you and do what I can to help."

Gratitude swelled in her chest. "You won't like my first request, Sergeant, but I want you to stay hidden with the horses while I go down into the camp. I need to gather what intelligence I can and I can more easily go unseen alone. Then, when we have the information we need, I would like you to go into Laki with me."

She could hear him shifting in his saddle again. "I like the second part better than the first."

Mira said nothing. She let Rajasi consider in silence.

"See that big tent. That is where they hold council. Any useful intelligence will likely be there."

"Thank you, Rajasi." She dismounted. "Let's go into those trees and find a place for you and the horses. That way I will know where to find you when I come back."

They found a good spot deep in the trees where no one was likely to stumble upon Rajasi and the horses. Mira left them there. She knew the sergeant itched to go down to the camp. If that desire won out and he was gone when she returned, she would cope, but she hoped it would not. Though she was starting to like the man, he had deserted Kashi, so she wasn't going to make her plans dependent upon him.

Mira did not leave Rajasi and the horses invisible. The limits of her power were still unknown to her and she saw no reason to stress it when she was this close to her goal. With Kazue by her side, she went down to the camp, moving with care to avoid alerting anyone to her presence. More than anything, she did not want to panic anyone. These men had enough problems without worrying about invisible assailants.

The night was clearly a time of tension in the camp. There was almost no one outside of the tents and structures. Those few she did see stayed in groups with their weapons drawn. The men she saw out moving through the camp spoke very little and she could almost feel their apprehension like lightening in the air. The uneasy silence seemed more appropriate for a cemetery then for a war camp. How much of the army was still here? If it was too decimated, her plans might not be as effective as she hoped.

Slinking through, she made her way to the big tent Rajasi had pointed out. There were lights in the tent and the shadows of seven men. She stopped alongside the tent and waited, listening.

"We have received word that Beikang is starting to evacuate." She was surprised to hear Shakari's voice. "We just need to keep the Hishae army distracted for a few more days."

"Then what?" Another voice demanded. "We run like cowards? They will cut us down from behind."

"Sergeant Moriki, if we plan our retreat carefully, we may be able to get out of here with our lives. Queen Isaye has little choice. Our weapons have been useless against them. There are powers working here that we do not understand."

"Major Shakari," another man spoke, this one with a more respectful tone. "Do we have an escape plan?"

"Not much of one," Shakari answered, a heavy sigh in his voice, and Mira's heart went out to him. "We must be ready to move in two days. We will leave just before dawn, when the birds are returning to the palace and the army is still down for the night."

Mira shook her head. How tired these men must be, harried both day and night by the enemy forces. Hishae's army could rest at night with the birds to keep Beikang's forces on constant vigilance. There were a few more words exchanged as the men parted ways in two groups of three. Shakari was not among them, which meant he would still be inside. For a moment, she was apprehensive about facing him, but he was almost a brother to her.

Mira entered the tent when the other men were far enough away that they would not hear her. Shakari spun at the sound of the tent flap opening. His face was pale and drawn. He pulled his sword from his sheath and took a fighting stance. Remembering her invisibility, she quickly made herself visible again. The expression that greeted her appearance was one of confusion, mingled with a touch of fear.

Shakari sheathed his weapon and rubbed his eyes, then peered at her again. "Mira?"

"Yes, Shakari. Major Shakari, I believe I heard."

"Mira! What are you doing here?"

"Hush." To try to induce his silence, she let Kazue appear and his eyes locked on the creature, his hand dropping toward his sword again. "Where is Kashi?"

Shakari looked at her. "Your eyes…"

"I know. Where is he? He should have been at this council."

Shakari shook his head and time slowed around them, drawing out his dreaded words. "He was taken by the birds."

"Killed?" She managed to choke the word out around the terror that squeezed her throat.

"I don't know. We've found no evidence of them killing anyone they take, and the major indicated that they are keeping prisoners. We've been hoping that all the men taken by the birds are being held prisoner."

Mira pushed away the image of the birds feasting on human remains in the memory Kazue had shared with her.

"What are you doing here?"

"I am here to stop Hishae." She held up a hand to stop whatever he was starting to say. "I have been given a great power, Shakari. For this purpose, specifically. I must try. Hishae has unleashed a power that can only be stopped with similar power and Kazue has given me that power." She gestured to the gargoyle so he would know who Kazue was. "If I fail, another will come. If I succeed, then Hishae's army will not be impervious to your attacks much longer. Is there any information you can offer me to help me get into Laki?"

"Mira, this is madness and I will not encourage it. I order you to leave here at once."

She laughed and made herself and Kazue invisible.

Shakari sucked in a startled breath.

"I said it was madness too, once. I will take my leave now. You will know if I have succeeded."

"Wait."

She turned, making herself visible again.

Shakari picked up a long scroll and rolled it out on a table.

Mira joined him.

"There are tunnels underneath Laki. No one knows when they were built. This map of them was made before construction of the sister palace began. It was thought that they would make a good escape route should the city fall under attack. We have not been able to get close to the entrances, but I have a feeling you can." He examined the map in silence for a few seconds, then pointed out a series of large rooms in one section of passages. "This area was converted to a prison. If they are holding prisoners, they will likely be here."

Mira nodded, trying to drive the information into her memory while he re-rolled the scroll and held it out to her.

She took the map and then leaned in to kiss Shakari on the cheek. "Thank you."

"Be careful and if…"

Mira met his eyes, her heart aching at the sorrow she saw there.

He forced a smile. "*When* you find Kashi, don't tell him I gave you that."

She smiled. "I won't tell him," she said as she turned invisible again.

Mira fled the camp as quickly as she dared. Several of the dark birds were circling over the camp, but Beikang's warriors kept hidden away. The very presence of the creatures permeated the air with a sense of hopelessness. Were they enchanted to radiate such emotions, or was it just an inevitable response given the state of things? Either way, she found herself resenting Rajasi a little less for his desertion. The air around the camp was so oppressive that she could not wait to be free of it.

Despite her efforts, she arrived back at camp around midnight, winded from her fast trek. Rajasi stood when he saw her approaching, his hand dropping to his sword until he was certain of her identity. He eyed the scroll she was carrying, but he did not ask about it. Instead, he handed her some water, which she drank down gratefully. When she had settled, he offered her food, which she accepted as well, then she created a small, focused light in the air and began to roll out the scroll on the ground. Rajasi helped her pin down the corners with rocks and branches, then they both fell to examining the map.

"By lord and by lands, Mira, this is fantastic! How did you get this?"

"Magic," she lied absently.

Rajasi rolled his eyes at her and turned back to the scroll. "With the invisibility, we could walk right through the outer edge of the camp and enter here," he pointed to an entrance in the west wall.

Mira shook her head. "We should enter here," she pointed to an entrance near the main gate.

"That will be a lot riskier."

"Yes, but if they are holding prisoners, they will probably be in this area." She pointed to the rooms Shakari had indicated. "We can get there much faster this way."

"Why do you say that?" Rajasi was eyeing her curiously now.

"These rooms were converted to a prison."

"And you know that how?"

She met his eyes. "Magic."

Rajasi grinned and looked back at the map. "You are a terrible liar," he replied, his tone hinting at amusement. "All right, my lady, we enter there. It is your mission after all."

"Good." She knocked the weights off the corners and folded the map into a small square that she could carry with her. "We will leave tomorrow afternoon. Get some rest."

"Why afternoon?"

Mira sighed. "You really do make a troublesome companion, questioning all my decisions." Rajasi only grinned proudly and she continued. "We need the rest, but if we wait until night, we are more likely to be heard. The Hishae army does not have to remain awake with the birds to watch over things at night so noises in their camp are more likely to be noticed."

Rajasi nodded. "Good plan. I like adventuring with you. There are so many advantages I don't usually get to factor in."

"Such as?"

He smirked. "The view, for one."

Mira shook her head at him and settled in to finish eating. Rajasi watched her with a thoughtful expression that might have bothered her once. Now she was focused on much more important things than the attention of one man. She tried to focus on her ultimate goal of finding and stopping the magic Hishae was using, but her mind kept drifting back to Kashi. The memory of the birds eating the soldier on the roof was powerful in her mind, but she clung to a glimmer of hope.

"You think they have the captain?"

Startled, she glanced at Rajasi, dread weighing heavy on her and tying her tongue.

"It isn't hopeless," he said. "I ran into another deserter before I caught up with you. He said that Hishae's major, Hideo, promised Queen Isaye that all prisoners would be released when she relinquished her kingdom."

Mira pushed aside the surge of hope and focused on the strange unease that had coursed through her when Rajasi spoke the major's name.

"Hideo," she whispered. The name was poison on her tongue, gaining sinister power with the nearness of the man. She smiled, sensing a lethal intent behind that smile that wasn't entirely coming from her. "He is in Laki, isn't he?"

Rajasi met her gaze, fidgeting with a dagger. "I hope you never have reason to hate me, because something about you is rather frightening. Perhaps the ability to split a man open with a thought."

Mira gave him an impatient scowl.

"Yes, he is here. I would guess that he's taken up residence in the sister palace."

Mira nodded. "He is the one we must find."

Rajasi shook his head, wincing when he absently broke the skin of one fingertip with the point of the dagger. "How do you know?"

"I can feel it," she replied, the sensation leaving no room for doubt.

They did not speak again that night. Mira tried to question her own certainty, but it was like questioning the magic itself. She just knew. It did frighten her that she knew nothing of the other types of magic Hideo might have found. How would she know how to stop those powers? All she could really do was trust in Kazue and the changes he had wrought in her. Entering the underground tunnels did not scare her. Not knowing how to stop the other power did, though nothing scared her as much as the possibility that she might not find Kashi.

She curled up next to Kazue, basking in the powerful comfort of his presence. She knew now that it was the magic he carried that created that sensation of safety. At one point, she might have resented the fact that the creature could manipulate her emotions. Now she just let the comfort wash over her, allowing her to drift into a peaceful slumber.

CHAPTER TWENTY ONE

Around noon, Mira and Rajasi reviewed the map again, trying to be sure they both understood the route they planned to take. Ideally, they would be able to turn visible in the passageways, but it was likely there would be patrols, so memorizing the route would help keep them from becoming separated.

When they were both comfortable with the route they had chosen within the passages, it was time to figure out how they would get through the camp. Mira made them invisible and they moved out into the open. They left the horses behind. There would be no place any closer where they could risk leaving them. They went to the nearby hilltop and gazed down on the opposing camp before the city.

"Maybe we should try going around the side then working our way along the main wall," Mira suggested.

"Why don't we just cut straight down the middle? That would get us there the fastest."

She glanced in the direction of his voice, forgetting for a second that they could not see each other. Looking back down on the camp, she frowned. "But we're more likely to get separated that way without the line of the wall to keep us on the same track. How will we know when the other has reached the door?"

Rajasi was silent for a long time and she almost wondered if he had left her, then she heard cloth tearing. She jumped when a hand bumped into her arm, then she reached for his hand and took the strip of cloth from it.

"See that rack of weapons near the main gate?"

"Yes." She marked the spot in her mind.

"When we reach that spot, we will each discreetly drop the piece of cloth. If there is already a piece there, we know the other person has arrived."

"All right," Mira replied. It seemed like a sound enough plan. "Rajasi?"

"Yes, my lady."

"You know you can call me Mira."

"Yes, my lady, but I'm sure Kashi would rather I didn't get that familiar."

Her chest clenched at the mention of Kashi. She pushed him to the back of her mind again. "What color is the cloth?"

A snort of laughter exploded from the space beside her and she looked around in alarm to see if anyone in the nearby Beikang camp had heard. "By lord and by lands, Rajasi. Must you try to get us killed before we even reach the enemy camp?"

There was another snort of laughter, muffled this time. Mira shook her head in exasperation and wished she dared to make him visible so she could see to hit him over the head with something.

"Sorry, my lady," he breathed finally. "It's brown."

"What?" He chuckled and she sighed. "Yes, the cloth. Thank you. Shall we?"

"Ladies first."

Mira swiped out with a hand and met forcefully with something that grunted in surprise. "Stop fooling around and take my hand. No wonder we aren't making progress with men like you in the mix."

A hand touched her arm, slid down it, and took hold of her hand. He sounded much more serious when he spoke this time. "You're probably right. Let's go."

She led the way down the hill. Kazue somehow always knew where she was, so she did not worry about him. He would be at the door when she was. It was odd walking down toward the bridge over the river holding Rajasi's hand, but she did not want to risk getting separated before they even got to the camp. Once in the camp, they would be able to maneuver better apart.

"My lady," Rajasi's whispered, the seriousness gone again, "can I tell Kashi about this when we find him? You know, how I got to hold your hand?"

Mira sent a shock into his hand and he let out a tiny yelp of surprise. The man was insufferable, but his words left her with a sense of hope. "*When* we find him," she whispered back, "why don't you let me do the talking?"

There was a soft chuckle in reply, then they both fell silent as they closed in on the Beikang troops hidden behind barricades near the bridge. They walked as quietly as they could. The Beikang camp was much more sedate and quiet then their counterpart across the river, so the risk of being heard was greater here.

They crept past the barricades, then moved out onto the bridge. She tried not to gag as they walked past the rotting head of Tatsuo that lay near the middle. Did Rajasi feel as exposed and vulnerable as she did? Oddly, the sergeant seemed to have absolute faith in her power, while she continued to wait fearfully for that moment when it would fail her. The Hishae soldiers, sitting insultingly out in the open playing dice and drinking, did not act as though they noticed anything out of the ordinary. In a few places, the wood of the bridge creaked and Mira held her breath each time, but no one heard it over the sounds of their own talk and activity.

Once across the bridge, Mira squeezed Rajasi's hand before releasing it. She dreaded this part. She was alone now, amidst an army of Hishae troops. Her heart began to beat loud in her ears as she wove her way into the camp. The heat of the day grew more intense and the smells of unwashed bodies and waste gagged her. There were three men in her immediate path, but there was enough room to move around them. She got close enough to smell their individual reek of sweat and dirt, then one of the men turned into her. She sprung away, narrowly missing contact, then a tent flap opened behind her and she jumped to the side as another man stepped out.

Mira tripped and fell, landing with a grunt. The man who had just emerged looked in her direction with a puzzled expression and she held her breath, remaining still. Finally, he shook his head and headed in the other direction. She allowed herself to breathe again as she got back to her feet. A low growl caught her attention, and she looked down to see a mangy dog growling at the spot where she stood. Lifting a hand, she checked that she was still invisible, then she began to move away from the animal. One of the men passing by kicked the dog and it scurried away, tail between its legs, her scent forgotten.

Finally, she reached the weapon rack and was disappointed to find no cloth lying there. When she was sure no one was looking, she dropped the cloth she held on the ground in the shadow of the weapons. That done, she slipped into the doorway that was their goal and waited. Her apprehension grew with every passing moment, then a piece of brown cloth seemed to appear from nowhere on top of the one she had dropped. Mira breathed a soft sigh of relief as his reaching hand bumped her shoulder. Something moist touched her other hand and she ran a finger up from Kazue's nose and stroked his head.

"Tell me when you think no one is looking," she whispered.

It did not take long. Hishae's warriors were not being especially vigilant. If she succeeded, then that arrogance would make them easier to destroy. Mira used her power to lift the latch on the inside of the door and opened it. She felt Kazue move past, then Rajasi, and she followed them into the corridor within the wall. She glanced around to inventory their surroundings.

The passageway was sparsely lit with torches, which meant it was probably being patrolled, but there was no one in sight now. A few feet away was the trapdoor down into the underground passages. It was standing open, which promised the potential for patrols below as well. It was encouraging, however, that they were obviously using the underground passages for something.

"Do we stay invisible?"

"Yes. Let's get down below and see what it's like before we risk changing that." She began making her way to the opening.

Unable to see her, Rajasi bumped into her and she reached out, managing to grab his shirt to keep from falling into the opening. He grabbed hold of her to help her balance

"Sorry," he whispered, when she had righted herself. "Can Kazue get down there?"

Mira eyed the opening for a moment. "Yes, I believe he can. I'm going down."

"Wait, why don't I go first."

"I appreciate the offer," she replied, squeezing his arm, "but I can take down an enemy at range with a single bolt of power. I think I should go first."

"You're not good for my ego."

She laughed softly as she stepped down onto the ladder, though her nerves made the laugh sound a bit manic. Despite her power, descending into the dim passage made her stomach turn. When she reached the bottom and moved away from the ladder there was a thud next to her and a puff of dust as Kazue landed. She was comforted to have him there, even if she could not see him now.

There were torches along the dirt walls here as well, but they were even more widely spread than the ones above. She looked down the direction they were planning to go and listened intently for any sound other than that of Rajasi descending the ladder. She could hear nothing yet, but they had a long way to go.

"Ready," Rajasi's voice whispered behind her.

"I don't want to risk being seen, so I will make our feet visible. That way we can keep track of each other. No one is likely to notice our feet before we've noticed them."

"Do we kill anyone we find or just avoid them?"

Mira did not feel qualified to decide who should live and who die, but they had to have a plan. She would rather defer to Rajasi on this one thing. However, he was more likely to sentence all of Hishae's men to death. She took a deep breath and steeled herself.

"We avoid if we can. A patrol going missing is likely to draw attention. If we find prisoners, we may have to kill the guards to get to them."

"Good plan," he replied, the hint of pride in his tone making her chest warm with unexpected affection. "You could be a captain with a mind like that."

Mira made the soles of their shoes visible and started down the passage. Kazue went ahead of her, the very bottom of his feet also visible now. "I'll leave such things to those more inclined to war. All I want is to live through this."

"If that were true, my lady, you wouldn't be here."

Pride surged through her at his words, and a confusion of other emotions in response to the fondness in his tone.

How quickly he had grown used to her power and how easily he had accepted the atypical role she had taken, albeit without much choice. How many men would be so open? Would Kashi accept this new adaptation of the woman he had known?

She shook her head to clear it. There was no time to get distracted by such thoughts. Now was a time to focus. It did not matter how Kashi felt. She had to try to find any prisoners and free them. At least they would stand a chance of escaping then, even if the rest of her plan failed. The rest of her plan was rather weak anyway. She had to find and stop Hideo, so the plan was to find him and take it from there since she had no idea what she would face once she found him.

A wry smile touched her lips.

What would Rajasi think of that strategy? Great military mind at work indeed.

They crossed paths two different times with rather disinterested looking soldiers patrolling the passage as they made their way along. Both men looked half-asleep and noticed nothing as they passed the three invisible infiltrators. Both times, Mira made them fully invisible, but she wondered if it had even been necessary. It was not until they got close to where the converted rooms were that she heard any sounds of more significant activity. There were voices ahead.

Mira reached behind her, bumped into Rajasi's chest, ran her hand over to his arm and down to his hand, which she took hold of, then she made their feet invisible again. Rajasi gave her hand a squeeze and they continued forward cautiously.

There was an opening in the hallway on their right and Mira peeked into it. Four men sat at a table playing a game of some sort and a fifth stood leaning in a doorway at the back of the room, staring into the space beyond. She could hear moaning from the doorway beyond, then there was a clanking as of metal on metal.

"Got any food out there," a voice hollered from the other room.

"Shut up, you worthless pig," the guard in the doorway hollered back.

Five men, and who knew how many more in the room beyond. Mira watched them for a time, considering that they might have families at home. Any one of them might have someone at home who missed them as much as she missed Kashi. Her heart raced. There were prisoners beyond this doorway, that much was certain, and she had to get to them somehow.

"Just ignore them, Balin, it only excites them when you respond," one of the men from the table replied, not looking away from the game.

The man called Balin walked up behind the one who had spoken and scowled down at him. Mira smiled and reached into the room with her power. Without him in the doorway, she could drop them all into a deep slumber with less risk of someone in the next room noticing. The man called Balin fell to the floor with a thud, but it was not loud enough to be heard over the noises in the next room.

"Nice work," Rajasi murmured.

"They're only sleeping," she whispered and led him forward.

The next doorway opened into a large, poorly lit room lined with cells, most of which appeared to be occupied. Mira smiled, then her smile vanished and she let go of Rajasi's hand. They needed time and they couldn't have anyone waking up behind them and sounding the alarm. An aching spread through her chest.

"I hate to ask you this, but can you take care of them while I get to work in here."

There was a moment of silence in which she struggled with the intense regret of asking such a thing of him.

"I suppose that is the safest way. I'm not big on killing a man in his sleep though."

"I'm sorry. I wish we didn't have to kill them, but I'm not sure if I can keep them asleep," she whispered.

"They have been impervious to our weapons in the past."

She focused on one of the men, reaching out with her power somewhat awkwardly. There was something different about how her magic felt around him. She tore at the sensation, stripping it away like a layer of clothing. She did the same to the others.

"They may not be now," she replied, confident in her words.

There was a sound of movement. One of the men's heads lifted and his neck opened with a gush of blood. Mira looked away, swallowing down the bile that rushed to the back of her throat.

"Go to the next room," Rajasi whispered from somewhere near the table.

CHAPTER TWENTY TWO

Grateful, Mira moved into the room and hurried across to the next doorway. The adjacent room was the same as this one, large and full of cells. One guard stood across the room and Mira shot a bolt of power, splitting open his chest before he could react to the flash of light. Several of the more alert prisoners cried out in alarm and she put up her hood and made herself visible. To stop any additional outcry, she used her power to open a few of the cells closest to her.

"I am here to free you. There is a sergeant in the next room, go to him and wait there." As she spoke, she made Rajasi visible.

The room fell silent and she made her way from cell to cell, telling each the same. At several cells, there were men too injured to rise, so she stopped long enough to heal them. They did not question her power, though some looked fearful. She had let them all become visible now and Kazue patrolled along the perimeter, watching the freed prisoners as warily as they watched him.

"My lady," Rajasi called from the doorway of the adjacent room.

Most of the remaining prisoners looked at her in surprise.

Mira sighed and threw her hood back. "Yes, Sergeant?"

"I've found the captain."

Mira's heart clenched at the tightness in his voice. She started to follow him back into the previous room then stopped. It wasn't fair to the rest of the men here. Closing her eyes, she focused intently on the remaining doors as she had seen them and was rewarded with a satisfying series of metallic clicks as the rest of the doors in the room opened. She opened her eyes and nodded to Rajasi who led the way back into the first room. He took her to a corner cell where a figure lay still on the straw floor. She had never seen Kashi so pale.

Mira glanced around the room to inventory the doors, then she closed her eyes and opened all of them. Rajasi started to try to answer their questions as she hurried into the cell and knelt next to Kashi. She removed bandages from his leg and his hand to see the damage. There was a festering wound on his thigh and another where his hand had been split open between the index and middle knuckles. Mira laid a hand on his feverish forehead and focused her power, tears escaping down her cheeks at the thought of his suffering. Pus ran from the wounds as they began to close, followed by a rinsing of clean blood, and then they sealed completely.

Mira looked back at his face and found his eyes open, watching her. She met those beautiful grey eyes and smiled gently.

Kashi's expression was one of utter confusion. "Have I died?"

"Not so far," she answered, "though you were certainly not far from it."

"Mira?" He sat up slow and put the freshly healed hand to her cheek. "How can you be here?"

"It's a long story. We have to get moving." She stood and offered him her hand.

Kashi took her hand after a few seconds and let her help him to his feet. He looked unsteady at first, then he seemed to get his equilibrium back. He gazed down at his leg, then looked at the healed hand and flexed it with an expression of wonder.

"I don't suppose you brought any food."

Mira smiled, pleased that he had an appetite. "I think the guards had some."

She spotted Rajasi and motioned him over. The sergeant joined them with an uneasy smile for Kashi who stared at him for a long moment.

"We need to divvy out the food the guards had to those who need it most, Kashi included. Is anyone else injured?"

Rajasi shook his head. "I think you got them all. Good to see you, Captain."

"Sergeant," Kashi replied, his eyes narrowing with suspicion as he looked the other man over. "You weren't taken by the birds, were you?"

Rajasi lowered his gaze and shook his head.

Mira glanced between them. "I take it you deserted before the captain was taken prisoner?"

Rajasi shrugged, gave them a faltering smile, and headed back to the guardroom. Kazue walked over and stood next to Mira as she looked over the freed soldiers. They watched her guardedly in return.

"What happened to your eyes?" Kashi asked.

"I'll explain later." She smiled again, warmth surging through her entire being as she turned back to him. "I thought I might never see you again."

Kashi started to reach for her, hesitating at the last moment. She stepped into his arms and wrapped her arms around him, burying her face against his chest. She yearned for this to be the end. The thought of leaving him again was pure torment.

"Well, Captain, looks like you've found yourself one devoted woman."

There were several chuckles around the room and Mira's cheeks burned as she stepped away from Kashi.

Rajasi returned and handed Kashi some dried meat and bread.

"What's the plan?" Kashi asked, his expectant gaze on Rajasi.

Rajasi gestured to Mira. "I'm just the hired help."

Kashi regarded her, his expression one of fresh surprise.

Mira turned to the watching soldiers. "Sergeant Rajasi will lead the way out of here, though I suggest you take the time to refresh yourselves on what is available and arm yourselves. There are some weapons in the guardroom."

Rajasi moved over next to her as the men went in search of more food and weapons. He ignored Kashi's scowl as he leaned close to her, his eyes narrowed.

"I thought I was here to help you," he stated.

"You are, Rajasi. I need you to hold them back and give me a good hour. If I succeed, the Hishae troops will be vulnerable when you emerge. If not, it will at least be dark and many of you may be able to escape under the cover of night."

"Where are you going?" Kashi demanded.

She turned to him and frustration surged to the fore. He was going to make this difficult. "I am going to find Hideo."

"Fine, then I'm coming with you."

Mira could not find her voice for a moment. She had expected him to argue with her, not agree and assign himself as her companion. "No, you must go with the others."

Kazue, who had been watching them silently, looked Mira in the eye and then, to her shock, he growled at her.

Kashi grinned triumphantly. "I think he disagrees with you. Besides, I know the way to the palace from here."

Rajasi met her eyes and there was a touch of sadness in his smile. "You three better get going then. We'll do our part."

Mira leaned forward and kissed him on the cheek. "Thank you, Rajasi."

They stopped in the guardroom and Kashi claimed a dagger and sword. When he had strapped on the weapons, he picked up the food Rajasi had given him and Mira took his free hand. She peeked into the hallway, then led him out with Kazue following. Once outside of the room, she turned to him, smiled, and made them invisible. A twitch of his hand was all that betrayed his surprise.

"I wondered how you got in," he murmured.

"You haven't had much time to recover. Are you sure you're up to this?"

"Yes," he replied.

She could hear him tearing a piece of meat with his teeth. "Lead on then."

It might have been simpler to make their feet visible as she had done before, but for now, she liked that they needed to hold hands. They were almost under the palace now and soon she would have to face the next challenge of confronting Hideo. A little pleasure in the interim was not much to ask.

"You don't seem very surprised," Mira whispered.

"I am, in a way." There was a pause as he swallowed a bite of food. "When I left Barik, I spent a night at your brother's." There was a pang of loss at the mention of Dannesk, but she said nothing. The timing didn't seem right. "Your great aunt Gemma asked to speak with me. When I acquiesced, she started raving about you, and gargoyles, and magic. I told her she was mad and that she shouldn't mention any of it to you."

He was silent for a short time, making his way cautiously along the underground passages, and Mira was about to say something when he spoke again. "I remembered your eyes though. The strange gold flecks I noticed the day I left. It made me wonder."

Mira remembered quite well the day he left. The way he had kissed her. The memory made her cheeks flush.

"Do you know anything about the palace?" she asked, chasing away the distracting memory.

"It is a mirror image of the palace in Beikang. It was supposed to be a wedding present for the queen's son."

"Yes, when he married King Mahesh's daughter. I wonder why the change of heart."

Kashi's hand shifted and she thought he might have shrugged.

"So, where in the palace would you be if you were an evil major?"

Kashi started to reply and she squeezed his hand quickly. A patrol was heading toward them. She put the man to sleep quickly and drew the dagger from her boot. They could not let him continue or he would find the freed prisoners. She let go of Kashi's hand and made them both visible for a moment so they could keep track of one another as she knelt at the man's head, her heart racing. Kashi took hold of her wrist and pulled the dagger from her shaking hand. He looked at it and smiled, then handed it back and drew his own dagger.

"That was meant to be a gift for you. I would not see you bloody your hands with it like this."

She met his eyes then nodded, relieved. Kashi moved the man into a side passage and she looked away as he put his blade to the sleeping man's throat. She heard the steel whisper through flesh and took several deep breaths to control her nausea while she waited. When Kashi took her hand again she made them invisible once more and they continued forward.

"I was taken to see the major in a study on the first floor of the palace. It seems as likely a place as any to find him," Kashi whispered. "He had a strange crystal in the room with him. I wonder if it has something to do with the protections over the warriors."

Mira smiled to herself. That crystal had to be something, especially if the major was keeping it close at hand. She could sense Kazue ahead of her and his presence seemed to almost be tugging her along. "I think Kazue knows where he is," she replied.

They continued in silence. Mira followed Kashi through the passages, holding his hand securely in her own. The feeling she got from Kazue assured her that they were still on the right track. They rounded a corner and the pull from Kazue stopped at a rather ordinary looking door so she stopped as well.

"This way."

"That isn't the way they took me last time," Kashi argued.

"Kazue says this is the way."

She leaned against the door, listening until a moist nose bumped her hand. Trusting the gargoyle, she carefully opened the door. On the other side was a staircase leading up to another door. Mira let them become visible long enough to see that all three were through, then made them invisible again and shut the door.

At the other door, she did not bother listening. She waited for the moist touch of Kazue's nose, then she opened the door. They entered what appeared to be a small library. The shelves were almost empty, but no one had actually been living in the palace yet. This first room at least was furnished with elegance and taste, more so than Mira would have expected. She always expected a palace to be overly grandiose, though she had never been in one until now. The furniture was sage, patterned in pale silver. The tables were a pale swirling wood she did not recognize.

"Mira."

Kashi's whisper brought her attention back to the matter at hand. She gave his hand a light squeeze and crossed to the doorway on the other side of the room. It was late enough now that any activity in the palace, of which there should not be much anyway, would be settling for the night. Part of her hoped they would find Hideo asleep somewhere. He would be easier to dispatch that way. However, it was probably still a little early to get that lucky.

When Kazue touched her hand again, she opened the next door and they entered a large receiving room that was far more ornate, with an elaborate fresco on the ceiling and gold painted sculpted stucco framing the walls and ceiling. As they crossed the room, someone entered through the door they were approaching.

Carefully and quietly as possible, they moved around behind a chair so as not to be in the serving woman's path. Instead of heading through the room, the woman rushed to the chair they were behind and dropped into it. She then began to weep into her hands. Mira's throat ached with a twisting of sympathy and she put the woman into a deep slumber. They continued across the room to the door the woman had left standing open and entered a long corridor.

"I think I recognize this hall," Kashi said under his breath.

Kazue became visible then. Mira glanced at her legs then at where she knew Kashi was, but they were both still hidden. The gargoyle had apparently dismissed her magic somehow. Her nerves danced at the thought of letting herself and Kashi become visible, but Kazue would not have done so if it were not safe enough. She let go of the invisibility.

At the end of the corridor, Kazue stopped and regarded Mira, his eyes possessing a gravity that made her dancing nerves sing with fear. She looked back at Kashi. When he raised his eyebrows and nodded toward the door she nodded in return. Yes, Hideo was here. Now was the moment when they would see if this journey was a fool's errand or a hero's.

Mira reached for the door handle.

"Come in. I have been expecting you."

The strong voice from within made her start with surprise. Kashi's hand rested on her arm and she took comfort from his presence. She closed her eyes for a second, took a deep breath, then opened them, and opened the door.

The room was a large study, adorned with mostly empty shelves and a large, heavy carved wood desk off to one side. The walls and carpets were done in a rich variety of reds and golds, creating a feeling of warmth and welcome that Mira thought rather odd under the circumstances. Toward the opposite wall stood a heavy granite pedestal on which a large, shallow marble bowl sat. Within that bowl was a crystal shard that glowed with a pale light.

Beside it, running his fingers delicately over an almost transparent barrier that surrounded the crystal, stood a tall man with finely chiseled features framed by a curtain of silver hair. His eyes caught hers, eyes so pale silver as to be almost white. His skin was also surprisingly pale. He would be rather handsome, she thought, if he didn't have the complexion of a frozen corpse. He was almost the color of the crystal itself. The magic in it must have changed him. The pale clothing, in light blues and grey, only enhanced his surreal appearance.

Kazue followed them into the room and the man gave the gargoyle a long, emotionless look. His eyes flickered to Kashi for a fraction of a second, registering a hint of surprise, then rested on her again. She made herself meet his eyes. Now did not seem a good time to appear weak in any way.

"I expected you and the beast. I am surprised to see you brought the captain along. I would have thought he had enough the last time he was here."

Mira narrowed her eyes at him, hate sweeping through her and burning away some of her fear. "How is it that you expected us?"

"I could feel you coming, you and your beast." He walked to a window as he spoke and gazed out, turning his back on them in an unnerving display of confidence and arrogance.

"Yet you called in no protection," Kashi remarked as he moved a few steps closer to the desk, perhaps trying to spread out the targets. "You must be rather confident, Hideo."

Hideo turned and smiled at her. "Oh, I am. You see, I tried to get what you have. The magic of the gargoyles, but after much experimentation, it seems that it must be given willingly, and the beasts refused to cooperate."

His words sent a chill through her. "Experimentation?"

Hideo scowled at her impatiently. "Are you truly that naïve? The magic is passed through physical contact. I tried killing a few, a feat unto itself, but it did no good to touch them once they were dead." Kazue growled, but Hideo ignored the gargoyle. "Then I tried capturing them and touching them while they were restrained, but even that did not work. Apparently, it is not touching a gargoyle so much as being touched by one that passes the magic."

Hideo gave Kazue a long, calculating look and Mira stepped closer to the gargoyle, ready to defend him if necessary.

Hideo chuckled. "Amusing that it should choose you. Clearly gargoyles don't understand the worth of a woman."

She let the words go, she was not about to let him get her ire up over such a thing, but she saw Kashi's hand drop to his sword hilt. She held up a hand to stay him and Hideo watched this, cocking his head to the side a fraction much like a dog trying to understand something its master has said. His gaze drifted from Kashi to Mira and back again and a slow, sinister smile touched his lips.

"This is too wonderful. The two of you aren't here together by coincidence. You're in love, aren't you?" He smiled and dread coursed through her. "How delightful. This could be fun."

Mira glanced at the strange crystal, taking a careful step closer when he looked out the window again. She noticed tiny veins of red pulsing through the crystal, and the bowl it sat in contained a dark red liquid. She understood all too quickly, perhaps more because Kazue understood than because of her own intuition. This crystal held the power he had discovered and the liquid was his blood. He was as bound to it as she was to Kazue. Hope surged through her and she raised her hand, sending a bolt of power at the crystal.

The bolt hit the barrier, which she had erroneously assumed was merely glass and rebounded in a blinding surge of light. The deflected bolt struck the ceiling, creating a large, black hole there. An acrid smoke wafted from the singed edges around the hole. A faint light coming through the center from the room above.

Hideo chuckled. "Did you really think I would have let you come here if it was going to be that easy? You have not learned the first rule of engagement. Know thy enemy."

Her heart was pounding. She could have killed any one of them with that reckless attack.

"Is that so?" She spoke with an arrogance she did not feel. "What do you know of your enemy, Hideo?"

Mira did not really care what his answer was. What she cared about was that his attention was on her for now. If he was focusing on her, he was less likely to do something to the others while she tried to come up with a new approach. It was tempting to try a similar assault against Hideo himself, but she suspected the shield that protected the crystal was the same thing that protected his soldiers and would undoubtedly protect him. If she could destroy the shield, she was sure he would become vulnerable, but how?

He looked at her then, his sneer dripping with disdain. "What do I need to know? You're a woman. Gold in the eyes of a woman is merely a color."

She wanted to slap him for his words. Instead, she smiled. She could feel a building of anticipation from Kazue. Her smile made his sneer falter.

"You don't know your enemy very well then."

Hideo scowled and she saw a flicker of uncertainty as his eyes jumped from her to the crystal and back again. "What do you mean?"

"You have more than one," she stated.

Hideo hesitated, confusion in his eyes.

At that moment, Kazue leapt, landing on the transparent barrier over the crystal. The gargoyle threw back his head and let out a ground-shaking roar as Hideo's silver eyes widened in alarm. The barrier ignited with a flash of light so bright Mira could barely stand to look at the pedestal or the gargoyle. Then the barrier fractured and exploded, sending Kazue hurtling into the wall. The gargoyle hit the floor and was still.

Mira, Hideo, and Kashi, all thrown in different directions by the explosion, scrambled to their feet, all three staring at the now exposed crystal. Hideo's expression of surprise turned to horror and he lunged toward the object, forgetting the others in the room. He staggered suddenly, Kashi's dagger appearing in his back.

Turning, Hideo sent a bolt of power at Kashi who lunged behind the desk. The second bolt struck the desk, bursting it into splinters of wood and slamming Kashi into the wall. In the second before he struck the wall, Kashi met Mira's eyes and she knew it was up to her now. Then he hit with a sickening thud and slumped to the floor. With a wave of desperation, Mira looked at the crystal and suddenly she was standing next to it. Hideo was trying to get up from his knees and Mira felt a strange pity for the man. He had thought himself invulnerable. Such arrogance.

Hideo met her eyes then, the agony in his eyes as great as that she felt for the state of her companions, which remained uncertain given that neither Kazue nor Kashi had moved again. She stared down at him with a mixture of pity and disgust as she shook her head. Then she slammed her palm down on the point of the crystal.

Hideo screamed something, but Mira barely heard it over her own scream. The initial pain of the point driving into her flesh was nothing compared to the pain that followed. Her entire body became a vessel of excruciating pain as the two powers collided within her. It felt as though the crystal were draining the life from her body. Her blood mingled with that of Hideo's in the bowl and began to sizzle and boil like macabre soup. Mira's legs gave out and she slumped against the pedestal. Then the crystal began to emit a high, shrieking sound and she longed to cover her ears, but she could not move her arms.

Just when she thought she thought the sound might split her skull apart, the crystal shattered and Mira fell to the floor at the base of the pedestal. The shrieking had stopped, but she could still hear the echo of it in her ears and she could feel nothing but pain. Hideo lay a few feet away, the dagger still sticking from his back. She had a second to wonder if he were dead before she slipped into unconsciousness.

•

Kashi woke to an intense aching spread through his back and a sharp throb at the back of his skull. He struggled to his hands and knees and looked around the room, moving slow to mitigate the dizziness. The desk was reduced to finger sized slivers of wood, several of which were embedded in his left arm. Toward the center of the room lay Hideo. One arm stretched toward the granite pedestal and Kashi's dagger still protruding from his back at the center of a growing red stain. The major was breathing very shallowly and his eyes were closed.

At the foot of the pillar, Mira lay crumpled in a pool of blood. The broken remains of the crystal and the marble basin were on the floor around her. He did not see any signs that she still lived. Panicked, he hurried to rise, but dizziness forced him back to his knees. Relenting to his injuries, he crawled across the floor to her. As he got close, he saw that she was breathing, though even more shallowly than Hideo.

Kashi grimaced with the pain as he pulled her to him. There were some shards of the desk embedded in her shoulder and a large wound in the center of her palm that was bleeding heavily. Otherwise, she appeared unharmed, but she showed no signs of awareness when he moved her. He held her close and brushed a strand of mahogany hair away from her mouth with gentle fingers. His own hair fell around them in a curtain of black as he bent over her, holding her tight.

The sound of movement a few seconds later made his heart jump, the sudden rush of blood exacerbating his dizziness. He looked up to see the gargoyle approaching and hope sparked in him, remembering how she had healed his wounds. If her power came from the beast, perhaps the beast could help her. He held Mira away from his body so that the gargoyle could see her. The big head moved close to her face and the beast sniffed at her, then it licked her cheek and backed a few steps away.

Kashi met the creature's golden eyes. Mira's eyes were the same now and he found the molten gaze soothing somehow. The pain in his head began to fade. After staring into those eyes for several long seconds, he slumped to the floor beside Mira, deeply asleep.

CHAPTER TWENTY FOUR

When he woke again, Kashi was no longer on the floor of the study. Now he was lying in a comfortable bed in a lavish bedchamber staring up at a gilded ceiling. He remembered Mira, lying unconscious in his arms, barely breathing, and sat up in alarm.

The first thing he discovered was that his back still ached, but his head felt fine. The next thing he noticed was that he was not alone. As soon as he sat up, Shakari rose from a nearby chair and approached the bed.

Kashi met his half-brother's tired eyes. "Mira, is she—"

"She is alive," Shakari interrupted, though he did not meet Kashi's eyes when he spoke.

"Is she well?"

"She has a bad wound in her hand that is not responding to treatment." Shakari offered, his hesitant manner implying there was more.

Kashi narrowed his eyes, growing impatient. "And…"

Shakari shook his head. "She seems fine otherwise, but she shows no sign of waking. She doesn't respond to any outside stimuli. We were hoping you could shed some light on what happened in the study."

Kashi backtracked in his mind, considering all that

had led up to this moment. "I could use some clothes," he stated, climbing out of the bed.

"By lord and by land, Kashi," Shakari exclaimed as he moved out of Kashi's way, "you look like a herd of horses danced a waltz on your back."

Kashi frowned at Shakari and walked to the mirror. Turning his back and craning his head around, he saw that his back was black with bruising from his impact with the wall. It was a wonder nothing was broken. He looked at Shakari again. "Clothes?"

"Ah, yes." Shakari walked to a wardrobe and opened it, rummaging around. "Your uniform was beyond repair, but we managed to pull together some other clothes for you. They may not be a perfect fit," Shakari threw a handful of clothes and Kashi caught them, grimacing as the sudden movement sent fresh pain through his back. "Sorry."

Kashi shook his head, dismissing the apology, and began to dress deliberately so as not to cause too much pain. "What happened to Hishae's army?"

Shakari smiled then. "Well, the short version is that they suddenly became vulnerable to our weapons. A bored archer on watch started firing arrows over the river, despite orders not to waste ammunition, and one hit home. As soon as word reached me, I knew Mira had succeeded in her rather mysterious mission. We attacked then, though it really was not the most organized attack. While we were attacking from the front, Sergeant Rajasi appeared leading our captured soldiers and attacked from behind the camp. They surrendered rather quickly."

"What about the birds?"

"They vanished," Shakari replied with a look of wonder. "It was almost like they had never been there at all. One moment they were in the sky, the next they were simply gone."

"And Hideo?"

"He lives. His wounds have been tended and he is awaiting trial in the underground prison. Rajasi had us put him in the cell that he says he found you in."

Kashi managed a brief grin at that. The sergeant may have deserted, but in the end, he had come through. There was silence as Kashi finished dressing. He sat on the edge of the bed, surprised at how weary his body still was, and looked up to find Shakari watching him with a strange expression.

"What?"

Shakari shrugged and turned toward the window.

Puzzled, Kashi stood and took a few steps toward him, then stopped, discouraged by the awkward feel in the room.

"Kashi," Shakari started, taking a deep breath before he continued. "I am glad Mira found you."

Shakari turned then and Kashi smiled. Stepping forward, he embraced his half brother and Shakari returned the gesture, careful of his injured back. "So am I," Kashi replied, stepping back again.

Shakari grinned, then his expression turned serious. "I did want to ask you something?"

"Ask."

"When Mira came to me in the camp, she seemed desperate to find you, and when I found you in the study, you had her in your arms..." He trailed off when Kashi met his eyes with a look of defiance.

"I love her, Shakari, but I will not do anything to ruin her future. Is that what you wish to hear?"

Shakari shook his head, looking disturbed. "How could I have missed it before?"

"You didn't want to see it," Kashi replied. "Can I see her?"

Shakari looked hesitant. "Perhaps it would be best to speak with the physician first."

"Fine, let's go."

Kashi followed Shakari down the hallway where they intercepted the physician's assistant.

"Where can I find Master Okuro?" Shakari asked the youth.

The boy nodded back down the hallway. "He is in with the Lady Mira Yukori."

Pleasure lightened Kashi's steps. Now he would not have to put off seeing her any longer. Shakari led the way to a door and knocked. The door opened and a short man with thick, graying brown hair and kind brown eyes answered. He glanced at Shakari for a second then fixed his eyes intently on Kashi.

"You are awake. Good. How do you feel?"

"I am well enough, thank you," Kashi replied, resisting the urge to shove his way into the room.

"Good, good. Perhaps you can help me then."

The physician turned back into the room and Kashi stepped in past Shakari, following the older man to the bedside. Mira lay in the bed, her shortened mahogany hair framing a face that was startlingly pale. She looked peaceful though, and impossibly beautiful. Kashi longed to touch her pale face, to hold her and try to call her back from wherever she was, but he stood back and waited.

The physician reached under the covers and gently pulled out the injured hand. "This wound has been defying all of my efforts," he said, turning her hand so Kashi could see the blood seeping through the bandage. "It bleeds constantly, though the bleeding is slow and may be getting slower. I do not think it is the wound that keeps her asleep though. What happened to her, Captain?"

Kashi allowed the doctor to lead him to a chair near the window of the room and the three of them sat. Kashi related everything he could remember from when Mira and Rajasi rescued him to when he slammed into the wall and went unconscious. He told them that he had woken enough to crawl to her side, though he did not mention the gargoyle's interaction.

"What happened to the gargoyle?" He asked then, knowing Mira would be concerned for the creature.

"We don't know," Shakari replied. "It wasn't there when we found you."

Kashi glanced at Mira, troubled. He had hoped the creature would have done something to help her. It seemed to have healed his head somehow. Perhaps her current plight was beyond the abilities of the beast.

There was a knock at the door and Shakari went to open it.

"Sergeant Rajasi."

"I heard the captain was up." Rajasi's head peered around Shakari's shoulder and he grinned. "Hey, Captain."

Shakari let him in. Rajasi had a stitched wound above his left eye, but he looked well otherwise. The first thing that came to mind upon seeing the other man was Mira kissing him on the cheek down in the prison. Kashi stamped down a surge of jealously, forced a smile, and stood, shaking the other man's offered hand. Rajasi pulled him in and gave him a quick rough hug that left Kashi gasping in pain. Shakari grabbed the sergeant's shoulder and shoved him down into a chair as Kashi composed himself.

"His back is injured, you idiot," Shakari snarled.

Rajasi smiled sheepishly. "Sorry Kashi, I was just glad to see you in one piece."

Kashi waved away the apology and sat back down.

"I'm glad you showed up, actually," Kashi said once the surge of pain had died down to a dull ache again. "I suspect you can fill in some blanks leading up to your arrival in the prison."

Rajasi shifted uncomfortably in his chair and stared down at the floor, then over at the still figure in the bed. His eyes lingered on Mira's face longer than Kashi liked, but he could not really berate the man for simply looking at her.

"We know you deserted, Rajasi," Shakari said finally. "However, you seem to have made amends for those actions. Now we need you to fill in what you know."

Rajasi turned back to them finally and nodded. "All right. Since you know I deserted, I'll skip that part and start with when I met Mira." Kashi narrowed his eyes and Rajasi flushed. "The Lady Mira, I mean."

Kashi nodded then and Rajasi continued, telling them of his first encounters with Mira, of the displays he had seen of her power, and of how they had come to the camp. Shakari filled in his encounter with her in the officer's tent, then Rajasi went on to tell of their travel into the underground passages up to when they found the prisoners. Kashi was surprised to hear how much the two men had done to enable Mira's quest, but he could not be angry with them. From what he had seen, he had begun to believe that there really was no other way to stop Hideo.

"The Queen needs to hear all of this," Shakari stated.

"Yes, Major Shakari, I think that would be wise," Okuro stated. "I think you would be the best one for that job. Sergeant Rajasi, I imagine you could help. Captain Kashi, would you be so kind as to keep an eye on Lady Mira? I need to check on a few things."

"I think Marikashi should come with me," Shakari stated in his officer's command voice.

Okuro was not going to be intimidated. "I think the captain should not be overstressed until his injuries have healed more. He will stay here and keep an eye on my patient."

Shakari hesitated, glanced from Mira to Kashi and then to the unyielding expression the doctor wore and finally nodded. "Come along, Sergeant."

"I'll have some food sent for you," Okuro said before vanishing through the door behind the other two.

Kashi watched as the door shut gently behind them. When they had been gone for a short time, he walked over to the bedside, bent down, and kissed her on the lips.

"Come back to me," he whispered in her ear.

There was no response. With an aching in his chest that had nothing to do with his injuries, Kashi took a chair and set it by the window, turning it to face Mira, then he sat and prepared to wait.

•

Mira woke in a large, soft bed in a bedchamber so ornate her eyes found it hard to focus on any one element of the decor. Her body ached all over, but she was alive, and that was reason enough to smile. She stared at the blue and gold bed canopy for a long time, taking inventory of her condition. It seemed that everything was still there and the only thing that hurt more than the rest was the hand she had driven onto the crystal. She took a moment, focusing on her physical self, and let her power sooth away the pain. It worked on everything except her injured hand. Lifting the hand gingerly from under the covers, she found that it was securely bandaged.

Everything from her encounter with Hideo was clear in her mind. Her current situation made little sense unless the warriors of Beikang had been victorious once the crystal was destroyed. That thought felt good, but she also remembered Kazue and Kashi lying still on the floor of the room and a sudden rush of fear made her heart race.

Sitting up carefully, she looked around the room. It was much grander than any room she had ever slept in. Each bit of embroidery, every carved piece of wood, was done in immaculate detail, and on a beautiful blue chair, embroidered in gold, Kashi sat, his head back and his eyes closed in sleep. He looked well. Giddy bubbles of relief burst joyfully in her chest. The window behind him revealing the darkness of night and pale moonlight was the only source of light in the room.

Mira pulled back the covers. Someone had changed her into a sleeping shift and she passingly wondered who it had been, but that was unimportant. She stood carefully and put on the dressing robe that had been left on the bed stand. With soft steps, she walked over to Kashi and drank him in with her eyes. Having survived much more reckless adventures, she didn't worry about consequences as she leaned down and kissed him. Kashi's grey eyes opened and then closed again as he wrapped his arms around her and drew her close, returning her kiss with a passion that made her whole body burn with longing. She wanted to throw aside propriety and ask him to make love to her, but that was unfair. What they were doing now would be considered improper in society and she knew he was torn enough already. To encourage more would only rend him with guilt.

When he released her, she knelt next to the chair and regarded him with a smile, surprised to find tears running down her cheeks.

Kashi leaned forward with a grimace that betrayed some lingering injury from the encounter with Hideo. He smiled though, and gently wiped the tears from her cheeks.

"Are you all right?" he asked in a hushed voice as though still afraid of waking someone.

She nodded. "Of course I am. You're alive, aren't you?"

His eyes reflected a mixture of wonder and torment as he leaned forward and kissed her again, his lips soft on hers as though afraid of hurting her. When he moved away again, she stood and took his hand. She led him to the couch where they could both sit. For his sake, she tried to be proper and sit a small distance away, but

Kashi pulled her close and wrapped his arms around her. Mira leaned her head back against him and longed for time to stop.

"What of Kazue?" she asked, fear of what the answer would be chasing away some of the pleasure of the moment.

"I don't know. Like you, I woke up in one of the bedchambers here. Shakari said there was no sign of the gargoyle when they found us in the room." Though she feared for Kazue, it was good to hear Shakari's name with all that his presence implied. "Apparently destroying the crystal destroyed the birds and the protection over Hishae's troops. You made it possible for us to defeat them."

Mira smiled. She worried for Kazue, but her role in Beikang's success brought a powerful sense of satisfaction. "What of Hideo?"

Kashi chuckled. "Rajasi gave him my old cell under the palace for now. King Mahesh has ordered his execution. It will probably take place in the next few days."

Mira twisted around to look at Kashi. "I don't understand. King Mahesh is here?"

"Ah, yes, that is the interesting part." Kashi turned her back around and drew her against him before he continued. "King Mahesh is here. He has been for some time. Apparently, Hideo was keeping him prisoner and controlling him when public appearances were necessary to bring about the assault upon Laki. When he moved to Laki, he brought the King with him the keep him under control. I don't know how Hideo expected to conquer the kingdom by himself or how he thought to manage things if he succeeded. He must have been mad."

"Perhaps he was, but that kind of power can be rather heady," Mira replied, sympathy taking the edge off her hatred.

Kashi was silent for a time and she watched the dark begin to turn grey with the advent of dawn. Perhaps her words worried him, but she could not lie, not to him and she could not hide the pity she had for Hideo.

Kashi fingers cupped her chin gently and turned her face toward him. He had leaned away a bit so he could meet her eyes. "I have always loved you, Mira. When we were younger, I used to lie awake at night making plans for our future. What our manor would be like. How we would go for glorious rides together on our own lands. It was not until I went to the academy that I fully understood how ridiculous those plans were. Even then, I had foolish fantasies for a time that we would just run away together."

"I would run away with you, Kashi." She held his gaze, hoping he could see how much she meant those words.

Kashi chuckled and pulled her close again. "I think it's too late for that now."

Mira snuggled in closer still and laid her head against his chest. "I can still hear your heart beating, Kashi. It isn't too late as long as that is true."

There was a firm knock on the door and she moved discreetly away from him. He rose and returned to the chair he had been in when she woke.

"Come in," she called.

The door opened and Shakari poked his head into the room. When he saw Mira, he smiled broadly. "You're awake," he exclaimed as he entered.

She rose and smiled.

Shakari crossed the room in a few long strides and hugged her gently. Surprised and pleased by the gesture, she returned it with enthusiasm.

"Did Kashi tell you?" Shakari asked vaguely as he backed away and looked her over.

"What?"

"The Queen is residing in the palace now. She arrived a few hours ago and would like an audience with you. With both of you," he added with a stern look at his brother, "when you are well enough."

Mira shook her head. "No, he didn't mention that part. I am as ready as I will be, though I would like to clean up first if that can be arranged."

Shakari nodded. "I will have a hot bath and appropriate clothing arranged for you. Kashi, we can do the same for you if you would come with me."

Kashi nodded and stood.

Shakari smiled at her then, an almost awkward admiration in his sparkling eyes. "There was a missive from Lord Valen Barik this morning. He was notifying the queen that he had sent men to watch over you and Ina, but that he thought you might need more protection." He chuckled to himself at that. "He also reported the passing of his father and his pending marriage to the Lady Johnis. I thought you would like to know."

Mira smiled and nodded. It was good to know that Ina was being looked after in her absence and that Valen was finally free of his father. "Thank you."

Kashi followed his half-brother from the room, glancing back at Mira with sad longing before the door closed behind him. She sighed and sat back on the couch, clinging to the memory of his arms around her for as long as it would last.

When a serving girl arrived to lead her to the bath, she requested food be brought to her. Once bathed, she ate ravenously of the fine meal they brought her, finding that she was near to starved. Finally, she climbed into the elegant gown that had been brought for her with the assistance of the lady's maid. It fit remarkably well. It was rather nice to feel like a woman again. The lady's maid also managed to make her oddly cut hair look almost elegant. When Mira regarded the finished product in the mirror, she was surprised at the pale beauty of the woman looking back at her.

The warm emerald gown was detailed with a pale green silk and a rich gold thread. The cut of the gown and the style of her hair managed to make her look less thin then she had become. The only thing she was uneasy with was the way the gown enhanced the gold of her eyes. Gazing into them, a surge of yearning for Kazue swelled inside her. The gargoyle had been with her for almost every moment of the journey that brought her here. To meet the Queen without him seemed like a surprisingly daunting task.

"Whose gown is this?" She asked, drawing herself away from thoughts of the missing gargoyle.

"Princess Lilamayi," the woman replied.

Mira spun from the mirror. "I can't wear this."

"The princess and you are about the same size. Her ladyship would be offended if you refused."

She was not about to add offending royalty to her list of firsts. "If you put it that way, then I am honored to wear it."

The surgeon came by a short time later to help change the bandages on her wounded hand. He thought the bleeding might have slowed a bit more. She wasn't sure she agreed. After he left, she stood at the window and gazed out, not wanting to muss the dress by sitting. When the summons finally arrived, her legs were getting rather tired and she followed the lady's maid from the room with butterflies fluttering wildly in her stomach. Though the prospect of meeting the Queen had gotten to be less daunting then the idea of standing much longer.

When they arrived at the audience chamber, Kashi was waiting outside, attired in a proper uniform and looking as magnificent as she could ever remember him looking. To her surprise, his long black hair hung loose around his strong features, rather than bound up in the typical warrior's knot she had grown accustomed to. She walked up to him and took his hand with her good one, squeezing it gently. Shakari slapped her hand, giving them both a warning glance, which they responded to with sullen looks. There was no time to say anything before they were announced and guided into the room by Shakari.

There were very few people in attendance, gathered quiet around the perimeter of the chamber. Mira recognized Rajasi and smiled at him. Rajasi grinned back discreetly then resumed his serious expression and gave Kashi a nod. At the head of the room, two grand chairs had been arranged at the top of the dais. In one of the chairs sat Queen Isaye, her dark hair bound in elaborate braids around the delicate tiara on her head. Her face bore the fine lines of age and dark shadows under her eyes made her look rather tired. Recent events had been hard on everyone.

The other chair held King Mahesh, whose thick beard was not quite adequate to hide his unnatural gauntness. His regal attire hung loose on his frame. The blue eyes that looked down at them were haunted in a way that only time could heal. It appeared that Hideo had not cared for him well. Standing to either side, down and back of the main dais, were the Queen's son, Prince Hikaru, and the King's daughter, Princess Lilamayi.

Mira curtsied low as Kashi bowed before the dais, a few steps behind Shakari.

"Thank you, Major Shakari." The Queen nodded to Shakari and he bowed, then moved to one side.

"Lord Shakari Arkesh and Captain Rajasi Taeko have both been rewarded for their parts in bringing this conflict to an end," Queen Isaye began. "However, it has been brought to my attention that you, Captain Marikashi Arkesh and Lady Mira Yukori, were the prime instruments of our salvation."

Neither of them spoke. She had not asked either of them to do so and Mira hoped nothing more was expected. She hadn't much practice with meeting royalty.

"Captain Marikashi Arkesh, rewarding you will be easy. For your service, I grant you a manor, and all of the titles and privileges associated with such. The details of this reward will be handled by my steward. Once you have settled, I will also see to it that a proper betrothal is arranged."

Kashi bowed deep. "You honor me, your Majesty."

Queen Isaye gave him a gracious nod and turned to Mira. "You, Lady Mira Yukori, are not so simple. Do you still have your... abilities?"

Mira met the queen's discerning gaze steadily. "It seems, your Majesty, that the power I was given and that of the crystal destroyed each other."

Queen Isaye nodded and her expression relaxed, her entire countenance becoming more tranquil. "Well, the healing might have been useful, but it is probably for the best. I offer you the lands that your family has long held and a position on my council should you wish it, Lady Mira. I would also like to find you a suitor worthy of you and the service you have done me. I dare say Lord Valin Barik would have been a good match, but I am afraid that he made other plans while you were on your rather unexpected adventure."

Mira's heart began pounding in her chest as she glanced at Kashi, who had chosen that moment to attempt a discreet glance in her direction.

"Is there something you wish to say, Lady Mira?" The Queen asked pointedly and Mira stopped breathing for a moment. "No?"

Mira took a deep, trembling breath and met the Queen's now curious gaze. "I do not wish to keep you, your Majesty, but might I suggest a solution to this betrothal problem."

Queen Isaye regarded her with a thoughtful curiosity, the barest hint of a smile touching her lips when she glanced between them. "Please, continue."

"If I were promised to the captain… Lord Marikashi Arkesh, you could be done with both of us."

Mira stifled a smile when she caught the sparkle of amusement in the Queen's eyes. She drew her gaze away from Mira to look at Kashi. "Lord Marikashi, would you be amenable to such an arrangement?"

Kashi glanced at Mira and her heart fluttered under his gaze, then he turned and met the Queen's eyes. "I could not be more amenable, your Majesty."

Elation began to fill Mira as a smile tugged at the corners of Queen Isaye's lips. "I suppose that solves the issue then. The two of you will be wed. I command it. You are dismissed."

Mira managed, through no small effort, to contain her elation until they were out of the room. Then she turned and met Kashi's embrace enthusiastically, kissing him. They stayed like this until Shakari came through the door and grabbed their shoulders to try and move them apart. They ended their kiss, but Kashi continued to hold her, smiling down at her. Mira thought she might burst with delight. She wanted to laugh and shout and dance. Shakari finally herded them out of the area and they spend the remainder of the day with the Queen's steward handling the paperwork around placing the Yukori holdings in Mira's name and awarding Kashi his own lands.

CHAPTER TWENTY FIVE

That night, Mira could not sleep for the excitement that filled her, so she stole away into the palace when the halls were quiet and made her way to one of the towers. She knew such nocturnal wandering was inappropriate under the Queen's nose, but she needed to feel the freedom of the outside air.

The night was surprisingly quiet for a city occupied by military. Mira glanced at the sky and was pleased by the gargoyles that flew there now, in place of the strange birds that had filled it for a time. She gazed out among them, searching for the one she had grown so familiar with. The one whose presence was like an extension of her own. She longed for the company of Kazue, yearning to share the night with the one to whom she owed her current happiness.

Mira waited for a long time, watching the gargoyles fly as the moon slowly crossed the night sky. She was about to abandon the tower when she heard wings beating through the air behind her. She turned with a surge of hope. Kazue lit upon the tower with extraordinary grace and she gave a cry of delight and ran to greet him. Standing before the creature, she wrapped her arms around his neck and hugged him tight. Kazue wrapped his wings around her and the warmth and comfort of him infused her.

"You can keep him, but he has to sleep on the floor."

Mira laughed and turned. Kashi had joined them on the tower. She went to him and moved to kiss him, but he held her away with his hands on her shoulders and gazed intently into her eyes. After a moment, he smiled.

"You look good in gold."

Then he did kiss her and Mira was happy to let him. She wrapped her arms around him, placing her hands over his badly bruised back. With a thought, she healed his injuries and Kashi stiffened in surprise. Then he lifted her and swung her around.

Putting her back down, he looked her in the eye with mock severity. "You lied to the Queen?"

"I know it was wrong, Kashi, but you don't think she would let this kind of power walk around loose, do you?"

"No," he answered honestly. "I'm glad you lied."

Mira shrugged and looked over at Kazue who sat watching them with his endless patience.

"We could give him a couch to sleep on."

Kashi laughed. "He's bigger than most couches."

Mira smiled and kissed him again.

ACKNOWLEDGEMENTS

As always, there are many people in my life I'm leaving out here for brevity sake. All of you are still very important to me and I am always thankful for you.

To my mom Linda for your loving support and for helping me work out and refine my ideas.

To Kai for your support and for being the most amazing creative partner.

To Rick and Ann for being two of the best of friends anyone could ask for and for being willing to give honest feedback on my books.

To Aradia for knowing I would succeed from the first time we met and being an inspiration in your dedication to your own art.

To my cover artist, Heather, my editor M Evan, and my interior designer, Brian, thank you for your fantastic work and for being such amazing people to work with.

To my fans, for being awesome people and for pushing me to finish this book.

To my sixth-grade teacher, Mr. Johnson, for being so pleased and excited when I told you I was going to be an author and to my eighth-grade algebra teacher, Mr. Siebenlist, for almost letting me flunk because you were so delighted that I was writing books in class rather than notes.

AUTHOR BIO

Nikki started writing her first novel at the age of 12, which she still has tucked in a briefcase in her home office. She now lives in the magnificent Pacific Northwest tending to her sweet old horse and a wondrous cat-god. She feeds her imagination by sitting on the ocean in her kayak gazing out across the never-ending water or hanging from a rope in a cave, embraced by darkness and the sound of dripping water. She finds peace through practicing iaido or shooting her longbow.

•

Thank you for taking time to read this novel.
Please leave a review if you enjoyed it.

•

For more about me and my work visit me at
http://nikkimccormack.com

OTHER NOVELS by NIKKI McCORMACK

CLOCKWORK ENTERPRISES
The Girl and the Clockwork Cat
The Girl and the Clockwork Conspiracy
The Girl and the Clockwork Crossfire

FORBIDDEN THINGS
Dissident
Exile
Apostate

THE ENDLESS CHRONICLES
The Keeper

www.ingramcontent.com/pod-product-compliance
Lightning Source LLC
Chambersburg PA
CBHW070439120726
47910CB00003B/851